CRITICS ARE CHARMED BY JANA DeLEON!

TROUBLE IN MUDBUG

"DeLeon brings her spunky style to a novel that's plenty of fun to read. The characters are easy to indentify with and demonstrate their multifaceted personalities in their actions and words. DeLeon is excellent at weaving comedy, suspense and spicy romance into one compelling story."

—*RT Book Reviews*

"Funny and exciting Deleon manages to keep you guessing and laughing from start to finish. . . . I would recommend this to anyone."

—Night Owl Romance Reviews

"A lighthearted romp . . . loaded with humor, intrigue and romance."

—Genre Go Round Reviews

"Interesting characters and a fun and entertaining mystery make *Trouble in Mudbug* a novel I highly recommend."

—Romance Reviews Today

UNLUCKY

"The quirky characters keep the action moving and I'm sure Mallory has been sitting next to me every time I go to the casino."

—Barbara Vey, *Publishers Weekly*
Beyond Her Book Blog

"With original, smart and comedic writing, DeLeon delivers a three-dimensional hero and heroine, a community of offbeat secondary characters, a complex and intriguing plot with a hint of paranormal and a fascinating peek into the world of casino poker."

—*RT Book Reviews*

"Ms. DeLeon has an excellent knack at weaving the total story together. She gives the right amount of mystery and suspense with plenty of romance and lots of laughter thrown in. I enjoyed every page and found it hard to put down. I think many people will be putting *Unlucky* on their keeper shelves."

—Once Upon A Romance

"Ms. DeLeon provides a great plot and a lot of mystery. The heat that sizzles off of Mallory and Jake keeps you turning the pages to see what will happen next. And right when you think you have it all figured out, you realize you don't. Things are never as they seem on the bayou!"

—The Romance Reader's Connection

RUMBLE ON THE BAYOU

"*Rumble on the Bayou* is a wonderful, poignant and fun mystery.... Filled with likable and interesting individuals, this first-rate debut novel is a truly fantastic read."

—*RT Book Reviews*, 4 ½ stars;
Reviewers Choice Nominee

"Jana DeLeon's debut had me chuckling from the opening pages, and I never stopped laughing. It's a fresh, fast-paced, fabulously funny mystery where sexy blondes have brains, small towns swarm with crazy characters, and everyone's afraid of the gators!"

—Diana Peterfreund, author of *Secret Society Girl*

"Racy, rambunctious, rollicking."

—Carolyn Hart, author of *Dead Days of Summer*

"A very impressive debut novel. *Rumble on the Bayou* kept me enthralled from the first page to the last!"

—Fresh Fiction

"Debut author Jana DeLeon has created a whole passel of down-to-earth, wonderful characters, and a page-turning, interesting mystery. *Rumble on the Bayou* is a perfect blend of secrets, intrigue, romance and laughter."

—*Affaire de Coeur*

Other books by Jana DeLeon:

TROUBLE IN MUDBUG
UNLUCKY
RUMBLE ON THE BAYOU

Mischief in Mudbug

JANA DELEON

LOVE SPELL   *Love Spell*   NEW YORK CITY

To the military men and women,
who risk their lives every day for freedom—
Thank you!

LOVE SPELL®

October 2009

Published by

Dorchester Publishing Co., Inc.
200 Madison Avenue
New York, NY 10016

Copyright © 2009 by Jana DeLeon

ISBN 10: 0-505-52785-5
ISBN 13: 978-0-505-52785-1
E-ISBN: 978-1-4285-0754-8

The name "Love Spell" and its logo are trademarks of Dorchester Publishing Co., Inc.

Printed in the United States of America.

10 9 8 7 6 5 4 3 2

Visit us online at www.dorchesterpub.com.

ACKNOWLEDGMENTS

To my friend, Tracey Stanley, for being a constant reminder that there are truly good people in this world. To my fabulous critique partners and friends, Colleen Gleason, Cari Manderscheid, and Cindy Taylor for keeping me on task and propping me up with wine and homemade cookies. My parents Jimmie and Bobbie, brother Dwain, sis-in-law Donna, and incredible niece Katianne, for all your support. My mentor, Jane Graves, for all your support, whether it was a plot problem or career advice—I'm lucky to have you. To my agent, Kristin Nelson, for taking a chance on something different and always believing in my ability to write, even when I sometimes forget. And to my incredible editor, Leah Hultenschmidt, for your brilliant editorial comments that always take my story to another level. And a huge THANKS to the cover artists for the absolute best covers in publishing—I love the shoe!

Mischief
in
Mudbug

Chapter One

Sabine LeVeche placed her hands over her crystal ball and looked across the table at Thelma Jenkins. It didn't take psychic ability to know that Thelma's problem was her husband, Earl, same as always, which was a good thing, since Sabine didn't have an ounce of paranormal gift in her body. But today, she would have given anything for the ability to know where Earl had squirreled away his secret stash, *if* the money even existed.

"Can you see the money?" Thelma asked.

Sabine held in a sigh. On any other day, she would have pretended to see the money in a suitcase or a box or under a bush, something that would send Thelma off happily on a witch hunt to buy Sabine two weeks of peace and quiet. After all, Thelma didn't need the money. She just couldn't stand the idea of Earl keeping something from her and was convinced he'd been skimming off their gas station profits all fifty years of their marriage.

At least that's how Thelma presented it.

The reality was, Alzheimer's was fast taking Earl away from this earth, and Thelma was desperately looking for something to distract her and fill her time. Looking for the mythical treasure of Earl fit the bill nicely.

Sabine focused on the crystal ball and tried to re-member all the tales she'd told Thelma before and come up with something different. "I see the money . . . no, wait, he's taking the money into a jewelry store. He's exchanging it for diamonds . . . a bag of uncut di-amonds."

Thelma sucked in a breath, the prospect of hunting for diamonds obviously even more exciting than a box of dirty money. "When did he do that?"

Sabine shook her head. "I can't tell for sure, but he placed the diamonds in a red shoe box and put it in the attic." She squinted at the ball. "The image is fading." She held her hands over the ball another couple of sec-onds, then looked up at Thelma. "It's gone."

Thelma stared at her, her brow wrinkled in concen-tration. "The attic, huh? Was it the attic in our house?"

"I couldn't tell for sure, and remember, Thelma, there's no way of knowing if the diamonds are still there. Earl could have moved the diamonds or even sold them sometime after the vision I saw. But my guess is he hid them where he had easy access, so that would limit it to your house." God forbid Thelma got arrested for breaking into every house in Mudbug, Louisiana, and digging through their attics.

"What a load of bullshit!" The voice came from out of nowhere, and Sabine felt her spine stiffen. She stared at Thelma, but the blue-haired woman just stared back at her.

"Did you hear that?" Sabine asked as she glanced around her shop, Read 'em and Reap, hoping that someone was hiding behind one of the many shelves of candles, tarot cards, and other paranormal paraphernalia. But as she peered in between the shelves, she didn't see a thing.

"Hear what?" Thelma asked, glancing around the shop. "There wasn't anyone here when I came in, and no one's come in since."

Sabine nodded. That's what she'd thought, but then where had that voice come from? Her imagination was great, but it usually didn't talk out loud.

"You didn't leave the back door open, did you?" Thelma asked.

"No. In fact, it's broken. I keep calling the landlord about getting it fixed, but he says everything has to go through the owner's estate attorney, and he never hurries. Right now, I couldn't open it without a crowbar."

Thelma reached across the table and patted her hand. "You've been under a lot of stress lately, dear, what with people trying to kill Maryse and all. You probably need a vacation."

"You're probably right," Sabine agreed.

"Give it a rest." The voice sounded again and Sabine jumped up from her chair. "That asshole Earl has been teasing Thelma for years over that money."

"Who's there?" Sabine looked frantically around her shop.

Thelma stared, her eyes wide with shock. "I didn't hear anything," she whispered. "Do you think it's the spirits?"

No, Sabine didn't think it was spirits. Obviously someone was having a bit of fun with her. The voice sounded familiar but made Sabine's nose crinkle like she'd encountered something unpleasant.

"So tell me where the money is," Sabine said loudly, figuring if she played along with the charade, she'd eventually expose the trickster. "You seem to know more about it than I do."

"She doesn't need the damn money," the voice answered. "She already has more money than Bill Gates and still won't pay for a decent hairdo. Why give her more?"

Sabine sucked in a breath. She looked over at Thelma, whose eyes were wide with either fear or excitement. "Is the spirit still talking?" Thelma whispered.

"Oh, yeah," Sabine said, wondering momentarily if Thelma was going deaf. How could she not hear that? Sabine walked across the room to look between the shelves. Finding them empty, she strode to the front of the store and peered behind the counter. Empty. "They're still talking. They said you don't need the money and you have a bad hairdo."

Thelma gasped and put one hand on her puffy blue hair. "Why, that's just downright rude. I didn't think spirits were rude once they crossed over."

"You'd be surprised," Sabine muttered, thinking about Helena Henry. Her best friend, Maryse, had gotten more than a handful when her dead mother-in-law turned up as a ghost even harder to get along with than Helena had been as a living, breathing human.

"Oh, for Christ's sake," the voice boomed again. "Tell her the money is in her mattress. She's been sleeping on it for years."

Sabine sucked in a breath. No, it couldn't be. God wouldn't play that unfair. "The money's in your mattress," Sabine said as she rushed over to the table and pulled Thelma out of her chair.

"My mattress?" Thelma repeated as she allowed

herself to be hustled to the door. "No wonder Earl never wanted to get rid of that lumpy piece of crap."

Sabine nodded and opened the front door to the shop, pushing a confused but excited Thelma out the door. "I'm sorry, Thelma," Sabine said, "but something's come up that I have to take care of. I'll call you tomorrow."

Thelma shook her head. "You young people are always rushing around to something. Slow down, Sabine, all you've got in this world is time and when it's done, it's done."

Sabine slammed the door shut, locked it, and flipped the "Closed" sign around in the window. *When it's done, it's done.* Like hell. Her heart pounding, she turned slowly around and faced her empty shop.

"I know you're there, Helena," Sabine said, then felt a wave of nausea sweep over her at her own words.

"Well, I'll be damned! You *did* hear me," Helena said. "For a minute there, I thought you'd actually gone psychic."

Sabine's gaze swept from side to side, casing every square inch of her tiny store. "I can hear you, but I can't see you. Where are you exactly?"

"I'm standing next to your table. See?"

Sabine looked at her table but didn't see anything out of the ordinary—until her crystal ball began to rise from its stand and hover a good two feet above the table. "I see the ball, but I can't see you."

"Hmm. That's weird, right? I mean, is that supposed to happen?"

"How am I supposed to know? You're the ghost."

"Sure, sure, always trying to make me responsible for everything. Hell, all this paranormal stuff is your bag. I didn't ask to stick around after I died, and no one handed me an instruction manual when I crawled out of my coffin."

Sabine yanked her cell phone from her pocket, punched in a text message, then slipped her phone back into her pocket. She stared at the ball, still suspended in midair, not even sure what to say, what to do. Aside from drinking, nothing else really came to mind. She was saved from reaching for the bottle by a knock on the door.

Sabine hurried to unlock the door and allowed Maryse to enter. "That was fast," Sabine said. *Thank God.*

"Luc and I were having a late breakfast across the street at the café," her friend said, the worry on her face clear as day. "What's wrong? Your text message seemed a bit panicked."

Sabine pointed to the hovering ball. "I sorta have an issue here."

Maryse looked over at the table and frowned. "Helena, what in the world are you trying to do—give people heart attacks? That's not funny."

"Oh, admit it, Maryse, it's a little funny," Helena said. "You shoulda seen the look on Sabine's face."

Maryse shook her head. "I don't need to see that look. I've worn it for weeks now. Would you stop freaking people out and find something to do?" Maryse turned to Sabine. "Please tell me she did not do that in front of a customer."

Sabine shook her head, squinting at the area surrounding the hovering ball, trying to make out a body or form or outline or anything, but she saw absolutely nothing.

"I have plenty to do," Helena argued, "and I was doing some of it. I was helping that fool Thelma find Earl's money. She's been bitching about that money for forty years. Everyone down at the beauty shop is tired of hearing about it."

Maryse sighed. "And how were you planning on helping—hitting Thelma on the head with that ball? It's not like you could whisper it in her ear. No one can hear you but me."

Helena laughed and Sabine cleared her throat. "Actually, Maryse," Sabine said, "that's the issue. I *can* hear her. I just can't see her."

Maryse stared at Sabine, her jaw slightly open. "You can hear her?"

Sabine nodded. "Loud and clear, unfortunately."

"Oh my God," Maryse said and sank into a chair. "That can't possibly be good."

"Hey," Helena said, "no use being rude about it. I'm not doing anything to Sabine."

Maryse glared at the ghost. "Yeah, you weren't doing anything to me either, but not long after you appeared, people started trying to kill me."

Sabine sucked in a breath and stared at Maryse. "Oh my God! You don't think . . . I mean . . ."

Maryse cast a worried look from the hovering ball to Sabine. "There's no way of knowing for sure, and God knows, this is one of those times I wish I was a decent liar. But it's like you told me before, if it involves Helena, it couldn't possibly be good."

Sabine sank into the chair next to Maryse, her head beginning to swim. If Helena was appearing now . . . or doing a voice-over, however you wanted to look at it, Sabine knew it couldn't possibly be a coincidence. She rubbed her fingers on her temples and silently willed her head to stop throbbing.

Maryse laid her hand on Sabine's arm. "What is it? What are you not telling me?"

Sabine stared at her friend, hoping her voice wouldn't sound as shaky as she felt. "I have an appointment with Dr. Breaux in an hour to discuss my biopsy results."

Maryse reached for Sabine's hand and gave it a squeeze. Sabine closed her eyes and focused on breathing. Any moment, Dr. Breaux would walk through his office door, sit down at the desk across from them, and give her the news. After Helena's appearance at her shop, Sabine hoped she was ready for what Dr. Breaux would say.

When the abnormalities had appeared four times before, Dr. Breaux had always called her with the good news. The fact that he'd asked her to see him in person coupled with her new ability to hear Helena Henry had the acid in her stomach working overtime. If more people could see or hear the shameless specter, antacid company profits—or alcohol sales, depending on preference—would shoot through the roof.

Sabine hadn't even thought about Helena being the Angel of Death, until Maryse had pointed out the timing of Helena's appearance and Maryse's run for her life. Even though Sabine had always wanted to have a paranormal experience, if Helena Henry was the only option, she'd just pass altogether. A nice, boring job at the bank posting deposits and counting pennies would be preferable.

"It's going to be fine," Maryse said, and Sabine knew her friend was trying as hard to convince herself as she was Sabine.

"Uh huh." Sabine opened her eyes and took a deep

breath, not at all convinced. "And what about the Helena factor?"

"It's just a coincidence . . . a fluke. Luc hasn't been able to see or hear her since that night she sent him to save me."

"Really? I didn't know that."

"We didn't know it, either, until she showed up at the café this morning while we were having breakfast and Luc never noticed her, not even when I pointed her out. Probably you'll never hear her again, much less ever see her."

"And if I do?"

Maryse sighed. "I'll pray for you. I mean really pray . . . down on my knees, begging for mercy sort of praying. I'll even do it in church *and* wear a dress."

Sabine smiled. She would almost pay to see the very skeptical and comfort-loving Maryse begging God for relief, wearing a dress and heels—if it didn't require Helena Henry appearing to prompt the action.

"Let's hope it doesn't come to that," Sabine said.

Maryse was about to reply when Dr. Breaux walked into the office. He gave both of them a nod and took a seat behind his desk. "I wanted this meeting with you to discuss the results of your latest tests." He looked at Maryse, then back at Sabine. "I'm afraid the news is not good."

Sabine sucked in a breath, unable to ask the question that raced through her mind.

"I'm so sorry to tell you, Sabine . . . you have acute myeloid leukemia. Now, as far as leukemia goes, this is the best one to have. Seventy percent or more of patients go into remission after treatment, and unless the leukemia returns, they go on to have long, productive lives."

Sabine blew out the breath she'd been holding, and her eyes blurred as she was overcome with dizziness. *This can't be happening.* She leaned all the way forward, trying to breathe, as the room began to spin. She felt Maryse's hand on her back, but somehow the touch seemed surreal, as if in a dream. *It's astral projection. I don't have a paranormal ounce of blood in my veins and yet today I've heard a ghost and projected my spirit out of my body.* She dragged in a deep breath and tried to focus. *You're losing it, Sabine.*

"Sabine," Maryse's voice cut into her labored breathing. "Do you need me to get you something . . . a cup of water . . . ?"

Sabine lifted back up to a reasonable position, her head still spinning. "No, I'll be fine. At least, I think I will."

"Of course you will!" Maryse's hand tightened on hers and her friend leaned forward in her chair, an intent look on her face. "Do we know what caused this?"

Dr. Breaux shook his head. "I don't have any way of knowing for sure. It could be a result of the chemical dumping you discovered going on in the bayou, or it could be completely unrelated."

Unbelievable. Sabine wanted to scream with the injustice of it all. All her life, she'd been so careful—no coffee, no substitute sweeteners, no diet sodas, no smoking . . . all the things that might cause cancer. Aside from her occasional glass of wine, she didn't have any vices to speak of. And now there was a chance she'd contracted the horrible disease from picking flowers on the bayou.

Sabine looked over at Maryse and saw the fright on her friend's face, plain as day. Oh, she was trying to hide it, but Sabine knew better. Inside, Maryse was on the verge of a heart attack. Sabine drew in a deep breath and looked at Dr. Breaux. "And the treatment?"

Dr. Breaux sat back in his chair and sighed. "Begins with chemotherapy. If we don't achieve the desired effect, we add radiation therapy to prevent the disease from moving into the brain and central nervous system."

"That sounds harsh," Sabine said.

"You're only twenty-eight and in good health. I'm not saying the treatments will be easy, but you are in the best of possible shape to handle them."

Sabine swallowed. "And if that doesn't work?"

"A bone marrow transplant is always an option," Dr. Breaux said and gave them a pained look. "Unfortunately, the most successful match for a treatment like this is a close relative."

Sabine clutched the arms of her chair until her fingers ached. *A relative? Could this situation get any worse?* Sabine's parents had died in a car accident when she was just an infant. A distant great-aunt on her mother's side of the family had raised her, but no amount of searching, either through earthly channels or paranormal, had yielded any information at all about Sabine's father or any other relatives of Sabine's mother. She might as well be searching for the fountain of youth.

Dr. Breaux cleared his throat. "I know your great-aunt is dead, Sabine, but I looked into things, hoping to find another relative—at least on your mom's side."

Sabine shook her head. "I've already looked, Dr. Breaux. You know I've exhausted every channel."

Dr. Breaux nodded. "I know you've exhausted all of *your* available channels, but sometimes if one is, um, *creative*, one might find information by matching medical records."

Sabine stared at Dr. Breaux. "So did you find someone?"

"Yes," Dr. Breaux said. "Your aunt had a nephew."

Sabine straightened in her chair. "A nephew? How is that possible? I asked, over and over again, and she always denied having any family at all."

Dr. Breaux looked down at his desk for a moment, then back up at Sabine. "My guess is she didn't want people to know."

"Who is it?" Sabine asked, almost afraid to hear the answer.

Dr. Breaux sighed. "Harold Henry."

"Jesus H. Christ!" Maryse jumped up from her chair. "Harold Henry? Are you kidding me?"

"I'm afraid not," Dr. Breaux replied.

"I'm related to Harold Henry?" Sabine asked in dismay.

Maryse slumped back into her chair. "Not that it matters. Harold won't work. Even if he wasn't in jail *and* he agreed to do it—which would never happen— he's old and has fifty million things wrong with him. High blood pressure, heart problems, and God knows what else."

"I agree," Dr. Breaux said. "Harold wouldn't be a very good choice, even if he was a match." He hesitated for a moment, obviously not wanting to say the next thing on his mind. "But Hank might be. You're the same blood type, anyway, so that's a start."

Maryse groaned and covered her head with her hands. Harold and Helena's son, Hank Henry, her ex- and always-disappearing husband, made professional illusionists look like amateurs with his ability to vanish into thin air.

"And there's no other way?" Sabine asked, starting to feel more than a little desperate. "Can't we look for another match, outside of my family?"

"Of course we can look," Dr. Breaux said. "I've already started the process, but I don't have to tell you the odds of finding a perfect match outside of a family member or the odds of success with anything less than a perfect match. I want the best possible odds."

Sabine nodded. "I understand. So what do we need to do now?"

Dr. Breaux picked up her file. "We'll start the chemo right away. There's an opening next week if you can arrange it. If there's any chance you can locate another family member . . . just in case . . ."

Sabine sighed. "I've been searching for my family since I was old enough to read, Dr. Breaux. Unless there's a miracle, I don't see it happening now when it hasn't all these years."

Dr. Breaux gave her a sad nod. "I understand, Sabine."

"But we'll be happy to try again," Maryse said. "Hank can't hide forever, and maybe it's time to try less traditional methods." Maryse stared at Sabine, obviously trying to communicate more than her words. "Who knows, something might appear now that didn't before."

Helena! Well, it was certainly a less than traditional route, and God help them both—it was the best idea Sabine had heard in years.

Chapter Two

Raissa Bordeaux stared across the table at Maryse and Sabine, an uncertain look on her normally focused face. "So let me get this straight," Raissa began, "Maryse started seeing her dead mother-in-law weeks ago, and now you see her, Sabine?"

Sabine glanced over at Maryse, looking for permission to tell Raissa everything. Maryse nodded, and Sabine began her explanation. "No. I can only hear her. We're not sure why I can't see her, but Maryse still can." Sabine hoped her mentor—a *real* psychic—might have some answers.

Raissa's bright green eyes glowed with interest. "Okay. So both of you can hear her, and Maryse can see her, so what exactly do you need from me?"

"Does that sound normal to you?"

Raissa laughed. "Hell, no. It's probably the most bizarre thing I've ever heard."

Sabine sighed and tried to control her disappointment. "Darn. We were really hoping you would know what was going on with the audio/video display."

"This one is a first for me," Raissa said.

"Okay," Sabine replied, "then this is our next problem. You know I've been trying to locate my family."

Raissa nodded.

"Helena once created an image of my parents for me

to see. She said she looked on the 'other side' and asked for them, and they appeared. Unfortunately, she can call them and see them, but they don't answer when she talks to them." Sabine frowned at the thought of being so close, yet so far away from an answer. "We thought that if Helena could create the image again, you could draw it, and it might give us more to go on. I've never even had a photo of them, so this could be a huge breakthrough."

"You want me to draw a portrait of your parents from a dead woman's image?"

Maryse laughed. "You know, Raissa, for a psychic, you seem to be having an awful lot of trouble with this."

"I get visions, not apparitions." Raissa shook her head. "Sabine, I thought you'd finally put this behind you. Why are you starting it all up again now?"

Sabine swallowed. "I *need* to find a family member."

Raissa's face cleared in immediate understanding, then sympathy. "You have cancer, don't you?"

Sabine nodded, struggling to maintain composure.

"Oh, Sabine," Raissa said, "I am so, so sorry. How are you planning to use the drawing?"

"I don't know yet, exactly," Sabine admitted. "Show it around? Maybe run an ad in the newspaper?"

Raissa was silent for a moment, then looked at Sabine. "Several years ago, a client mentioned a private investigator here in New Orleans who specializes in missing persons. I think he's usually working on more recent cases—consulting with the police, that sort of thing. But if you'd like, I could contact him and see if he's available to help you. I remember his rate being quite reasonable."

Sabine nodded. "If you can recommend someone, that would be great. I started saving to buy a house, but this is a little more important."

"I can help, too," Maryse added. "Since I've got the grant with the medical research company in New Orleans, I don't need my own lab equipment anymore. I still have a lot of the money from my inheritance."

Raissa nodded. "If you need any more, I've got a bit stuck back myself. And let me know if you need someone to cover at your shop. I can always shift my clients around."

Sabine felt tears gather in her eyes and she sniffed. "Thank you both so much. I don't know what I'd do without you."

Raissa smiled. "That's what friends are for, right?" She looked over at Maryse. "Well, if you two think this ghost can produce the image, I'm game to try it. Hell, it would probably be the most interesting thing I've ever done. Is the ghost here now?"

Maryse rose from her chair and opened the front door of Raissa's New Orleans' shop, then motioned to someone on the sidewalk.

"What the hell were you thinking?" Sabine could hear Helena the Horrific Ghost bitching before she ever entered the shop. "Leaving me standing out on the sidewalk like some vagrant. That's not respect, I tell you."

Maryse waited for Helena to enter the shop, then closed the door behind her.

Raissa looked over at her. "What? Is she not here?"

Sabine shook her head. "Oh, no, she's here, believe me. I might not be able to see her, but I could hear her bitching from three parishes over."

Maryse nodded her head in agreement. "That's why we left her outside. Trying to have a conversation with Helena around is like trying to watch a movie with a two-year-old."

"I see how it is," Helena ranted. "You expect me to do you favors, but you want to insult me. And what the hell are we doing here anyway . . . talking to another nutbag?"

Sabine closed her eyes and sighed. "Raissa is an artist, Helena. I want you to reproduce that image of my parents so Raissa can draw it."

"Hmm. A new approach to your lifetime of futility. Why don't you let this go, Sabine?"

"I have my reasons, Helena." Sabine and Maryse had already agreed that the less Helena knew, the better. The ghost would be certain to want to "help." And Helena's help was something they were hoping to do without, except on a very selective and clearly instructed basis. "Can you produce the image or not?"

"Of course I can produce it. Tell the nutbag to break out her charcoal."

Sabine looked over at Raissa and nodded. "She's ready whenever you are."

Raissa pulled a drawing pad and pencil from a table behind her and flipped to a blank sheet. "Ready."

"Go ahead, Helena," Sabine instructed.

There were several seconds of dead silence, and for a moment, Sabine was afraid that Helena wasn't going to be able to pull it off. Then a small orb of light began to glow just to the side of the table. Raissa gave a small start when the orb appeared and watched in fascination as it grew in size and detail, ultimately depicting a man and woman standing in the center of the light.

Raissa stared at the image, her eyes wide, then finally asked, "How long can she hold that?"

"We're not sure," Sabine said.

Raissa laughed, her expression still mingled with excitement and disbelief. "Then I best get to drawing."

Raïssa closed the door to her shop a little early that evening. She didn't have any late appointments scheduled, and walk-ins would just have to wait until the next day. Maryse and Sabine had left, happy as clams, a couple of hours before with a fistful of photocopies of Raissa's drawing. The original and a couple of spare copies, Raissa had locked away in her filing cabinet for safekeeping. Her door secure, Raissa closed the blinds, emptied the cash and receipts from the register, and carried it upstairs with her to her studio apartment above the store.

The apartment was cool in contrast to the store, where the door admitted summer heat and humidity along with the customers. She shrugged off her black robe, a necessity for her customers even though what she wore made no difference as to how she did her job, and pulled on shorts and a T-shirt. There was a nice chilled bottle of Pinot Grigio in her refrigerator and she was tempted to pour herself a glass, or two, and pile up on the couch with a good book, but she knew her mind was whirling too much to relax even if she drank the whole bottle.

She settled for a bottled water and sat at her tiny kitchen table. God knows she'd seen things that any twenty people would never run across in their lifetimes . . . and that was a good thing. But nothing had prepared her for what she'd witnessed today. She'd drawn a sketch of two dead people from a hologram created by a ghost. That and a plane ticket would get her a spot on Jerry Springer.

Or an even smaller apartment with padded walls.

She reached across the tiny table for her laptop and connected to the internet. There was something about the man in that drawing that looked familiar, but for the life of her, she couldn't figure out what.

She did a quick search for private detectives around the area. She clicked on the first link and studied the list of names and numbers. Atwater, Baker, Cooke . . . none of them was right. Deacon, Farris, Howard, Lawther . . . no, further down. Villeneuve—that was it. Raissa reached for the cordless phone on the cabinet behind her and dialed the number on the listing. The detective answered on the first ring.

"Villeneuve," he said, his voice strong and crisp.

"Hello, Mr. Villeneuve. My name is Raissa Bordeaux, and I'm interested in hiring you to locate some family members."

"Are the family members missing, Ms. Bordeaux, or are you performing a historical search?"

"More of a historical search, I suppose, but my goal is to find living relatives."

"What do you have to go on?"

Raissa sighed. "Not much, I have to admit. A couple of surnames and a drawing of two family members."

"I assume this is your family?"

"Actually, no. It's a friend of mine who's looking. I'd love to help her, but I simply don't have the knowledge or connections to research something like this. I understand you're an expert at this sort of thing, and I think you being from the area is an advantage. I've already exhausted all the resources I have."

"And what sort of resources would those be, Ms. Bordeaux?"

"I'm a psychic. I talked to dead people."

Beau Villeneuve walked into a café in Mudbug, Louisiana wondering why he'd ever agreed to this job. He didn't need the money and never would thanks to a reclusive grandfather who hoarded every penny he'd ever made.

So the job was never about the money, which allowed him to be selective . . . pick only the cases that interested him. The harder the better. And that was the crux of it, really. Boredom. Some days he wished he'd never left the FBI, but that was another thought for another day. Maybe another year.

And there weren't too many cases more challenging than missing-family searches. He had yet to take on one that turned out well. When people disappeared without a trace, there was usually a reason, and it was rarely a pleasant one. Plus, people who had gotten away with disappearing for ten, twenty, thirty years were never happy to be "found." He'd discovered that first-hand.

Still, Beau had recognized the determination in Raissa Bordeaux's voice. If he didn't take the job, she'd just move on to the next detective who would. A detective who most likely wouldn't have the experience and skill at working these family situations. A detective who most likely would open a rash of shit for the searcher and have no idea how to deal with it. And Beau just didn't want that to happen. Raissa seemed genuinely concerned for her friend and really wanted to help.

He grabbed a local newspaper from the rack next to

the door and took a seat at a table in the corner of the café with a clear view of the door. Raissa had laid out the case the night before at a local pub. He wasn't sure what he'd expected when he'd met with the psychic, but she hadn't looked or talked like a nut. In fact, he'd admired the way she'd presented the facts, minimal as they were, in such logical order. The only question she wouldn't give him a straight answer to was where she got the image for the drawing.

She'd claimed she'd had a vision, but Beau wasn't buying it. Regardless of any so-called psychic ability, she was one hell of an artist. The drawing was highly detailed and ought to give him something to work from. He'd studied it for over an hour the night before, thinking about the job. Thinking about the people depicted. Like Raissa, he had the nagging feeling in the back of his mind that he'd seen the man somewhere, but knew that was probably unlikely as the man in the photo had died more than twenty years before.

Assuming Raissa had her facts—and her visions—straight.

He was two cups of coffee down and halfway into a story about an alleged UFO sighting when the door to the café opened and a young woman walked in. Raissa's description hadn't done the woman justice.

Certainly she was tall and thin with long black hair, but Raissa hadn't mentioned the perfect skin with a beautiful tanned glow, or the grace with which she walked, almost like watching a dancer. *Get a grip, Beau. Women are not part of the equation. Not then, not now, not ever. You don't need the money. You should turn down the job.*

Against his better judgment, he raised a hand as she

scanned the café. The vision nodded and headed toward his table. Beau felt his heart rate increase with every one of her choreographed steps. *Maybe she isn't near as impressive up close. Maybe she has buck teeth and a speech impediment.* But when she reached the table, she gave him a shy smile, her pale blue eyes not quite meeting his own.

"I'm Sabine LeVeche," she said, the words rolling off her tongue like music.

And that's when Beau knew he was in serious trouble.

Sabine slid into the booth across from the detective, her heart racing because of the task at hand and the appearance of the man who was going to perform it. He was so young, so rugged, so manly. Sabine had no idea what she'd been expecting, maybe some gray-haired man wearing a Sherlock Holmes hat . . . but that was ridiculous. Still, she'd only worked with a private detective once before and the chain-smoking, mid-fifties burnout hadn't even remotely resembled the gorgeous man across from her.

She took a deep breath, hoping to slow her racing pulse, and pushed a folder across the table, praying that her hands didn't shake. "Mr. Villeneuve, I know Raissa gave you some information about my family, but this is everything I have. Twenty years of research."

He reached for the folder and flipped through the sparse set of papers Sabine had given him. "Not a lot to show for twenty years." He looked over at her. "That must be very disappointing."

"You have no idea."

Beau studied her for a moment, a contemplative expression on his face. Then his expression shifted back to business mode, and whatever it was that Sabine had thought he was going to say was apparently pushed back. "So tell me what you *do* know," he said. "I like to hear the story firsthand if I can. It gives me a better feel for the situation and sometimes opens up avenues of investigation that might not have been explored."

Sabine laughed. "If you can find an avenue I haven't explored, then you're the best detective in the world, Mr. Villeneuve."

"Call me Beau."

"Okay, Beau. I guess I'll start at the beginning, what I was told of it anyway. I was only six months old when my parents had a fatal car accident."

"You weren't in the car?" Beau asked.

"I was in the car. Some folks around here called it a miracle, and I suppose it was, but apparently they were riding with the windows down and I was thrown clean when the car rolled. The fireman who worked the scene probably wouldn't have found me at all, except they'd brought their dog with them. He set up a howl, and they found me perched in a clump of marsh weeds, not a scratch on me."

"Wow! That's incredible."

Sabine nodded. "The police did a search to locate the closest relative, trying to find someone to care for me until the state could decide what to do. They came up blank on my father. His name didn't appear in records anywhere except for a driver's license that had been issued a little over six months before. They finally got lucky with my mother and came up with my great-aunt in Mudbug."

"And she took you in?"

"Yes. Aunt Margaret was a nurse. She never married and, to hear the talk, never even dated much. All I know is she took me in. Gave me a home, food, clothes . . . took care of me."

Beau nodded. "And your mother? What did your aunt have to say about her?"

Sabine frowned. "Not much. She didn't really know my mother or her parents that well. Apparently they were from the dirt-poor branch of the family that lived deep in the bayou—in huts, really. All Aunt Meg knew was that my mother's parents had died young, probably when she was a teenager, and she didn't know of any other children at all."

"Was there any other family?"

"Not that Aunt Meg was aware of." Sabine frowned, recalling her recent conversation in Dr. Breaux's office.

"What's wrong?"

"Well, my whole life Aunt Meg always said she had no other living relatives, but I just found out this week that was a lie."

Beau leaned forward and stared at her. "Why would she lie?"

Sabine shrugged. "Since my aunt passed away years ago, I can only guess it's because the relative she failed to mention was her nephew, a loser of monumental proportions. Harold is in jail right now for an assortment of charges, attempted murder being two of them, and who knows what else the cops will find now that they're looking."

"Then it's just as well you weren't obligated to exchange Christmas cards or anything."

Sabine smiled.

"I need to tell you up front that I journal all my cases from start to finish, but I promise any documentation I acquire or create will always remain confidential. Writing things down helps me reach logical conclusions, and I tend to remember things more easily if I write them longhand."

"Do most detectives work like that?" Sabine asked.

"I can't speak for other detectives, really. I started keeping journals when I was a kid. The habit just stuck, I guess." He looked down at the table and fiddled with a packet of sugar.

Sabine, sensing he was somewhat embarrassed, continued. "Well, that's basically it in a nutshell." She reached for the gold heart-shaped locket that was always around her neck. "This locket belonged to my mother. That information in that folder and this piece of jewelry are all I really know about them."

Beau looked back up at her. "And a drawing from beyond."

Sabine nodded. "Raissa's very talented. I'm fortunate to know her."

Beau narrowed his eyes at her. "Do you really buy into all that psychic stuff?"

Sabine laughed. "She didn't tell you?"

"Tell me what?"

"Raissa's my mentor. I own the psychic shop across the street."

Beau hopped into his vehicle and stared at Sabine as she unlocked the front door of her shop. Read 'em and Reap. Good God Almighty! He'd stepped into the middle of a nut parade. And the worst part was, against his own better judgment, he'd picked up a banner and agreed to march. No doubt about it—he was going to make a colossal fool of himself over a beautiful woman who walked like a ballet dancer. Maybe he needed to reconsider his vow of bachelorhood and settle down with a nice accountant or something. Women like Sabine LeVeche could only get him into trouble.

Sabine turned before entering the shop and gave him a wave and a smile. Beau waved back and started his truck, hoping the drive back to the city would clear his head and help him make sense of the mess he'd just gotten himself into. Not one psychic but two. And he had actually agreed to embark on a search for dead people with his biggest lead supposedly coming from the dead people themselves. For a man who was more than a skeptic, it was an irony he wasn't quite ready to fathom.

As he drove out of town and onto the highway to New Orleans, he pulled Raissa's drawing out of the envelope and took another look. He knew he'd seen that face somewhere before, but not exactly that face and not in person. For the life of him, that's all he could remember. Given the sheer number of photos he'd viewed when he was an FBI agent, God only knew when he'd seen a picture that resembled the man in the drawing. Hell, there was nothing to say he'd even seen it while working at the FBI. Raissa had claimed she thought the man looked familiar, too, so for all he knew it could have been a likeness in a local newspaper.

But for some reason, that didn't feel right.

He took another glance at the drawing and frowned. Somewhere buried in the depths of his mind was the answer. He slipped the drawing back into the folder and concentrated on the road ahead of him. As soon as he got back to his apartment, he would pull out his journals from his FBI years. Maybe something in them would spark his memory. Beyond the basics of background searching, the drawing was his best lead for now.

Unless, of course, Raissa or Sabine could call up more spirits to give them an address.

Sabine opened the tiny window in the corner of the attic of her store's building and stuck her head out, hoping for a breeze. She coughed once, wheezed a couple more times, then pulled her head back inside and stared at Maryse, who was already tugging on boxes tucked in the far corners of the room.

"I can't believe you haven't looked at any of this stuff since last time," Maryse said.

"Please, you act like my aunt stored the secrets of the world in those boxes. We've been through this before and didn't find a thing."

"We were eighteen. What might be important now is something we might not have noticed or understood then."

Sabine sneezed and tugged another box from its hiding spot. "I guess so. But if all I end up with is a cold, you're making me soup every day."

Maryse waved a hand in dismissal. "You live across the street from every restaurant in town and they all deliver. Besides, I burned the toast this morning. Luc won't even let me use the microwave."

Sabine laughed. "Smart man." Her scientific-minded friend gave a whole new meaning to the term "nondomestic."

"I don't have to take this abuse from both of you.

And if I find an anti-aging formula in here or a *Farmer's Almanac* for 2015, or something equally as cool, I'm not letting you in on it."

"Who the hell reads the *Farmer's Almanac*?" Helena's voice boomed from the doorway.

"Farmers," Sabine shot back. "What do you want, Helena?"

"I saw the 'Closed' sign for the shop and thought I'd come see what you were up to."

"We're cleaning out the attic," Sabine said.

"Hmmmpf," Helena grunted. "Looks like this shit's been here for a hundred years. You're not much of a housekeeper, are you, Sabine?"

Sabine stared at the empty doorway. "I guess your attic was spotless?"

"Of course. I paid people to clean it twice a year."

"Never mind." Sabine rolled her eyes, and Maryse grinned. Sabine turned around and opened a box of ancient clothes. She pulled out the first couple of garments, then waved one in the air. "Hey, Maryse, you think one of the playhouses in New Orleans would be interested in these?"

Maryse looked up from an old steamer trunk that she was struggling to pull into the middle of the room. "Cool! I think they'd be thrilled."

"Some of this material is fantastic, and so well-preserved. I might keep a couple myself and make something of them."

Maryse nodded. "If anyone can make it wearable, you can. That pink would look good on you." She pointed to a pretty calico dress.

Sabine held up the dress and studied the color. "I don't know. This is the same color as that T-shirt I wore to that breast cancer walk in New Orleans last month. A picture of me, Mildred, and a couple others ended up in the newspaper and the shirt made me look all washed out."

"None of you look good in the newspaper," Helena said. "Look at that shot of Maryse the local paper had. Maryse looked like the running year of bad weather."

"Well," Maryse said, "the next time a ghost wakes you up in the dead of night because a man is crawling through your bedroom window to kill you, *and* you have to run down the street in your pajamas *and* bare feet, *and* you just miss dying by a half a second, *then* you can tell me how bad I look."

"She's got a point." Sabine glanced over at the doorway, an idea forming in her mind. "Helena, are you planning on sticking around for a while?"

"Yeah, although the beauty shop is a hell of a lot more interesting than the two of you. Now, if Maryse would let me in her house when Luc was there . . . that would probably be something to see."

"Not on your life," Maryse said and glanced over at Sabine, who was holding up a large lime green dress with ruffles from top to bottom. "What's with the gigantic ruffle thing?"

Sabine grinned. "I was thinking that Helena ought to wear it. Then I could see her. Or her clothes anyway."

"Oh no," Helena said. "I'll wear a hat or something or a wristband, or even one of those cone bras like Madonna wore in that video, but I'm not wearing that monstrosity. No one over the age of four should ever wear ruffles, especially across their butt. And green? Jesus, I'd look like moving shrubbery."

"I hate to admit it," Maryse said and laughed, "but she's right."

"Probably so," Sabine agreed, "but I'd still like to see it."

"No way," Helena said.

"You know," Sabine said, "I could still work in that exorcism Maryse and I discussed before. You wouldn't want me to sic the power of God on you, would you, Helena?" Sabine knew an exorcism wouldn't do a thing to the ghost, but Helena still wasn't sure.

"Fine," Helena huffed. "Throw that damned thing toward the door."

Sabine tossed the ruffled nightmare toward the doorway and grinned at Maryse as Helena grunted and complained while tugging.

"Are you happy now?" Helena asked.

Sabine took one look at the doorway, now totally eclipsed in a sea of jiggling green, and howled in laughter.

Maryse shook her head. "That is just wrong."

Sabine wiped at her eyes, tears of laughter blurring her vision. "You ought to see it without Helena in it. Oh my God, that is just the funniest thing I have seen in forever."

"That's it," Helena said. "I'm taking this thing off."

And that's when the sound of glass breaking downstairs made them all freeze.

Chapter Three

Sabine froze, straining to hear any further noise from downstairs. She eased up beside Maryse, who was standing stock-still, her eyes as wide as an owl's.

"What the hell," Maryse whispered. "I thought the shop was locked."

"It is," Sabine said. "Do you have your cell phone? Mine's downstairs."

Maryse shook her head, her eyes wide. "I forgot it at home. Shit."

"Oh hell," Helena said. "I'll go check it out. Not like anything can happen to me." And with that, the green blob floated out the door and down the narrow attic staircase. Sabine peered after her, still not taking a breath.

There was dead silence for several seconds, but it felt like an eternity. Great. Just when Helena flapping her jaws would have been appreciated, she had to go silent. Sabine couldn't take just standing there for another moment. She looked over at Maryse, who nodded. As quietly as possible, they began to creep down the stairs but didn't make it two steps before the ancient staircase creaked, the noise seemingly amplified in the dead silence of the building.

They stopped short, but it was too late. A crash came from the storage room at the back of the shop and then a terrifying scream. Sabine rushed down the remainder of the stairs and rounded the corner in her upstairs apartment, grabbing a butcher knife from the kitchen counter as she took the next set of stairs down into the shop. She skidded to a stop at the back door, and Maryse stumbled into her from behind, sending them both sprawling.

Sabine hit the wood floor hands and knees first and felt a piercing pain in her palms. She jumped back up, looked at her hands, and saw tiny shards of glass embedded in her skin. Someone had broken the window in the door. Helena was nowhere in sight. Neither was the screaming intruder.

"It's ten o'clock in the morning," Maryse said, staring at the door. "It's broad daylight, Sabine. I mean, I know this is the back of the building, but what kind of person would risk trying to break in right now?"

"I was just wondering the same thing." Sabine peered out the broken window and looked up and down the alley. "And where in the world is Helena?"

Maryse's eyes widened. "At this point, God only knows." Maryse reached over to open the door, but it didn't budge. "The landlord still hasn't fixed this?"

"No. And I guess it's a good thing. That's why they couldn't get inside." Sabine looked over at Maryse, who stared at the door, a worried look on her face. "What's that look?"

Maryse sighed. "I was just wondering how much of this has to do with you hearing Helena, like she's some bad-luck curse or something."

"She can't control the universe, Maryse. I know her appearance or rising or whatever it was brought you nothing but trouble, but that's no reason to think she's responsible for this."

Maryse didn't look convinced. "Maybe not, but in all the time you've lived here you've never had a problem."

Sabine nodded. "Yeah. I guess I need to call the police, right?"

"It won't do any good, given the caliber of our law enforcement, but you should still get something on record." Maryse glanced around the room at the broken glass. "I guess I can't clean up the glass until after the police taken a look, but I'll move those boxes of inventory over in case it starts to rain. Once the cops are done, we can figure out something to do about the window until your useless landlord bothers to fix it."

Maryse had just shifted the first box away from the door when a huge shaking mass of green fabric burst through the wall. Sabine jumped back in surprise, then realized what she was seeing. "Helena, you scared the crap out of me!"

"Sorry." The ruffled horror slumped onto a box against the wall, and the cardboard sagged under her weight. "Can't breathe."

Sabine stared at the wheezing pile of green. "You're dead, Helena. Why do you need to breathe?"

"You know," Helena said between pants, "I'm well aware of that without you and Maryse constantly reminding me. And don't ask me why I need to breathe. You're the one who's into all this paranormal crap. You tell me."

Sabine sighed. "Did you see anything?"

"Of course I saw something. You think I went running down the alley in this dress for nothing?" Helena coughed, then wheezed out more air, sounding like a leaky air compressor. "There was someone out back. They broke the window in the door."

"Who was it?"

"I don't know," Helena said. "Whoever it was wore a turtleneck, a ball cap pulled down real low, and black sunglasses."

"A turtleneck?" Maryse asked. "In Mudbug in the summer?"

"I'm just telling you what I saw," Helena said. "He was a little taller than you, Sabine, and moved fast. I couldn't even come close to catching him."

Which meant absolutely nothing, as two-year-olds and eighty-year-old invalids were also known to move faster than Helena. "Was that you who screamed?" Sabine asked.

"No. It was him, but I have no idea why. I ran downstairs and when I saw the arm reaching in through the broken window, I hauled ass through the wall to get a better look. Then he screamed and took off running. Must have cut his hand or something."

Sabine looked over at Maryse, her lips already quivering. One look at her friend, collapsed against a storeroom shelf, and Sabine lost it. Laughter resounded in the storeroom and Sabine clutched her side. "Don't you see . . . oh my God . . . now *I* can't breathe . . . the dress, Helena . . . you ran through the wall wearing the dress."

"It's like one of those B horror movies," Maryse said. *"Revenge of the Bridesmaid's Dress."*

There was dead silence for a couple of seconds, and then Helena started to laugh. "I didn't even think about it. I'd completely forgotten about the dress, even though the damned thing was impossible to run in. What a sight that must have been."

"I would have definitely screamed," Maryse said.

"Me too," Sabine agreed. "So how far did you chase the man? Did you see a car or anything that I could tell the police?"

"He ran to the far end of the street and into the park. When I got to the end of the trail, he was already gone. I saw a white pickup truck hauling ass out of the park. That must have been him. But he was too far away for me to see a plate or anything."

"Well, then I guess I better call the cops and tell them I chased an intruder into the park."

"Sure," Maryse said, "and the first thing you can explain is just how you chased an intruder through a door that's been wedged in place since the Civil War."

"Crap," Sabine said.

Maryse nodded. "Been there, done that crap."

"Hey," Helena interrupted, "while you two dream up some bullshit story for the cops, why don't one of you help me out of this damned dress? I think it's stuck."

Sabine reached over with one hand, grabbed the dress, and pulled, but the dress didn't budge.

"I swear when this is off of me," Helena griped, "I am going back to my MTV eras of fashion."

Sabine took a firm hold on the dress, right at the zipper, and yanked as hard as she could, ripping the dress in two. "As long as your fashion quest doesn't include this dress, I think we'll be okay. I don't think I ever want to see this again." She tossed the dress in a box of rags next to the back door, and the light in the room dimmed. She took another look at the broken window. "Oh, no. Here comes the rain, and we left the window open upstairs."

"You go get the window," Maryse said. "I'll get the rest of the boxes out of the line of fire."

Sabine hurried up the stairs and into the already darkening attic. She felt the wall for the light switch, certain they'd left the light on when they'd gone after Helena. She found the switch and flipped it up and down. Nothing. Great. "Maryse," she yelled down the stairwell. "Can you bring me the flashlight from the storeroom, please?"

"No problem. Be there in a minute," Maryse yelled back.

Sabine inched into the room and started shuffling toward the tiny stream of light coming in the open window. She'd made it halfway across the room when lightning flashed across the sky and through the open window, striking a metal rack against the wall. Sparks flew from the rack as the sound of thunder exploded around her. Sabine lurched backward and tumbled over something big. The large object rolled with her and they both crashed to the floor, Sabine's head banging against the hardwood planks.

Sabine had no idea how long she'd been out when she felt heat on her face. Opening one watery eye just a bit, she saw a single beam of light that seemed to stretch out infinitely in front of her. *Oh my God. I'm dead.* She clenched her eyes, squeezing the tears out, then opened the lids again.

And saw Helena Henry leaning over her, encased in the beam of light.

"I *am* dead!" Sabine cried.

"Oh, give it a rest," Helena said. "You're just as alive and strange as you were ten minutes ago."

Sabine struggled to rise from the floor and felt a hand on her arm.

"Don't move yet," Maryse said. "You must have banged your head good. You were out completely."

Sabine stared into the darkness behind the beam of light. It sounded like Maryse, but that couldn't be if she was dead. Suddenly the attic light flickered on and a dim glow filled the room. Sabine blinked twice and looked up at Maryse's worried face. Relief washed over her and she laid her head back down, hoping the dizziness would pass soon.

"I thought I was dead," Sabine said. "The flashlight looked like a hallway . . . you know like those stories you hear from those people who died, then returned. And then I saw Helena. Jeez, I must have banged my head hard."

Maryse peered down at Sabine and bit her lip. "You saw Helena?"

"Yeah, but I must have imagined it, right?"

Maryse motioned behind her and a couple of seconds later, Helena Henry stood right next to Maryse, peering down at her.

"Oh, no," Sabine said. "It wasn't my imagination. I see her . . . but what the heck is she wearing?" The hair was the same, all poufy and gray, and the streetwalker makeup looked just as it had in the coffin. Unfortunately, Helena's outfit matched the makeup. The leather bodysuit, complete with cone bra, stretched in directions it wasn't intended to, straining to hold in all of Helena. It was a partial success.

Maryse grimaced. "Helena's going through an unfortunate rebellious phase in her fashion journey through the ages."

Sabine blinked again and stared at the ghost. "What year did we all dress like hookers?"

"Oh for Christ's sake!" Helena bitched. "I am *not* dressed like a hooker. Didn't you people ever watch MTV? I'm wearing a Madonna outfit."

"From the nineties, maybe, but that's questionable," Sabine said and rose to a sitting position.

"I'm working my way through the generations." Helena crossed her arms and glared.

Sabine looked over at Maryse. "Thank God I missed hair bands of the eighties."

"The seventies weren't any better." Maryse leaned in a bit and whispered, "Cher."

Sabine rubbed her temples and groaned.

Maryse placed her hand on Sabine's arm. "Do you think you can get up? We still need to call the police, and I'll bet you'd like an aspirin about now."

Sabine moved her head from side to side. "I think so. I don't feel dizzy, anyway."

Maryse offered her hand and helped pull Sabine into a standing position. She felt a rush of blood into her head and pressed at her temples. "An aspirin is sounding better and better." She looked over at Helena and blinked. The cone bra was starting to blur. She stared harder but the ghost began to slowly fade away, until nothing was left at all.

"She's gone," Sabine said.

"Who's gone?" Maryse asked. "Helena's standing right here."

Sabine clenched her eyes shut for a moment, then looked again. Nothing. "I can't see her anymore. What does that mean?"

Maryse slowly shook her head. "I don't know, but I don't like it. Let's get out of here."

Sabine stepped forward and looked down at the trunk that had caused her fall. It was flipped over backward, the contents spilled out onto the floor. "Guess that was one way to get that thing opened."

"Yeah," Maryse agreed, "but not exactly what I was shooting for. Don't worry about the mess. I'll pick it up later."

Sabine started to move, but then something within the scattered hats and ancient purses caught her eye. She leaned over a bit, straining to focus in the dim light.

"What is it?" Maryse asked.

"There's something in the bottom of the trunk." Sabine knelt and reached inside the trunk for the object. It felt like paper wedged into the bottom of the trunk. Sabine gently worked the paper from side to side, careful not to tear it. Finally, it came loose and she pulled it out.

Maryse leaned over to see. "It's a diary page. See the date at the top? She's talking about the crop prices dropping."

"A diary? My aunt didn't keep a diary."

"That you know of," Helena pointed out. "It's a generational thing. Lots of women kept diaries during the Vietnam conflict. All the men going off and us left here to manage. Some took comfort in writing it all down."

"Did you keep a diary?" Sabine asked.

"Hell, no," Helena said. "Put all your feelings down on paper just so someone can get a hold of it later and pass judgment? I don't think so. I was damned happy when Harold went off to serve . . . not so happy that he came back. How would that look to people if I'd written all that down?"

"If they knew Harold, it would look really smart," Sabine pointed out.

Maryse leaned over and peered into the trunk. "Is

there more? I mean there can't be only one sheet. And how did it get wedged in the bottom? I thought it was solid."

"Good question," Sabine said. She stuck her hand into the trunk and slid one long fingernail into a gap between the bottom and the side. "There's a false bottom. It must have come loose when I fell. Let me see if I can work it out." She stuck another fingernail in the gap and gently pulled on the bottom. It held firm for a moment, then broke loose from the sides of the trunk. A stack of journals fell out on top of it.

"Holy crap!" Maryse said.

Sabine stared at the books. "I can't believe it. All those years and I never knew she kept a diary. But why would she hide them like this? Why not tell me before she died?"

Maryse shook her head. "I don't know. But I think we ought to take them all downstairs and find out." She picked up one of the journals and flipped through the hundreds of pages of handwritten text. "It may be, Sabine, that your aunt knew more about your family than she admitted."

Sabine nodded and started to gather up the journals. She'd already had the same thought. It was the next thought that worried her. If her aunt knew something about Sabine's family, why had she hidden it from her all these years?

Late that night, Sabine grabbed a bottled water and two more aspirin from the kitchen, then crawled into bed with the book she'd been trying to finish for two weeks. It had been a long and exhausting day, what with the break-in, the absolutely useless time spent with the local police, and then the trip to the hospital that Maryse had insisted on to check out her head. She'd tried to nap that afternoon with limited success and had instead spent a good portion of the time scanning through some of her aunt's journals. Unfortunately, she hadn't found anything of relevance, but the logical, systematic way her aunt had documented such a volatile time in history made Sabine think that had her aunt been born in a different era, she would have made a great scientist, or maybe even a detective.

She propped herself up with a stack of fluffy pillows and snuggled into the pale pink sheets and comforter, figuring she had twenty minutes tops before sleep caught up with her. She opened the book and started at the marked spot. The hero had just saved the heroine from a killer and his arms were still wrapped around her. A fleeting image of Beau Villeneuve clutching Sabine and moving in for a kiss flashed through her mind. Where the hell had that come from? She lifted her water and took a sip. Like she needed a roadmap to answer that question. Beau Villeneuve was quite frankly the best-looking man she'd come into contact with in . . . well . . . forever.

And she couldn't have met him at a worse time.

Sabine was pretty sure he didn't buy into the psychic connection, but she might have still made a run at him had her situation been less complicated. She set her book on the nightstand and sighed. *Who are you kidding? You've never made a slow stroll at a man, much less a run.* Twenty-eight years in Mudbug, Louisiana, and she'd spent most of her time trying to talk to dead people instead of the living. And then when she finally got the opportunity to talk to the dead, she was saddled with Helena Henry. Not exactly what she'd had in mind.

Beau Villeneuve was just another piece to the puzzle that wasn't going to ever form a clear picture. Sitting across from him in the café, she'd felt a tug that she'd never felt before . . . a desire to know this man, inside and out. But with her life hanging in the balance, the last thing Sabine was going to do was complicate an already impossible situation by developing feelings for a man she might not be around to see grow old. It wasn't fair . . . not to her and especially not to him. She turned off the lamp and lay down, hoping she dreamed about anything besides death, ghosts, family, and the good-looking man who would never know she was interested.

It felt like she'd barely fallen asleep when Sabine bolted upright in her bed, her pulse racing. There was noise downstairs in her shop. She glanced at the alarm clock and saw it was just after midnight. Much, much too late for anyone to need anything legitimate. And with the attempted break-in that morning, she wasn't about to take any chances. She eased out of bed and pulled open her nightstand drawer. Within easy reach and already loaded rested the nine millimeter she'd purchased years before.

Mudbug might be a small town, but Sabine was a single woman living alone. Residents of Mudbug may call her crazy, but no one was going to call her stupid. She lifted the pistol from the drawer and crept out of the bedroom. The stairwell door creaked just a bit as she eased it open, and she froze. The only sound she could hear was the ticking of the old clock in her living room.

Then she heard rustling downstairs and knew whoever it was hadn't fled. Which wasn't good. When faced with the possibility of a homeowner in a small town in Louisiana, most thieves would flee—unless they were on drugs. But then, most thieves didn't try to break into buildings in broad daylight, either, even if it was the back door.

Unless theft wasn't their primary objective.

Clutching the pistol, she crept down the stairs, hoping they didn't creak under her weight. She reached the bottom without incident and peered around the corner into the shop. A silhouette stood silently by the cash register. She squinted in the dark, trying to make out the figure, and as her vision shifted just a bit, she realized the person wasn't trying to break into the register, as she'd originally thought, but was instead writing something on the pad of paper she usually kept under the counter.

Now or never. Please God, don't let him have a gun, too.

She took a deep breath and tightened her grip on the pistol. Her heart pounded in her chest, making the silence seem ever more sinister, more empty. With a silent prayer, she flipped on the shop lights and stepped around the corner, her gun aimed directly at the figure. It took a moment for her to focus and realize that the man standing at her counter was someone she knew.

"Jesus, Hank! You scared the shit out of me. What in the world are you doing in my shop in the middle of the night? For that matter, what are you doing in Mudbug at all?"

Hank Henry, disappearing husband extraordinaire, remained frozen in surprise and fright, his hands in the air. Finally, he found his voice. "You're not going to shoot me, are you?"

"No . . . well, probably not." Sabine looked closely at him, trying to figure out what he was up to, but all she saw was the good-looking guy Maryse had been unfortunate enough to fall for and marry.

He stared a moment more, then apparently deciding she probably wouldn't shoot him, he lowered his hands and sucked in a breath. "Jesus yourself, Sabine. I already got shot once in the last month. I'd really like to avoid it again if I could."

Sabine tried to hold in a smile but only partially managed to. Hank, in an unusual fit of heroism, had taken a bullet that wasn't meant for him. It had definitely improved his rating with Maryse and Sabine, but Hank was far from out of the woods. There was still that two-year disappearance, and Sabine wasn't yet ready to forgive Hank completely for all the trouble he'd brought to her friend . . . bullet or no.

"Well, if you stop putting yourself in situations to get shot, you might have a better chance at keeping your innards intact," Sabine said. "You darn near bought it."

Hank swallowed. "Yeah, I can see that. Damn, Sabine, what are you doing with a nine? That's a helluva gun for a chick."

"I'm a helluva chick, Hank. You still haven't answered my question—what are you doing in my shop and how did you get in?"

"I still have a key from back when I was with Maryse." He pulled it from his pocket and slid it across the table to Sabine, a sheepish look on his face. "I need to talk to you, but couldn't risk being caught by the Mudbug cops. I haven't exactly got all my past transgressions worked out. Although, the way things look now, I would probably have been safer with ole Leroy."

Sabine had to laugh. Deputy Leroy Theriot was more likely to shoot himself in the foot than actually apprehend a criminal. "You ever thought of using a phone?"

"Yeah, but this was sorta important and I felt kinda funny doing it over the phone. Please, Sabine, I need to use your restroom first, but then I really need to talk to you."

Sabine sighed. "Restroom's on the far right wall. The break room is through the door behind the counter. Meet me in there when you're done. I'll make some tea."

Hank relaxed a little and headed off. Sabine stepped into the break room and pulled a box of decaffeinated tea from the cabinet. It was far too early for coffee and if she could hear whatever Hank had to say and get rid of him soon, there was still a chance of sleeping again. She nuked two cups of water in the microwave and dipped the tea bags in them until the water turned a deep, rich brown. Sabine took in the sweet smell of cinnamon and spice and smiled.

She had just set the cups and sugar on a tiny table when Hank entered the room. She motioned to the other chair and he took a seat, reaching for the cup of tea and the sugar spoon almost immediately.

"Thanks for the tea, Sabine. And I'm really sorry I scared you. That's not what I was trying to do. I thought I'd make it here before you went to bed, but I got held up. So then I thought I'd just leave you a note and hide out somewhere around town until you woke up and could meet me."

"And what is so important that you risked the Mudbug police department and a nine millimeter bullet?"

Hank looked down at his cup. "I heard about the cancer."

Sabine froze. "How? No one is supposed to know."

"I was in that attorney's office, Wheeler, when Maryse called trying to hunt me down."

Sabine stared at Hank. "Maryse told you about my cancer?"

Hank looked stricken. "Oh, crap, you didn't know. She probably didn't want to get your hopes up in case she couldn't find me or something. Shit. I can't seem to do anything without causing trouble." He sighed. "Maryse didn't tell me. She told Wheeler to explain why she needed to find me. I guess he thought I wouldn't do the right thing if I didn't have all the facts."

Sabine rolled this over in her mind, trying to bunch all the facts together into something that made sense, and all at an hour she should have been curled up in her bed not thinking at all. "So Wheeler told you everything, and then you came here. Why, exactly?"

Hank grinned. "Well, *cousin*, I thought if we were a match, I would give you some bone marrow."

Sabine sat back in her chair, stunned. She stared at Hank Henry, the most selfish, most irresponsible person in the world, and tried to come up with any reason whatsoever for this charade. Hank just stared back, the grin still in place, his expression completely sincere. Well, that tore it all.

She felt the tears well up in her eyes and reached

for a napkin. "I can't believe you'd do that for me, Hank."

Hank looked a bit embarrassed. "Oh, hell, it's nothing but a test for now. We don't even know if I'm a match or if you'll ever need me. You're a really good person, Sabine. You've always looked after Maryse, and I know neither of you believe me, but I *do* care about her."

Sabine sniffed. "Just not enough to be her husband."

Hank sighed. "I'm not in any shape to be anyone's husband. I've got too many issues, Sabine. All I could do is bring her down. And the reality is, I care about Maryse a lot, but I don't love her like that DEQ agent does."

"How do you know about Luc?"

"I've seen them together out on the bayou, but they didn't see me." Hank smiled. "They look good together, Sabine. Right. Like two pieces that fit perfectly together. And after everything I put her through, I'm really glad she's happy."

Sabine sniffed again. "Me, too."

"So . . . I wanted to let you know that I saw a doctor in New Orleans this morning to do the tests. Wheeler called in a favor, so it's all sorta anonymous . . . you know, given my situation. The doctor will send Wheeler the results and he will contact you. If that's all right, that is."

Sabine smiled. "That's fine, Hank."

Hank rose from his chair. "Then I guess I best be clearing out of here before anyone sees me."

Sabine rose and followed him to the shop entrance. Hank opened the door just a crack, but before he could slip through, Sabine grabbed his arm. "Thank you, Hank."

Hank stared at her for a moment, then leaned over to kiss her forehead. "You're going to be fine, cousin. I can feel it." He smiled and slipped out the door and into the night.

"Thirty damn years," Helena's voice boomed, and Sabine spun around. "Thirty years for him to grow a conscience, and technically, I'm not even around to see it."

Sabine sighed. "Where are you, Helena?"

"At the counter."

Sabine saw her stapler hovering a foot above the counter. Great. "Exactly how much did you hear?"

"Well, since I saw Hank sneaking into your shop and followed him in, everything. Nice pistol, by the way."

Sabine groaned and leaned against the shop wall. "I could have shot him, Helena! Why didn't you yell or something?"

"If you'd have gotten to the actual shooting part, I would have said something. Maybe. Probably."

"He's your son, Helena, and he did take a bullet that wasn't intended for him. Can't you cut him a little slack?"

"I'm not ready to move on yet. Seem to be having that problem everywhere." Helena began to laugh.

"If you're done enjoying the show, I'm going back to bed."

"So," Helena said, "I guess now I know why you dragged me to New Orleans and had that nutbag draw your parents. You're looking for a match, right?"

Damn it. The very conversation she'd been hoping to avoid. Sabine sighed. "Yes."

"Well, why the hell didn't you say so? I'm sure I can help."

Sabine rubbed her temples with her fingers, trying to stop the rush of blood into her head. "That's sorta what I was afraid of."

Chapter Four

Beau slammed the journal shut and tossed it onto the floor with the rest of the pile. Nothing. Eight hours of reading his own scribbles and he wasn't any closer to identifying the man in the drawing now than he had been when he started. At this point, he'd welcome a spiritual intervention. Hell, right now it might be the only way to locate the man.

Her father was the key to it all, Beau was certain. There was little information on Sabine's mother. It seemed she'd never held a job and didn't drive, but her name was accurate and he'd traced her back to high school photos. No secrets there. Mom was who she said she was, and Sabine's aunt had been correct in thinking the Sabine's mother was the last of her family line.

But her father had no past to speak of except a license that wasn't even a year old. Skinny amount of data for an American, even for that day and age. After hours of searching boxes full of handwritten payroll records, Beau had tracked him to a warehouse job on the docks in New Orleans and had located the ancient building in a seedy part of downtown that used to house the apartments where her parents had lived. It had been condemned for years, so there was no information to be gained on that avenue.

The social security number he'd used for the application hadn't matched the name on the license. In fact, the number belonged to a man who had died some ten years before Sabine's father took that job. Beau had already figured the name on the license wasn't the man's birth name, but he had yet to discover why it had been changed. If he could discover anything at all. Even more interesting was the fact that no one had put out a missing person's report for a man of his description at the time.

True, the father could have been from another state. Communication between police departments wasn't anything like it was today, but still, surely someone knew that this man, his wife, and his infant child were in New Orleans and set off alarms. But according to Sabine's research, no one had. Not in Louisiana anyway.

Beau rose from the couch, walked into the kitchen, and pulled a beer from the refrigerator. It was two a.m. and long past reasonable drinking time for most people, but then the great thing about being self-employed and independently wealthy was that you didn't have to live like most people. Beau was a night owl, pure and simple. Even during his time at the FBI, he'd always requested and always received night surveillance on takedowns. Ten years and not even once had someone tried to slide into the vampire role with him.

And then the thought of vampires led him right back to Sabine LeVeche and her strange way of living. What exactly caused a seemingly normal woman to launch off into believing in tarot cards and ghosts and rubbing rocks together for luck? Beau understood the overwhelming desire to know where you came from, understood it personally, but talking to dead people was one avenue he'd never even thought for one second to explore. He walked back into the living room.

What was Sabine doing right now, he wondered? Was she eating catfish and throwing back beers? Was she sitting in her apartment pouring over the limited information she had on her parents for the millionth time? He shook his head. More likely she was sleeping. Which sent him off on a whole other line of thought.

The mental picture of Sabine lying on a giant canopy bed draped in white gauze flashed across his mind. Her tanned body in crisp clarity against the bright white background, a giant ruby in the center of a silver headband the only vivid color in the image. The headband was also the only clothing she was wearing. Well, except for all those dangly bracelets like she'd had on at the café.

He shook his head and grabbed the television remote, frustrated he'd allowed his imagination to run away with him. Undressing a client was a line Beau had never crossed, not even in his fantasies. Then a horrible thought crossed his mind. If there was any truth at all to this psychic mumbo jumbo, could Sabine see his thoughts if they were about her? Shit.

He flipped channels, looking for something worth watching. This was the huge downside of being a night owl—there was rarely anything good on TV. He was just about to give it up as a loss and log on to the internet when a History Channel special on war criminals caught his eye. The commentator narrated the background of the people pictured in the photos on screen, going into great detail about their many crimes against the American people. He started to feel a tickle at the back of his neck.

He stood stock still in the middle of the living room, staring at the television, but the picture was no longer clear. The photos on the screen began to blend together in a kaleidoscopic blur. The commentator's words ran together into a single noise. And then, in a flash, it hit him . . . exactly where he'd seen the man in the photo.

In the FBI's most wanted files for war criminals.

He dropped onto the couch and took a huge gulp of his entire beer. Jesus, his memory was a pain in the ass; sometimes it was on, sometimes off. But when it was on, it was usually a hundred percent. He'd known when he took this job that it was probably going to end badly. Innocent people normally didn't make themselves disappear. But the guilty made a career of it. Granted, there was no way the man in the drawing could be the criminal he remembered. The age was all wrong. But he would bet anything they were blood relatives. He set his beer on the coffee table, the desire for it completely gone.

He glanced at his watch. One other person would still be up about now. Someone who had access to the FBI database and probably wouldn't mind giving him a little help on this. He reached for his cell phone and pressed in a number.

"Turner," the man answered on the first ring.

"Hey, it's Villeneuve."

"Villeneuve! How the hell are you?"

"Doing good, man. How 'bout yourself?"

"Can't complain, and wouldn't waste the time on it if I could."

Beau laughed. "I hear ya."

"So what the hell are you calling me in the middle of

the night for? I know it's not to discuss football, politics, or religion."

"I wish. This case I'm on just took a turn that makes politics and religion look like better options for discussion."

Turner whistled. "Doesn't sound like much fun. What can I help with?"

"I need access to some files . . . FBI files. Nothing that will raise any eyebrows. All old shit—back during Vietnam."

"Sounds okay to me, man. Hey, if you're coming now, do you think you could pick me up a burger and another six pack?"

"I think I could manage." He closed his phone, grabbed his keys and the case folder, and headed out of his apartment. *Maybe I'm wrong. Maybe my memory is totally off and the guy in the drawing has nothing to do with a wanted criminal from a long since dead war.*

Then the vivid recall of the young man in uniform flashed across his mind, imprinted there as if he'd seen it just seconds ago. Everything in perfect clarity, right down to the three freckles on the bridge of his nose.

That perfectly matched the three he'd seen on Sabine.

Sabine clenched the steering wheel of her car, well aware that it was far too early in the day to be up and moving, much less driving around downtown New Orleans with Helena Henry.

"By the hotdog stand is good," Helena said, directing Sabine to a corner about a block away.

For the life of her, Sabine couldn't figure out exactly what Helena wanted to do here. "What are you up to,

Helena? You wake me up first thing this morning, even though you know I didn't get hardly any sleep last night. Then you insist I drive you to New Orleans—"

"First thing! Are you kidding me? It was eight o'clock already."

"I have a head injury, and I'm not a morning person. Besides, I was busy almost having to shoot intruders last night, remember?"

"No shit. Well, while you were busy playing Cops and getting your beauty rest, I was formulating a plan of action."

Sabine groaned and pulled up to the curb. "Why does that worry me so much?"

"Jesus, for such an artsy-fartsy liberal sort, you're just as uptight as Maryse. I'd think a so-called psychic would have a broader mind."

"Well, it might help if I knew what I was supposed to be broadening my mind to."

"You'll see. Just circle the block. If I'm not here when you come back, circle again."

Sabine stared at the empty but very vocal passenger seat. "And how the heck am I supposed to know if you're here?"

Helena laughed. "Oh, you'll know. But just in case I need to give you some getaway instructions, you might want to roll your windows down. Okay, I'm outta here."

There wasn't so much as a stir of the air as Helena left the car, but a minute later, a floating hotdog that appeared to be eating itself gave her away. Dead people could eat? Good God. Sabine pulled on her sunglasses and slid down in her seat. What the hell was she thinking? Hooking up with Helena? Letting Helena help?

Helena's brand of help had almost gotten Maryse killed.

You're desperate.

Sabine pulled away from the corner and hoped that whatever Helena had gotten her into wasn't illegal. But she didn't hold out a whole lot of hope. Helena had never believed the "rules" applied to her when she was alive. Death had given her an entirely new avenue on life . . . one that could get her living, breathing accomplices in a whole boatload of trouble.

Sabine circled the block and approached the hotdog stand again, keeping an eye out for any stray floating hotdogs. Nothing. She pressed the gas and circled once more, hoping no one had noticed her circling and called the police. She was almost to the end of the block when she saw a group of policemen rush out of a building a block away. "Police Substation," the sign on the building read. Great. Just what she needed was the police only a block away with Helena breaking God knows how many laws just down the street.

They could start with stealing hotdogs.

She stopped at the corner and watched as the cops came to a halt in the middle of the street, looking both directions, confused expressions on their faces. A bad feeling washed over Sabine. Something wasn't right. What in the world were they all doing standing in the street? What were they looking for?

A horn sounded behind her and she jumped. She lifted one hand to wave at the angry motorist and started to make the turn, and that's when she saw the hotdog stand hurtling down the sidewalk toward her car. Which might not have been so odd in itself, but the fact that there was minimal slope to the road and no wind at all made the situation far from normal. Not to mention the small matter of the cart owner running ten yards behind and yelling at the top of his lungs.

The horn behind her sounded again and Sabine panicked, torn between pulling over for the other motorist to pass and hauling ass back to Mudbug as fast as her old Sentra would manage. Abandoning the last semblance of common sense, she jerked the wheel to the right and stopped the car at the curb, waving as the honking motorist drove around her and gave her the finger.

"Prepare to haul ass!" Helena's voice sounded above the fray.

Sabine whirled around in her seat just as the hotdog stand launched off the sidewalk behind her and landed in the street, sending hotdogs flying in all directions. The police had locked in on the commotion and were running toward the stand, closing in on her parking space by the second. *To heck with this.* Sabine put the car in gear, but before she could stomp on the gas, a mailbag flew through the open passenger's side window and landed on the floorboard.

"What the hell are you waiting for?" Helena yelled, her voice booming right next to Sabine.

Sabine floored the car and squealed away from the curb. She glanced in her rearview mirror just in time to see the cops chasing the hotdog stand onto the other side of the street. Barely slowing, she rounded the corner and accelerated onto the highway from the service road. She'd driven at least a mile down the road before she took a breath and looked over at the passenger seat.

A hotdog hovered just inches from her face. "Want one?" Helena asked.

Sabine pushed the hotdog away. "No, I don't want one. What the hell is the matter with you? You stole something from that police station, didn't you? All those cops were looking for you . . . but I don't understand why or how."

A chunk of the hotdog disappeared and Helena said, "Me eifer."

"Don't talk with your mouth full. Jesus, I would think someone of your upbringing would have some manners."

"What's the point? No one to see them but you and Maryse."

Sabine lowered her window a bit, grabbed the remainder of the hotdog and tossed it out onto the highway.

"Hey! What did you do that for?" Helena yelled.

"Two can play at the no manners game. And why in the world are you eating? You're—"

"Don't say it. I know I'm dead. I'm eating for the normal reason—I'm hungry."

"How can you be hungry?" Sabine shook her head. "Never mind. I don't even want to know. You've completely negated an entire lifetime of studying ghosts. Cone bras, eating hotdogs. It's simply too weird for me to process."

"If it's too weird for you, then I must be the anomaly of ghosts. Not for nothing, Sabine, but you're not exactly running with the normal crowd."

Sabine sighed, not even wanting to think about the irony of that statement at this very moment. "Start answering questions, Helena. Why were all those cops trying to find you and what's in that bag?"

"Just a police file that I thought might come in handy."

"You stole a file from that police station? Oh God. No wonder they were looking for you."

"I know. I guess maybe that barcode strip thingie set off the alarm."

"Are you crazy?" Sabine asked. "No. Never mind. You don't need to answer that."

"I don't know why you're getting all huffy. This would have been a lot harder before when I couldn't touch things. Remember, Maryse had to break into the hospital for those medical records herself."

Sabine rubbed her forehead with one hand, not even wanting to recall Maryse's foray into breaking and entering into the hospital's medical records room. It was one of those things Sabine still couldn't quite believe her straitlaced scientist friend had gotten roped into. Until now. She stared at the highway, a flashback of the runaway hotdog cart still vivid in her mind. At the moment, Maryse's actions didn't seem near as strange since Sabine was currently making a getaway with stolen police records and pilfered hotdogs.

Sabine stared at the bag once more but couldn't hold the question in any longer. "What file did you steal, Helena?"

The bag on the floor rustled a bit and a manila folder appeared to float out of it. The file spun in mid-air so that Sabine could see the typed words on the side. She took one look at the lettering and groaned. "You stole the police file from my parents' wreck?

What were you thinking? As soon as they figure out what file is missing, they're coming straight to my door."

Helena laughed. The mailbag flipped upside down, dumping a stack of manila folders and two more hot-dogs onto the floorboard. "They'd have to figure out exactly which one I was after first."

Chapter Five

Sabine gave Maryse a smile as she slid into the booth across from Sabine at Carolyn's Catfish Kitchen. "You're late . . . but why is that not a surprise?"

"Hey," Maryse protested. "You're the one that's always late, not me."

"Not since you've got a hunky DEA agent in your bed. You've ceased to be the morning person you used to be and it's almost noon. In fact, you're not much of a night person anymore either."

A light blush crept over Maryse's face. "Luc's next assignment is going to take him out of town, probably for a month or better. I'm making sure he doesn't forget what he's got waiting back home."

Sabine laughed. "Okay, I would sorta get that except that it's so obvious that Luc is over the top in love with you. I don't think he's going to forget a single square inch of you." She reached across the table and placed her hand on Maryse's. "I am so happy for you, Maryse. Seeing you and Luc together makes me believe there's hope for me, too. If I make it that long, that is."

Maryse squeezed Sabine's hand. "Do *not* think that way. There is no way in hell I'm letting you leave me here alone with Helena. And besides, as my best friend, you owe it to me to wear some tacky pink taffeta dress for my wedding."

"Pink?"

Maryse grinned. "Fuchsia. Glowing so bright you could see it from space. Maybe with a lime green bow."

"Yuck!"

Maryse sobered. "Seriously, I don't want to hear any talk like that, okay? You start the chemo soon and that will probably be the end of it. With any luck, I'll be able to help you out on that part of things."

"You're right. I'm sure within no time at all I'll be back to my exciting life."

Maryse cocked her head to one side and stared at her friend. "You sound like that's a bad thing. I thought you were happy with your life."

Sabine sighed. "I am. I was. Oh, I don't know. I guess my life seemed fine before I found out it might end prematurely. Then I guess I started thinking about it and well . . . there's a whole lot I haven't done."

"Okay, like what?"

Sabine frowned, not exactly ready with an itemized list. "Oh, I don't know—see a live play, scuba dive, leave this state, have an entire day at the spa . . ."

"Sounds easy enough. "

"You're kidding me."

"Not at all. Today, I want you to get a notebook and start jotting down all the things you want to do. Anything you can think of. Then we'll start tackling them. I can't guarantee we can do them all, depending on what you come up with, but I'm game to try." Maryse cast her friend a nervous look. "Unless you're still wanting to be abducted by aliens. That's sorta not on my list of things to do ever."

Sabine laughed. "I was ten years old when I said that. And believe me, Helena has been enough of a journey into the unexplained to last me a lifetime. I was actually thinking about giving up the shop and becoming a bank teller or something."

"Helena tends to have that effect on people."

"You have no idea," Sabine muttered and lowered her eyes to the table.

"Oh, no. I know that look. I wore it too many times over the last month. What have you let Helena talk you into?"

"Well, she said it was just an errand in New Orleans, and technically all I did was drive . . ."

Maryse groaned. "What did she do?"

"She stole the police file on my parents' wreck and a bunch of others from the station. The barcodes tripped the alarm, and half the cops in downtown came running out after her."

"Oh, God. Why didn't you call me for bail?"

"Oh, we didn't get caught. Helena caused a runaway hotdog stand accident and used the diversion to hop in the car with the stolen files and at least five hotdogs. I'm never going to get that smell out of my car."

"Helena is enjoying death way too much. It's really not fair at all." Maryse shook her head. "Okay, so I get the police file thing . . . in a Helena thinking sort of way, but what's up with the hotdogs?"

"Apparently, Helena is hungry. Don't even ask. I have no idea."

Maryse raised her eyebrows and stared at Sabine for a couple of seconds. "Alrighty then. So what did you do with the files?"

"I made a copy of my parents' file—wearing gloves, of course—then mailed them all back to the police. Then I called that detective Raissa found to let him know about the file."

"Bet that went over well. How did you explain having a copy?"

"I just said a well-meaning friend thought she'd help me out. And since she'd already broken the law, I figured he might as well take a look at the spoils." Sabine felt a blush creep up her face as she recalled her earlier conversation with Beau.

Maryse studied her for a moment. "So you never actually told me about this detective. What's he like?"

Sabine felt her face heat up even more. "He's nice. Seems very competent."

"Uh huh."

Sabine looked down at her coffee, concentrating on stirring the already mixed sugar. "He's got experience in this sort of detective work."

"Uh huh."

"And he seems nice."

"You already said that."

Sabine sighed and looked up at her grinning friend. "So what do you want me to say—that he's hot? Well, he is. The hottest guy I've ever seen in person, okay? Are you satisfied?"

"Not yet. But I'm getting there. And what do you propose to do with this hot detective?"

"I don't propose to do anything with him, except give him information to help me. Jeez, just because I find some guy hot doesn't mean I should jump on him like some floozy."

Maryse laughed. "You are the furthest thing from a floozy that I could locate in Mudbug. You know, for all your fussing at me to get out of the bayou and into society, you're not exactly the pinnacle of the social scene, either. When was the last time you got any?"

"Maryse! What a question."

"That long, huh? Well, I can't really bitch at you as I was on a two-year draught myself after Hank left, and Mudbug doesn't exactly have the best to pick from. But you've had some dates off and on. Nothing came of those?"

"No. A couple were buttheads. A couple were nice, but there just wasn't any spark."

"I get you. And this Beau . . . there's a spark there?"

"More like a volcano waiting to erupt."

Maryse whistled. "I know that feeling. Do yourself a favor and don't put it off. That eruption is something out of your wildest imagination."

Sabine shook her head. "I can't go there."

"Why not? Why are you so afraid of letting go?"

"It's not the eruption that scares me. It's the cooling off. How can I start something with a man, knowing good and well I may not be here to finish it?" She brushed at her eyes with her fingers. "I heard from Wheeler just before lunch. Hank's not a match."

Maryse sobered. "I'm really sorry. I had hoped there was an easy answer to all this. And I understand your apprehension about moving forward when you don't know if you're going to hit the wall, truly I do. But you don't know what the future holds . . . none of us do. Disease is not the only thing that can take us away from this world—you saw that with me over the last month. But putting your life on hold waiting for a death that might not come for another fifty years is like already dying."

Sabine felt the tears begin to form in her eyes. "I hate it when you're right."

"So if this detective is interested, you're not going to turn him down, right?"

Sabine shrugged. "I'll add it to my list, but it's not at the top."

"Really? Because I was hoping to get at least one thing crossed off the list today. Please tell me the spa day is at the top of the list. I could sooooooo use a massage."

"Not exactly."

Maryse stared at Sabine, her hesitation clear as day. "Why do I get the feeling I'm going to regret this?"

Sabine gave Maryse an evil grin, unable to resist teasing her friend since she'd just shoved reality down Sabine's throat. "I was thinking bungee jumping."

Maryse shut her eyes and clenched her hands. "That made me dizzy just thinking about it. You know I'm afraid of heights."

"And you know I'm afraid of relationships."

Maryse put her head face down on the table and covered it with her arms. "What time are we going?"

"I think before supper would be best."

"Yeah, I'd hate to waste a good meal on plummeting out of control toward the ground wearing a rubber band on my ankles." Maryse lifted her head and looked back at Sabine. "Fine. I'll do it as long as you promise not to turn down anything the detective offers."

"Oh, no. I'm not locking into that agreement. What if he sells insurance on the side, or even worse . . . Tupperware?"

Maryse laughed. "Okay, but if he's peddling anything but expensive plastic or disability insurance, it's a go." She studied Sabine for a moment. "You know, I've never seen you this riled up over a guy. Not since Johnny Arceneaux put that frog in your lunchbox in first grade."

Sabine smiled. "Well, you know how much I love frogs." The door to the café opened and Sabine glanced over, then froze as she saw who was standing there.

"What's wrong?" Maryse asked. "It's not Helena, is it?"

"No," Sabine whispered. "He's early."

"Who's early?"

"The detective. I was supposed to meet him here in a half hour. He's early."

"Great! Now I can see what all the fuss is about."

"Don't you dare."

Maryse grinned and turned all the way around in her seat. She held for a couple of seconds, then spun back around to face Sabine, her eyes wide. "Holy shit! You are in *big* trouble."

The instant he walked into the restaurant, Beau zoned in on Sabine like he had preset radar. She was sitting in a corner booth with another woman, who had turned around when he walked in and given him a comprehensive up and down before turning back to Sabine. He briefly wondered if he'd passed the friend's test, then got agitated at himself for caring . . . or wondering . . . or whatever he was doing.

No strings, Villeneuve.

His entire adult existence centered on keeping things simple, uncomplicated. He'd learned that one the hard way. He carried his own baggage, and he wasn't interested in carrying anyone else's. It had always been his experience that women were the most complicated people on earth. And their baggage usually came in matched sets. Hell, if the line he had on locating Sabine's family turned out to be accurate, she would soon be faced with more baggage than a freight train.

Unless you can talk her out of wanting to know.

Sabine waved at him and he smiled. Quickly catching himself, he put on his game face and crossed the restaurant, resolved to talk Sabine out of this quest of hers. It couldn't possibly bring her anything but misery. And if there was any way at all, he intended to spare her the disappointment he'd suffered.

As he stepped up to the table, the other woman sitting with Sabine rose and extended her hand. "I'm Maryse Robicheaux, Sabine's best friend. It's nice to meet you." She looked over at Sabine and grinned. "Sabine has been telling me everything about you."

A light blush crept up Sabine's face and she glared at Maryse. Beau shook Maryse's hand. "Beau Villeneuve."

"Well, this has been fun," Maryse said, "but I have to run."

"Oh, no you don't," Sabine argued. "You said you had another thirty minutes."

Maryse smiled. "But that was before you made plans for us tonight. Now, I need to see my attorney and remove you from my will." She winked at Beau and hurried out of the restaurant.

Beau slid into the booth across from Sabine, wondering how in the world she made jeans and a plain blue polo shirt look so elegant. Maybe it was her hair, twisted in a complicated knot, with shiny black locks framing her face. Or maybe it was the silver earrings shaped like a teardrop.

Maybe you should get your head out of the clouds and focus on business.

"Should I even ask what your plans are for tonight?" Beau asked.

"No. I was trying to play a joke on Maryse, but apparently it backfired. She always gets the last word. I don't know why I bother."

"I like her," Beau said, trying to block out the sweet smell of Sabine's perfume. "She doesn't dance around things, does she?"

"No. Finesse was never Maryse's strong point. I think she sees it as a waste of good creative energy and time."

Beau nodded. "She's probably right."

"Really? Then maybe you should try taking her shopping with you. We've been officially banned from two boutiques and a pet store."

"A pet store?"

Sabine waved a hand in dismissal, at least twenty bracelets jangling on her arm. "It's a long story and doesn't end so well for the turtle." She pulled a manila folder from a bright pink shoulder bag and slid it across the table. "This is the file I mentioned when I called."

"The file your friend 'appropriated'?" Beau scanned the police records inside.

Sabine sighed. "Yeah, that's the one."

"This friend wouldn't have been Maryse, would it?"

"Oh, God no! Maryse can be painfully direct and sarcastically entertaining but would never break the law. Well, almost never . . . okay, definitely not this time."

Beau smiled. "Convinced yourself yet?"

"Not completely. Was it that obvious?"

"Well, let's just say I didn't have to be psychic to get it."

Sabine laughed. "Good. Raissa and I already have

the spirit world covered. It's the real world I can't seem to make any headway in."

Beau sobered. "That's another thing I'd like to talk to you about. I've got a lead on your family."

Sabine's eyes widened. "You're kidding. So soon? I can't believe it!"

"Don't get excited just yet. It might turn out to be nothing."

"Still, a lead in a matter of days when I've come up with nothing for over twenty years is definitely something."

It's now or never, Villeneuve. Beau took a breath and pushed forward. "I guess what I wanted to say is, before I get too far, I just want to make sure you really want this."

Sabine stared at him. "Why wouldn't I?"

"Lots of reasons, and probably things you never thought of."

"Like?"

"Well, what happens if your family doesn't turn out to be the kind of people you hoped they would be?"

"You mean they might be conservatives?"

Beau smiled. "That's possible, of course, but what I had in mind was something a little worse."

"Fundamentalists? Yikes." Sabine's expression grew serious. "I understand what you're insinuating. My family could turn out to be people who don't share the same value system—and while I know on the exterior I may look a little questionable, I assure you I'm really a law-abiding bore."

Beau nodded. "And your family could be the kind of people that HBO makes movies of the week about."

"Like the weirdo that tried to break into my building in broad daylight . . . and with three—two—people right upstairs?"

Beau's senses went immediately on high alert. "Someone tried to break into your building? When?"

"Yesterday midmorning." Sabine gave him a rundown of the attempted break-in.

"Did you get a good look at him?"

Sabine shook her head and described the intruder's outfit. "The Mudbug police dusted for prints, but they only found mine and Maryse's."

"What did the police say? Has there been a problem with random break-ins lately?"

"I've never had a problem, and the only other break-in the police know about was at the hospital last week. The whole thing is very weird."

"Do you keep much cash around?"

"No way! I take everything but a hundred dollars of change for the register to the bank every day right before closing. Everyone in town knows that, and even someone who didn't only had to watch me for a couple of days to figure it out."

"Could be junkies. They're not always smart with their targets. And that would explain the break-in at the hospital, too," Beau said, but his mind was whirling with possibilities. He didn't believe in coincidences—especially not this kind. What if something Sabine had done had made someone nervous? It could be her search for her family or something else entirely, but either way, Beau wasn't about to dismiss the timing of the attempted break-in. It might turn out to be nothing, but it would be foolish to ignore. "This is exactly the sort of thing I was worried about. And things could get far worse the closer we get to the truth. What if these people you're looking for simply don't want to be found?"

"You're thinking what I don't know can't hurt me."

"Exactly."

Sabine studied him for several seconds, then sighed. "I understand what you're saying, and I appreciate that you're trying to protect me from what might be an ugly situation. The fact that you're having this conversation with me after informing me you have a lead tells me you're not happy with the direction the lead is taking you."

"No. I'm not."

"I wish I could tell you I didn't care and just let the whole thing drop, but that's just not possible. I know you're trying to protect me and that's very sweet, but the reality is, not finding my family could be far more detrimental to me than anything you come up with." She reached across the table and placed her hand on his. "Thank you for caring. Most people wouldn't even have given it a second thought."

The skin on Beau's hand tingled under Sabine's gentle touch, and he fought the urge to pull his hand out from under hers before he did or said something he'd regret. "I've had nothing but second thoughts since the moment I met you," Beau muttered, then sucked in a breath. "Oh hell, I said that out loud, didn't I?"

Sabine stared at him, her eyes wide. "I've thought of you, too."

Beau felt a queasiness in his stomach. *Back out while there's still room.* "So what are we going to do about it?" *Shit.*

The color rushed from Sabine's face. She pulled her hand away from Beau's and jumped up from the booth.

"We're going to pretend this conversation never happened. Thank you for the update, Mr. Villeneuve. I hope the file helps." She spun around and hurried out of the café without ever looking back.

What the hell? Beau watched the door shut behind her, then slumped back in the booth, replaying the conversation and Sabine's response over and over in his mind. *Unbelievable.* All those years of carefully guarding himself from crossing that line with a woman and the one time his resistance was too low, he'd run into the only person in the world more scared of relationships than he was.

Chapter Six

Sabine rushed out of the restaurant and crossed the street to her shop. She let herself inside and hurried upstairs without turning the sign out front to "Open." She didn't have any appointments that afternoon and anyone important had her cell phone number. In her tiny kitchen, she pulled a bottled water from the refrigerator and twisted off the top. Her hands shook as she lifted the bottle to her lips and took a drink.

"It's official," she said to the empty room, "you *are* a nutbag."

She dropped into a chair at her kitchen table and set the water down. Beau Villeneuve was the best-looking man she'd ever met in real life, and he was nice. He'd actually tried to talk her out of locating her family because he was afraid she'd get hurt. Even worse, most improbably, he was interested in her. Helena's rise from the dead had surprised her far less.

And you ran. Idiot.

She propped her elbows on the table, covered her face with her hands and groaned. A twenty-year search for her family she could handle. Helena Henry rising from the dead she could handle. Heck, she'd been teasing Maryse when she suggested bungee jumping, but even that she could have handled. But apparently a date was out of the question. Maryse was right—she was already dead.

She reached for the water and knocked a stack of her aunt's journals onto the floor. With a sigh, she reached over to pick them up. A sentence in one of the open books caught her eye. She lifted the journal and started to read.

September 2, 1963

A peculiar thing happened at work today. A woman and her husband came into the hospital with an infant who had an ear infection. I did my normal check on the baby, a beautiful little boy, while asking the mother our standard questions. When I asked her about breast-feeding, she got flustered, then looked at her husband. I'm not for certain as I could only see him out of the corner of my eye, but I swear he shook his head.

Although she'd been chatty before, the woman immediately clammed up and simply said no, she wasn't breast-feeding, with no further explanation. She answered the remainder of the questions with clipped responses, her gaze darting back and forth between me and her husband.

Dr. Breaux came in to do his exam and gave the woman a prescription and some written instructions. As he was writing out the instructions, an orderly came by and told the husband that he'd left the windows down on his car and it was starting to rain. It was obvious the husband didn't want to leave his wife alone, but with both Dr. Breaux and I standing there, it would have appeared odder for him not to.

Dr. Breaux finished shortly after the husband left and as I was wrapping up the baby in his blanket, I tried to chat with the wife, asking her some questions about her recovery after the delivery. She hesitated

*with her responses, and based on her answers, I am
suspicious that she never gave birth.*

*Before I could pry any further, the husband re-
turned and hustled the wife and the baby out of the
room. The tension coming off of them both was so
strong I could feel it, but for the life of me I don't understand what the problem was. If the baby is not their
biological child, why all the secrecy?*

*If they weren't honest about the child's parentage
with a doctor, what in the world were they telling people who knew she hadn't been pregnant? Perhaps the
child belonged to an unmarried relative and they were
protecting the woman's reputation. I hope that is the
case since the only other alternative I could come up
with for all the lying is that the baby was bought on the
black market.*

*The scene in the exam room played in my mind over
and over the rest of the day.*

Sabine sat back in her chair and stared out the
kitchen window. Black marketing babies. What a horrible thought, the level of desperation it would take to
go such a route to have a family. She shook her head.
And Sabine thought locating *her* family was hard.
Imagine a black-market child ever finding their biological family. It was a sobering thought, especially
given Sabine's current medical crisis.

Wondering if her aunt had ever come in contact
with the woman again, Sabine lifted the journal and
skimmed the pages, looking for any mention of babies.
It was a couple of months later before she found another entry.

November 4, 1963

Sissy and her husband, friends of mine from high school, came in today with their baby. She's about three months old and has a face like a cherub. Sissy could hardly contain herself. She had rheumatic fever when she was a child and knew that it would be unlikely she'd ever have a baby. They'd put their name on the adoption list the year before and her dream had come true. I was a bit surprised, as healthy white babies are in high demand and not so easy to get through the proper channels.

When her husband left the room to speak with Dr. Breaux, I made a comment to Sissy about their good fortune, and she confided in me that the adoption had been private. The woman had been poor and unable to care for the baby. Apparently the father had been killed in Vietnam. The woman had asked the priest at their church to find a good home for the little girl. I asked whether they had any personal information on the mother or the father, in particular their medical history. Sissy told me the priest had only said that the mother was a devout Catholic.

In less than two months, I've seen two healthy white babies being raised by women who didn't give birth to them and live in the same small town. I have a bad feeling about it, but I don't know what can be done. I worry that those mothers didn't give up their babies voluntarily. Or even worse, maybe the mothers are dead.

Something's not right about any of this. I am going to check the obituaries for the past year and see if I find any military widows who had recently given birth.

Hopefully, I am wrong in my suspicions. All I can do for now is pray for those babies and their mothers.

Sabine flipped through the rest of the journal and three more after that but didn't find another reference to the women or the babies. Frustrated, she placed the last journal on the table. There had to be an answer. Aunt Meg wasn't given to flights of fancy. If she'd thought something was wrong, then something had been.

Sabine tapped her finger on the stack of journals, but a good answer didn't magically appear. She glanced down at her watch and shook her head. No wonder. Before figuring anything out, she'd need some lunch. She was deliberating between a grilled cheese or ham sandwich when the chair across from her slid back from the table. It took her a second to register the indentation on the chair cushion and process exactly what that meant. "Helena, jeez, you scared me."

"You sure are jumpy lately."

"Two break-ins in one week are a little beyond my lifetime limit," Sabine said. "I'm allowed to be a little on edge if someone just strolls into my apartment and I can't even see them."

"I guess."

"Is something wrong, Helena?" The ghost's voice didn't sound right, and for the first time since that horrible cone bra sighting, Sabine wished she could see her.

"Today's the exhumation."

Sabine sucked in a breath. "I'm sorry. I'd completely forgotten." Maryse's week-long adventure in trying to remain alive had produced a whole lot of surprises, one of them being the exhumation of Helena's body. They were looking for evidence of murder, something the police and the coroner hadn't considered the first time around.

"Well, you've got other things on your mind," Helena said. "I know that. But Maryse is off at the lab in New Orleans still trying to save the world with one of her concoctions, so I didn't really have anyone else to talk to."

"Are you worried they won't find anything?"

"No. Yes." Helena sighed. "That's just it. I feel funny, but I'm not sure why. You know that feeling that you get before you go to the dentist or something?"

"Yes, I know that feeling well." *And ran out of a restaurant because of it.* "I think it's fear, Helena, even though you can't put your finger on what it is exactly that you're afraid of."

"Fear. Hmmmm. Maybe you're right."

"I think I am. This is a huge event for you. You're sure you were murdered, but what if the medical examiner doesn't find any evidence of that . . . where does that leave you? Not to mention that even if they prove you were murdered, that doesn't tell us who did it. And there's just the overall ickiness of knowing your body is going to be lying on a table somewhere. That would definitely make my stomach flutter."

"Yeah. I think no matter what, it's the 'where does that leave me' question that haunts me the most. What if I never leave here? What if this is it—death's cruel joke for the lifetime of bullshit I put people through?"

Sabine considered this for a moment. "I don't think you're being punished for being a bitch, if that's what you're asking. I honestly believe that you're still around because no one has solved your murder. Apparently the world is just not in balance until that happens, so you're stuck in the transition."

"But what if we never know? What if the man who killed me dies without ever being caught and I'm doomed to roam here like this forever? I mean, right now I have you and Maryse, but what about a hundred years from now or two hundred? Once you guys are gone no one will even know about me, much less care."

"You can't think that way. I'm sure this will all work out all right."

"You mean like your life is working out? Face it, life sucks and the earth barely tolerates our existence. Thanks for listening, Sabine. I'll see you later."

"Wait!" Sabine cried, but there was no answer and the depression in the cushion was gone. "Damn." She picked up the journal and opened it to the first entry she'd read. What if someone *had* killed those women for their babies? What if they were roaming the earth like Helena, still waiting for someone to set them free? What if everyone had forgotten?

And now Sabine was the only one who knew anything about them at all.

If ever there was a time that Sabine wished she didn't have a conscience, it would be now. She already had enough on her plate: Helena's murder, her missing family, her cancer, and now her completely unexpected and unwanted attraction to Beau Villeneuve. She probably wouldn't sleep for a year at this rate.

But what if others were stuck in between?

Sabine slumped back in her chair with a sigh. Even though she didn't have a psychic bone in her body, that didn't mean she didn't believe in the afterlife and spirits and, well, pretty much darn near everything. And even if she hadn't before, Helena was a pretty convincing argument. Sabine couldn't bear the thought of someone else's soul in limbo. She could at least spend a couple of hours looking into it.

She rose from the table and grabbed her purse. She'd start at the library. They had microfiche for the Mudbug newspaper for as many years back as there had been one. The obituaries would be a good place to start. Her aunt hadn't made another note about the women in her journals, so Sabine had to assume she'd either let the whole thing drop, hadn't found out anything in her own search, or hadn't been able to prove anything if she had. She picked up the journal from the table and slid it into her purse. At least she had a decent idea of the dates to start looking.

From his booth at Carolyn's, Beau had a clear view of Sabine's building. She'd left the restaurant almost an hour ago but still hadn't changed her shop sign to "Open," which meant she either didn't have any appointments for the rest of the day or she'd cancelled them because he had absolutely no skill at asking a woman for a date. And why should he? He'd shot more people in the line of duty than he'd asked on dates. Which, now that he thought about it, must say something about him, but he had absolutely no idea what.

He took one last bite of an absolutely heavenly banana pudding and rose from the booth. That attempted break-in at Sabine's still weighed on him. The hospital break-in didn't really concern him, as that was a choice spot for a drug user to try to get a fix if they couldn't find any other way. But there was nothing about Sabine or her business to suggest it was worth breaking into her building, especially in broad daylight. Even if the burglar had thought no one was inside, it was a huge risk, even from the back door. Again, the desperation of junkies came to mind but he didn't want to force that to fit. Not just yet. Nothing about Sabine had made him think she used illegal drugs, and she'd been vehement in her denial of keeping anything but a minimal amount of cash on hand.

Beau pulled some bills out of his wallet and set them on the table. He mulled over the possibilities, limited as they were, as he paid the bill. The timing of the attempted break-in coupled with his search for Sabine's family troubled him, but for the life of him he couldn't see where the two could have intersected. Sabine had never come up with anything remotely close to the angle he was working now, and all his activity so far had been restricted to FBI files and news articles. The family had no way of knowing that he was researching them. Not yet. So they had no way of knowing about Sabine.

Which meant her trouble was coming from something else. But what? And who would try a break-in in the middle of the morning, in broad daylight, and with occupants inside the building? It was damned odd, but if Sabine couldn't even handle Beau admitting his attraction, she sure as hell wasn't going to start unloading her secrets on him. And then there was always the chance that Sabine had no idea what had set this into motion. So many times in his work with the FBI, he'd seen cases of normal people thrust into the middle of something sordid without ever intending to step in shit. Certainly none of them realized it until it was too late.

Beau stuffed his change in his wallet and turned to

the exit. He looked across the street just in time to see Sabine lock the front door on her shop, hurry to her car, and drive away. What now? He exited the restaurant and paused outside on the sidewalk, making a quick assessment of the town. The entire downtown wasn't any bigger than a city block, but with the wooded areas and the bayou surrounding every side of the tiny town, there were too many possibilities for an unobserved approach to make Beau happy with Sabine's safety.

The hotel was the tallest building on the street. If he could manage a front room, he'd have a clear view of Sabine's building—the front of it anyway. He hoped she'd taken the necessary precautions with the back door after the last attempt. It was something he'd ask her about as soon as he had an opportunity. If she'd let him see the door and secure it, even better. Mind made up, he walked down the street to the hotel and stepped inside. A large woman with silver hair sticking up in all directions looked up from the counter as he entered.

"Hi," she said. "Are you here for the sales convention?"

For a fleeting moment, Beau considered lying, but quickly changed his mind. The town was simply too small and once his cover was blown he'd have an even harder time convincing Sabine to trust him than before. "No. I'm here doing a little work and need a room."

"Welcome. My name's Mildred and this is my hotel. 'Bout how many nights you need to stay?"

Beau considered this for a minute. "I'm not really sure. Are you full, or can I negotiate something for a day at a time?"

Mildred shrugged. "Fine by me. But the hotel's

completely booked a week from now. Think you'll be done with your work by then?"

Beau nodded. "I hope to be." He pulled his license and a credit card from his wallet and handed them to Mildred. It was only Tuesday and with any luck, he would either figure out what was going on or reassure himself that it was an isolated incident and be satisfied Sabine was safe.

Mildred ran his credit card and pushed the receipt across the counter along with a pen. "What kind of work do you do, Mr. Villeneuve?" she asked as she glanced down at his license.

"Research, mostly."

"Sounds fascinating. Medical?"

"No." Beau pushed the completed registration card back across the counter. "Family history stuff mostly. Is there a room available in the front of the hotel?"

Mildred pulled a key from the pegboard behind her and handed it to Beau. "Third floor." She studied him for a moment. "Anyone I might know?"

"It really wouldn't be appropriate for me to say without permission."

Mildred gave him a shrewd look. "Not for nothing, Mr. Villeneuve, but I've most often found that opening up family business long since dead is like stepping on a land mine."

"I couldn't agree more." Beau took the key and started toward the stairwell.

Sabine shoved the copies she'd made from the library microfiche into her shoulder bag and waved at old Mrs. Hebert, the librarian, as she exited the building. Three possibilities to fill two possible slots—

Amelia Watson, Sandra Franks, and Ruth Moore, all living in nearby bayou towns. No cause of death was listed, or surviving family. But at least she had a starting point.

She'd gone through the microfiche index for ten years preceding their deaths but had found no mention of any of the women. She'd ask Mildred and Helena if they knew any of the names, even though both would have been teenagers at the time of the women's deaths. Beyond that, Sabine felt she'd spent enough time chasing a "bad feeling." If Mildred or Helena had never heard of the women, then Sabine had already decided she would let it go without regret. Well, with almost no regret. Who was she kidding? She'd probably feel like crap but what other choice did she have? Maybe when things were more settled in her own life she'd pick it up again.

She glanced at her watch and realized it was getting toward suppertime and she still hadn't eaten lunch. No wonder she was starving. She briefly considered the limited options in her apartment. She really had to get to the grocery store. And since Maryse had known good and well that Sabine had been joking about the bungee jumping and Luc had left that afternoon for his undercover assignment, Sabine knew her friend would remain at the lab in New Orleans until all hours of the night. Which put her out of the running as a dinner date.

Sabine looked over at the hotel. There was always Mildred. Sabine hated the thought of sitting across a table from Mildred knowing that she was hiding her cancer from her, but if she didn't see her soon, Mildred would wonder and besides, she could go ahead and ask her about the three women and get that out of the way. The hotel owner had raised Maryse after her mother died, and ran herd over Maryse and Sabine from childhood to their early twenties, doing her best to keep them from doing something foolish. She was moderately successful except for their teenage years and Maryse's disastrous marriage to Hank.

Mind made up, Sabine started across the street for the hotel. She found Mildred behind the counter, wrapping up her daily accounting. The hotel owner looked up and smiled as Sabine entered the lobby.

"I haven't seen you in days." She gave Sabine a critical look. "How are you?"

Sabine took one look at Mildred and sighed. "Maryse told you."

Mildred walked around the counter and gave Sabine a hug. "Oh, honey," she said as she pulled back. "You know Maryse never could tell me a lie—not that I didn't know about, anyway. And not telling me something like this is the same as lying in my book. What I don't understand is why you didn't tell me yourself."

"It wasn't that I was trying to keep it from you, exactly. It's just that . . . well . . . I didn't want you worrying about me. We haven't even really gotten past everything that happened to Maryse, and I didn't want to throw something else on you this soon. And I know how you feel about my looking for my family. I knew you wouldn't be happy with me starting it up all over again, much less in full force."

Mildred sighed. "I guess I figure little good ever comes from digging up the past. I don't want you hurt, Sabine, and it just might be that finding them hurts more than never knowing them. I've always believed family is about sharing your life, not your blood, but I understand why this is different. I just wish there was another way."

"I love you, Mildred, you know that? But let's not put the cart ahead of the horse. We don't know what's in store for me, so there's no use worrying about a bunch of things that may or may not happen. Believe me, I spend enough time worrying for everyone."

Mildred gave her a sympathetic look. "I understand you trying to protect me, Sabine, but you know good and well that I'm no shrinking violet. If you or Maryse need me, I want to know about it and be right in the middle of everything, raising Cain and getting things done. That's what friends do."

Sabine brushed an unshed tear away from her eye. "No, that's what *mothers* do. Maryse and I are so lucky to have you."

Mildred smiled. "Yes, you are. So I assume that means you're taking me to dinner. I could sure use a mess of catfish and a glass of wine."

Sabine laughed. "As a matter of fact, I'd love to."

Mildred reached behind the counter and grabbed her purse. "Ready?"

Sabine nodded. "Can you leave? There's no one to cover the desk."

Mildred waved a hand in dismissal. "Julia should be here any minute. That girl is always five minutes late. Besides, we'll just be across the street so it should be fine."

They stepped outside, and Mildred pulled the lobby door closed behind her. "Now," Mildred said and gave her a shrewd look, "are you going to tell me what you really wanted to talk about?"

* * *

Beau eased down the remainder of the stairwell as the door closed behind the hotel owner and Sabine. He stared through the lobby window after them. He'd known from the beginning that Sabine was keeping something from him . . . most clients did. The trick was deciding whether it was something important to the investigation or merely something private and perhaps embarrassing to the client. Beau hadn't really gotten the impression that Sabine was holding back anything concerning her family, so that must mean it was personal.

And apparently something so dire she'd also kept it from the woman she considered a surrogate mother.

Which was very interesting when considered with all the other facts that Beau had. Like the fact that Raissa had just recently had the "vision" of Sabine's parents, but had been friends with her and known of her situation for years, or that a "friend" had stolen a police file of her parent's car wreck just this week but no one had ever done this before. And even though he knew she'd hired an investigator in the past, she'd claimed it had been years before and he had no reason to think she was lying.

So why the big push now?

Was Sabine's secret related to her search for her family? And if so, how? And was the break-in at her shop tied in to all of it, some of it, or none of it?

He crossed the lobby and looked across the street. Sabine and Mildred were entering the catfish restaurant. They were both smiling as if nothing was wrong, but from their earlier conversation, Beau doubted that was the case. More likely they were making small talk now and would have the bigger discussion once they had been served and were left to themselves. He deliberated for a moment walking across the street and getting a bite himself, but there was no way to do that without alerting Sabine that he was staying in town. The last thing he needed was Sabine to be suspicious of him or he'd never be able to help her.

His FBI buddy had gotten him all the information on the guy he'd remembered, and based on Beau's subsequent research, a picture of Sabine's family had started to take shape. He had nearly completed his investigation, more and more convinced that he'd not only identified her father but also located a whole host of living relatives. The kind that came with baggage. He'd dragged his feet on putting the final touches on the file, hoping to convince her to give up the search, but even if the earlier restaurant performance hadn't convinced him, he now knew for sure that Sabine had an ulterior motive for starting her search all over again and with such enthusiasm.

Whatever was up with Sabine LeVeche was serious business. He felt it in his bones. And even though he knew he shouldn't care, he wasn't even going to bother trying to pretend he didn't.

Chapter Seven

Sabine gave Mildred a hug and crossed the street to her building. They'd sat in the restaurant for hours, starting with catfish and ending with far too many cups of coffee. Now it was getting late and the hour coupled with the storm that was moving in had brought darkness to the dimly lit downtown area. Out of the corner of her eye, she saw a shadow move off to her left. She whirled around and stared into the inky darkness, trying to make out where the movement had come from. Two buildings down was a stack of crates outside of the general store on the corner. The owner's car was parked in front of the crates parallel to the sidewalk, even though the lines clearly were painted perpendicular. No matter, since there was so little activity this late in the evening.

She took a couple of steps closer to the end of the street and peered closely at the stack of crates. Was there something moving behind it? She shot a look back at the restaurant and bit her lip. There were only a few patrons inside and with the music playing and the general buzz of talking and serving, it would be unlikely anyone inside would hear her if she called for help.

Go back to your apartment, lock yourself inside, and call the police.

And tell them what? That you're spooked over some creepy

diary entry from forty years ago? Yeah, they'd love to hear that, especially after her phone call today, asking for an update on their nonexistent investigation on her break-in. Sabine got the impression that if Leroy and company never heard from her *or* Maryse again as long as they lived, it would be too soon. The Mudbug police were well-equipped to deal with drunk and disorderlies, or poaching, or off-season hunting, but breaking and entering and murder went a bit beyond their scope.

Then another thought crossed her mind—what if it was Hank? He wasn't exactly square with the local law, so hiding behind a bunch of crates waiting to talk to her wouldn't be a stretch. "Hank? Is that you?" Silence.

She bit her lower lip, then pulled her cell phone from her pocket. She pressed in 9-1-1 and slipped her phone into her palm, her thumb hovering over the Talk button. At least she could scream. They wouldn't have any idea where she was making the call from, but the police station was at the far end of town and surely someone would come running outside if she made the call. Surely.

She took a deep breath and headed toward the crates. One, two, three, four, five, she counted each step as she went, like knowing the number somehow made a difference. The crates were only twenty feet or so away and she stood stock still, trying to make out any shift in the shadows cast out into the street, straining to hear anything besides the wind blowing between the buildings.

Nothing.

She let out her breath and shook her head. *You're*

imagining things, Sabine, and the only thing you're accomplishing is scaring yourself. What was the point? If she wanted to lay wide-eyed in her bed all night, there was a twenty-four-hour run of horror movies on one of the local channels. At least that way she could have dry, non-blinking eyes and a pounding heart in the comfort of her pajamas and her bed. Not to mention a glass of wine to thin the blood and a double-fudge chocolate brownie to top off the sugar coma.

Then something moved again, just beyond the crates.

If she hadn't been looking directly at the shadows cast far out into the street, she would have missed the tiny sliver of movement, but she was certain she hadn't imagined it. Something was behind those crates. The shadow had seemed too long for an animal, so that left only one other option. And the only reason to lurk in the shadows was if you were up to no good.

She tightened her grip on her phone and leaned over to the side, trying to peer beneath the car. "Hank, is that you? If it is, come out. You're giving me the creeps."

And that's when he rammed her, his shoulder catching her right in the collar bone.

She'd grossly miscalculated, Sabine thought as she slammed down onto the sidewalk. He hadn't been behind the crates. He'd been hiding in the shadows on the side of the car, not five feet from where she'd stopped to listen. She screamed as she hit the ground, pain shooting through her shoulder as it took the brunt of the fall. She struggled to press the Talk button on her cell phone, but the fall had jostled it in her hand, and Sabine was certain the call didn't make it through.

She rolled over and jumped up as fast as possible,

knowing that a standing opponent was in a much better position to defend themselves than one lying down, but she was no sooner standing than the ski-masked figure shoved her, trying to knock her to the ground again. Sabine struggled to maintain her balance, and for a moment, she didn't think she was going to manage. But at the last moment, she managed to spin around and clock the masked figure in the shoulder with her heel.

The attacker stumbled backward. Through the slits in his mask, Sabine could see his eyes widen with surprise. He paused only a second to stare at her, then turned and ran into the woods at the edge of downtown. Sabine stared after him, sending up thanks for the seven years that she'd spent the time and money driving to New Orleans for martial arts lessons. Finally deciding that he wasn't going to try for a repeat performance, she picked up her cell phone from the sidewalk and hurried down the sidewalk to the police station.

No use sending up the alarm . . . especially not with Mildred right across the street and already worried about her. Her attacker was long gone and short of an Olympic sprinter or a bloodhound, there was going to be no catching him. Not tonight anyway. She paused for a moment before opening the door to the police station. This was really a waste of time, and she knew it, but regardless of their ability, it was still their problem. Maybe if odd things continued to happen around town, the city council might just figure out that an inept ex-fisherman and his otherwise unemployable nephew might not be the best choices to keep the city safe. She sighed as she pulled the door open.

Getting a competent police force was as likely as the town banning beer and losing religion.

Sabine exited the police station after what was probably the most frustrating thirty minutes of her life. Oh, there was a whole lot of writing—longhand—on legal pads, and the constant nodding and glances between Leroy and his idiot nephew, but it all amounted to nothing. The reality was, the business with Maryse had shocked the town but absolutely no one was willing to believe it was anything but an isolated incident—the ravings of a madman. And now that the madman was gone, there couldn't possibly be anything more than the normal redneck offenses going on in Mudbug.

At least that's what they wanted to believe.

There was noise across the street and she looked up in time to see the last of the patrons leaving the restaurant and the owner locking the door behind them. She glanced down at her watch and sighed. It was past time for her to be in pajamas, and she was going to regret every minute of her *Kill Bill* routine the next morning when her alarm went off.

"Is everything all right?" The voice sounded close to her and caused her to jump. Beau was standing next to his truck.

"Oh," she said, flustered. "I didn't see you there."

"Sorry. I didn't mean to startle you."

"No, it's not, I mean . . . I just didn't expect to see you here."

"I needed to talk to a few people around the area. The conversations went a bit longer than I thought they would, and I was hungry." He shrugged. "I decided to have dinner before I started the drive back. So . . . is everything all right?"

Sabine shook her head. "No. I don't think so, but I can't put my finger on it."

Beau stepped onto the sidewalk and looked closely at her. "What happened?"

"I saw someone lurking in the shadows on the corner when I left the restaurant." She let out a single laugh. "Listen to me—lurking in the shadows. I sound like a B horror movie." She looked at Beau, expecting to see him smiling, but his expression was serious and he didn't look happy.

"Lurking where, exactly?"

Sabine pointed to the end of the street. "The corner, just in front of the general store. I know I should have just minded my own business and gone home, but after the attempted break-in at my shop, I thought maybe someone was trying to break into the store."

"And you thought you'd apprehend a thief? Why in the world would you put yourself at risk like that? You've got a police station just down the block."

Sabine smirked. "Yes, and the state of our policemen is why I thought I was a better choice for the job. I might look fragile, but I assure you I can take care of myself."

"Really . . . you packing?"

"No. I mean, not on me. I *do* have a pistol if that's what you're asking."

"Not going to do you a bit of good in your sock drawer."

Sabine sighed. "Look. I appreciate your concern, really I do, but I'm trained in martial arts—seven years of training to be exact."

"So you learned that new how-to-stop-a-bullet ka-rate move. Is that what you're saying?"

"Oh, good Lord! Are you always this aggravating? So maybe I shouldn't have gone looking for trouble, although I hardly equate walking down Main Street with entering a war zone. Besides, I didn't get anything but a little dirt on my pants, but the guy sneaking around is going to feel the throbbing in his shoulder for a couple of days."

Beau studied her for a moment, then smiled. "Martial arts, huh? I assume you kicked him?"

"Yeah, I was off-balance so I used it to my advantage."

"I'm impressed. That's an advanced reaction. Well, at least let me walk you home. I know you don't need an armed guard, but you'll damage my chivalrous male ego if you turn me down."

Sabine stared at him, aggravated that she hadn't insulted his manhood, aggravated that he was impressed, aggravated most of all because she *liked* the fact that he was impressed. "Fine. If we run into trouble between here and the thirty steps to my doorway, you are free to take control."

Beau grinned. "I'll keep that in mind."

He fell in step with Sabine and they walked up the sidewalk to her building. For just a moment, Sabine thought he was going to take her hand in his and found herself disappointed when he didn't. *What the heck are you thinking? If he touches you, it's all over. Get your mind off the guy and onto bigger problems.*

They were halfway to her building, but the walk already felt like it had taken hours. She had to find something to take her mind off the gorgeous man next to her. Something to keep her from committing the ultimate sin—inviting him inside. She scanned the businesses on Main Street looking for inspiration. *Catfish, banks, dirty car, special on canned goods, massage—crap!* She blinked once and looked past the Mudbug Hair Salon & Spa. Rubbing naked bodies wasn't likely to make her forget anything—in fact in the split second it had crossed her mind, she'd added two or three more things to the list of what she'd like to do with Beau Villeneuve.

"Something else on your mind?" Beau asked.

"No." Sabine held in a groan, certain her face was flaming red. Thank God for a cheap town and dim street lights. "I mean, no more than any other day."

"You've got a lot going on. Maybe you ought to take a break."

"And do what? Even if I had unlimited funds and someone to take over my business for a while, geography isn't going to stop my mind from whirling."

Beau sighed. "No, it's not."

Sabine stopped in front of her shop and looked at him. "You say that like someone who tried it."

"Tried it and failed miserably." He looked down at the sidewalk.

Sabine bit her lip, knowing she should let this conversation end and go inside, but her curiosity had already gotten the better of her. "So how far did you travel to not forget?"

Beau looked back up at her. "In miles—who knows? Three continents, eleven countries, God knows how many cities, and a couple of islands that aren't even on the maps."

"Wow. You weren't kidding. I've never even been out of Louisiana."

Beau stared. "Wow. *You're* kidding."

Sabine held up two fingers. "Scout's honor. Unless you count the Gulf of Mexico for an offshore fishing trip."

Beau laughed. "Not exactly a world tour."

"No big deal, I guess. And the way things have been lately, there's plenty of excitement in Mudbug."

Beau's expression sobered. "A personal tour of the Australian outback is exciting. What's been going on in Mudbug lately is criminal, and that's just dangerous." He looked up and down the front of the shop building, then twisted the front door handle. "You sure you don't want me to take a look around? Everything looks okay, but . . ."

Sabine shook her head. "I'll be fine, but I appreciate the offer and the walk. Besides, you have a bit of a drive back to New Orleans."

Beau stared at her for a moment, as if he was contemplating saying something, or God forbid, doing something, but finally he nodded. "All right then. Goodnight, Sabine." He headed back down the sidewalk to his truck and Sabine let herself into the shop and made sure the new lock was turned all the way. She peeked out between the blinds and saw Beau sitting in his truck, looking at her shop. He waited a couple of seconds more before starting his truck and pulling away.

Sabine sighed. The triple threat—sexy, intelligent, and kind. Beau Villeneuve was the kind of distraction she just didn't need, but damned if she didn't want him anyway.

It was almost lunchtime, and Beau paced the microfiche room in the New Orleans library for at least the tenth time, holding his cell phone but not wanting to make the call. He'd verified everything he could and then spoken with the family's attorney. He was almost positive that he'd found Sabine LeVeche's family. After recognizing the man from Raissa's drawing in the Vietnam war criminal files, he'd dreaded the outcome. On the upside, the war criminal was an identical twin and hadn't been seen since the war. With any luck, the remaining brother was Sabine's grandfather, but Beau still didn't feel right about any of it.

The family's attorney had been short and dismissive when he'd first contacted the man the day before. Not that Beau blamed him. Based on his research, the family was quite wealthy and probably always had their share of nuts trying to get a piece of their money. Beau expected he'd have to contact the man again, but first thing that morning the attorney called asking for a photo of Sabine and the particulars of her upbringing. Less than an hour later, he'd called again, the incredulity in his voice apparent, stating that the family would like to meet Sabine at her earliest convenience.

No request for DNA testing, birth records, or any of the other hoops Beau had expected them to ask Sabine to jump through. Which bothered him even more. They knew something they weren't telling. No wealthy family accepted a long-lost granddaughter without some proof. It had to be something about Sabine's father. Aside from his driver's license, which didn't reflect his real name, no other form of ID was ever found in his car or in the apartment the couple was renting in New Orleans.

Supposedly, he was the oldest son of one of the wealthiest families in the parish. Yet he lived like a pauper with no past? People who abandoned their inheritance without looking back were running from the people who controlled the money. But why? What had those people done that was so horrible that an eighteen-year-old left the comfort of his family's estate and took a job working on the docks for minimum wage with a wife and infant daughter to support?

It couldn't possibly be anything good.

Shit. He'd been putting off the call to Sabine for hours. He couldn't put it off forever. Now that the family was aware of her existence, there was nothing to stop them from contacting her directly if they felt he wasn't moving fast enough for them. He started to press her number into the cell phone, then changed his mind. He scrolled through his call list and found the number he was looking for. He pressed the Talk button and waited for the woman to answer.

"Raissa? This is Beau Villeneuve. I need to talk to you about the research you hired me for. Can you meet me this afternoon?"

Thirty minutes later, Beau slid into a booth in a bar across the street from Raissa's shop. He gave the psychic a nod. "I really appreciate you meeting me." He gave Raissa the basics of his search and explained his current dilemma of how to approach meeting the family.

Raissa listened intently and when he was finished said, "I'm glad you called. I can see why you're not comfortable with this."

"I'm sorry to put you in the middle, but I didn't know who else to talk to. I mean, I've met Maryse, but she and Sabine seemed a little close for Maryse to be objective and, well . . ."

"And you didn't want to panic Maryse given the recent events in her own life." Raissa smiled. "Don't look so surprised, Mr. Villeneuve. You're a detective—former FBI. You'd be remiss if you didn't check the background of everyone Sabine is close to."

Beau nodded. "Please call me Beau. And you're right, of course."

"Well, Beau, I further deduce that once you started reading up on Maryse you were probably far too interested to stop at the surface level. She's had an amazing past month."

"Amazing is one way of putting it—so is frightening, overwhelming, and beyond statistically fortunate."

"It's certainly no secret that Maryse is lucky to be alive. The things that happened to her were fantastic but some of them could have been prevented. That entire situation still vexes me. I should have been more on top of it from the beginning. I knew something wasn't right—beyond the obvious. I could feel it in my bones."

Beau studied Raissa for a moment. "In your bones? No visions, no ghostly warnings?"

"The phenomenon doesn't work that way. It's usually very obscure, unplanned, and certainly not scheduled. To make matters worse, the dead are often confused and even when trying to help they can give mixed signals or the wrong information entirely. It's not an exact science."

"Some would argue that it's not a science at all."

Raissa inclined her head and studied him. "Some would also argue that the Holocaust didn't happen and that we never landed on the moon."

"Touché."

"Regardless of its fantastic nature, I still feel I should have picked up on something before things got that out of control for Maryse."

"How? Who would have thought those kind of things were going on in such a quiet little place? Who would ever have believed that such hideous secrets were hidden in a small town? Easier to hide in a crowded city where everyone isn't constantly in your business."

Raissa nodded. "There is some truth to that, of course. And people often migrate to large cities to 'disappear,' but in a small town, if you've very good, you can disappear in plain sight."

"What do you mean?"

"In the small town I grew up in, there was a drunk. He was upper forties to early fifties and everyone called him Walker because he was usually so drunk he couldn't even find his car keys, much less operate his car, so he walked everywhere he went. His house was at the end of an otherwise tidy little street of bungalows. But Walker's house was rundown—the roof sagging on one end, paint peeling from every square inch of wood. He didn't do much—picked up odd construction jobs from time to time, when he was sober enough. Then he usually went on a bender after that. Left town for a couple of days and came back snookered as ever."

Beau shrugged. "Okay, so almost every town has a drunk like Walker. Nothing special about that."

Raissa smiled. "No one in the town thought so either, until the day he disappeared."

"Disappeared?"

"His mail started piling up and people began to realize that no one had seen him for a while, although no one could put their finger on exactly when. A group of people went to his house and knocked on the doors and windows, but he never answered. His car was in the driveway, so he wasn't off on a bender. Finally, they called the fire department and had them break down the door, afraid he was dead."

"But he wasn't?"

"Not even close. The house inside was neat as a pin, although a layer of dust had settled over everything. There was no sign of Walker anywhere, and even more interesting, there was no sign of a bottle. The house was completely empty of booze. In fact, he didn't even own a shot glass, a bottle opener, or a corkscrew. When they went to leave, one of the men tripped over the kitchen rug and discovered a door in the floor beneath it. You'll never guess what they found in that makeshift basement."

Beau leaned toward Raissa, fascinated. "Bodies?"

Raissa laughed. "Nothing so evil. No, they found a printing press. Walker had been counterfeiting money. It took a while for the local police to sort it all out, but finally the truth emerged. No one knew exactly how long Walker had been manufacturing money, but a couple of people remembered when the 'benders' began."

"And they weren't benders?"

"Not at all. Walker waited until he had a good bit of the fake money ready, then took a trip to Las Vegas to launder it through the casinos. The police finally tracked down banking records where he'd transferred large sums of money from a bank in Las Vegas to the Cayman Islands. By the time Walker had disappeared, those transfers amounted to over three million dollars."

"Holy shit! What a story."

Raissa nodded. "All anyone in town saw was a drunk, and they didn't look any further."

"Hiding in plain sight," Beau said, his mind whirling. "It's brilliant."

"And simple. If Walker had been a recluse who rarely spoke and didn't get out among town, people would have gone poking around."

"Instead, he invented a personality that was loud enough for people to stop looking any further. They took it at face value and left it at that."

"Which is exactly what happened in Mudbug," Raissa pointed out. "And if I had to guess, might be what's happening with your search for Sabine's family."

Beau stared at Raissa for a couple of seconds. "You 'guess'?" He leaned in and lowered his voice. "Exactly how does that psychic thing work? I'm not saying I buy into it, but I'm not so hardheaded as to think I have all the answers, either."

Raissa studied him for a moment, then smiled. "You're attracted to Sabine, and you're worried about this less-than-normal way of life she has."

Beau sat back and put on his game face. "I didn't say anything like that."

"You didn't have to. And before you think the spirits are telling your secrets, I'll let you in on one aspect of my ability—a lot of it is simply the talent of reading people extraordinarily well, then putting everything together in one neat little package. Logic, deduction, an innate flair for understanding the psychology of human behavior. Not all is paranormal, Beau. A lot of what I do is no different than your FBI profilers would accomplish with the same information. It's just that sometimes, I have a little advantage."

"Okay, so maybe I find her interesting, and yeah, she's definitely not hard on the eyes . . . something you failed to mention, I might add."

"I wasn't aware that was part of your job-considering criteria."

"It's not. It shouldn't be. Oh, hell, I didn't ask to be attracted to her and don't want to be, if the truth's told. But it's too late to undo what's been done and that includes finding her family."

Raissa, who'd obviously been enjoying his flustering, sobered when he mentioned Sabine's family. "You're afraid they're hiding something."

"Barely legal teens don't usually run away from millions in inheritance to live in squalor."

Raissa sighed. "And people who have millions to leave in inheritance should have been able to find a missing teenager with relative ease—especially as he was less than a hundred miles from his hometown."

Beau nodded. "There's something else. It's Sabine. She's hiding something."

Raissa waved a hand in dismissal. "We're all hiding something."

"You know what it is, don't you?"

"Yes, I know some of Sabine's secrets. Do I know the particular one you've picked up on? I have no idea."

"And if these secrets are relevant to the case?"

"Then I would have already told you what I knew. I'm not a fool. I'd break a confidence if I thought Sabine was at risk from the things I knew."

Beau clenched his jaw, then released. He didn't like it but knew he wasn't going to get anything out of Raissa. "Okay. You know what's at stake. Knowing Sabine, how do you think I ought to proceed?"

"There's no going back now. Everything's already been set in motion."

"I know. That's the problem."

Raissa lifted her wine glass and swirled the red liquid around inside. She gazed at it as if in a trance, or looking for some magical sign. Hell, for all Beau knew, she might have been doing just that. Finally she frowned, sat the glass down, then looked him straight in the eyes. "Then I guess, unwanted attraction or no, you're going to have to keep an eye on Sabine for a while. You and Maryse are the only people they wouldn't question being part of the family reunion process, and you're much better equipped to handle what is likely to come than Maryse."

Beau narrowed his eyes at Raissa. "Exactly what did you see in that wine glass?"

"Nothing in particular. It's just that it suddenly struck me how much the color resembled recently spilled blood."

Beau walked from the pub to the parking lot, still uneasy from his conversation with Raissa. Everything the woman had said made sense, yet he was still hesitating over doing the one thing he knew had to be done. He passed the parking lot and kept walking, circling once around the block, his mind whirling with all the possibilities, most of them not good.

Finally, unable to come up with a good reason to delay any further, he pulled his cell phone from his pocket and pressed in Sabine's number. Maybe she wouldn't answer. Maybe she'd be watching a movie or painting her toenails and this entire conversation could wait until he was ready. Like maybe 2056.

But she answered on the second ring.

"Sabine," he said, "it's Beau."

"Hi, Beau," she said. "How are you today?"

"Er, fine. I'm fine. Um, Sabine, I have some news for you."

"Oh." Her previously pleasant voice took on a somewhat fearful tone. "What is it?"

"I think I've found your family," he pressed forward before he could change his mind.

He heard the sharp intake of breath and waited for her response.

"Oh my God," she said finally. "So fast? I mean, I'm glad, but I can't believe it. I guess I never really thought you'd find anything . . . after all these years, you know?"

"I understand. Sometimes you just need a fresh eye and a stroke of luck," he said, mentally cursing the television special on war criminals.

"I guess so. So what now? I mean, what am I supposed to do? Do I write to them, call them? I know I can't show up on someone's doorstep and expect them to be happy about it."

"That's all been taken care of for you," Beau explained. "The family is quite wealthy, and I was certain they'd want all contact made through their attorney. I've spoken to him already and provided him with the information I had. He's spoken to the family and apprised them of the situation."

"So what do I do now?"

"They want to meet you. If you'd like, I can set up

the meeting and go with you if that would make you more comfortable. I know this is very scary, and awkward, so please let me know how I can best help you."

"Yes . . . I, um, yes, that would be fine. I mean, set up the meeting and let me know what they say."

Beau felt his jaw clench involuntarily. "All right then. I'll call you as soon as I know something." He flipped the phone shut and shoved it in his pocket, trying to convince himself that everything had already been set in motion before his phone call. That call hadn't changed anything.

At least that's what he was going to keep telling himself.

Chapter Eight

Beau looked over to the passenger's seat and studied Sabine. "Are you sure you're ready for this?"

Sabine stared at the enormous iron gate and swallowed. Somewhere on the other side of the ten-foot stone fence was an estate, just forty-five minutes from Mudbug, where her family lived. Living, breathing relatives. Her dad's people. It all seemed like a blur. Twenty-odd years of searching with absolutely no results and now she had an entire family . . . grandparents, aunts, uncles, cousins, maybe even a dog. It was more than overwhelming. It was like waking up into a whole new existence.

She realized she hadn't answered and looked over at Beau. "I think so. I don't know. Maybe not?" She covered her face with both hands. "I'm sorry. You must wish you were anywhere but here with me."

Beau gently pulled her hands down and placed his hand on top of hers. "There's nowhere else I *need* to be. That's all that matters."

Sabine looked up at him. "I can't tell you how much I appreciate you doing this. I should have waited until Maryse could come."

"But that would have been another two days, right?"

Sabine nodded. "Yes. She would have cancelled her

plans, but the man she is speaking with is a scientist and could have information leading to the break she's been looking for in her own research. He's only going to be in the country a couple more days, and going to Houston was the only opportunity Maryse had to talk to him."

Beau didn't look completely convinced that the reason was good enough to dump her best friend on the eve of discovering her long-lost family, but Sabine couldn't help that. What she couldn't say was that Maryse's research had led her to a medication that could possibly eliminate the side effects of radiation treatment.

A medication Sabine herself would most likely benefit from in the very near future.

The truth was, Maryse had begged Sabine to put off this meeting until she could be there, but Sabine had already waited for so many years that even another two days felt like a lifetime. Besides, she had the rest of her life to introduce Maryse to her family. However long that turned out to be.

"They know I'm coming?" Sabine asked.

"Yes."

"And they know why?"

"I told their attorney everything," Beau assured her. "He spoke with the family and they asked him to arrange this meeting. There shouldn't be any surprises. At least not on their end."

Sabine caught the tone of his voice as he delivered the last sentence. It had been a sticking point between them, but other than the bare minimum, Sabine had insisted that Beau hold off giving her any detailed information about her family. She wanted to get a clear impression of them without the bias of any information Beau had uncovered during his investigation.

No surprises. Yeah right. She took in a deep breath. "Okay. Let's do it."

"You're sure?"

Sabine nodded. "I'm sure."

Beau squeezed her hand, then lowered the truck window and pressed a button on a speaker mounted in front of the gate. A man's voice sounded over the speaker, asking his name. Beau gave the man the information and a couple of seconds later, the gate began to open. Beau put the truck in gear and pulled through the gate and into an enormous courtyard. Acre after acre of sculpted hedges, row after row of beautiful flowers—a palette of color set against a lush lawn.

Beau guided the truck around a bend in the drive and the house came into view. Sabine gasped. It looked like something out of *Gone with the Wind.* A front porch complete with white columns reaching from the ground to the roof spanned the width of the main house. Wings stretched out from both sides of the main structure, making the entire thing at least the length of a football field.

Sabine finally found her voice. "Oh, my God. I know you told me the family was wealthy, but I had no idea . . ."

Beau stared in awe. "I had no idea either. I mean, there's wealth and then there's this. I haven't ever come in direct contact with this before."

Sabine swallowed. "Me either. Not even close." She said a silent prayer of thanks that she'd forgone her normal eclectic dress and decided on her navy pantsuit, a splurge at a designer shop having a good sale.

Beau circled a twenty-foot fountain and parked in front of the house. A middle-aged man wearing a brown suit came out to meet them. "I'm Martin Alford, the Fortescues' attorney."

"Beau Villeneuve," Beau said and shook the man's hand, "and this is Sabine LeVeche."

The man turned to Sabine and studied her for a moment. "Ms. LeVeche. It's a pleasure to meet you. I was very surprised when I got Mr. Villeneuve's phone call. We'd given up hope of ever hearing anything about Adam."

Adam Fortescue. Her father, although that wasn't the name that had been on the driver's license he carried in his wallet the day of the accident. It had been two days since Beau had given her the news that he'd located her father's family and she still couldn't wrap her mind around it.

"I'd given up myself," Sabine said.

The attorney nodded. "I can imagine this has been a shock for you as well . . . to find your family has been so close all these years."

"A huge one," Sabine agreed.

"Well," the attorney said, "are you ready to meet them?"

Sabine took a deep breath and looked over at Beau, who nodded. "I'm ready."

The attorney smiled. "This way, then. They're anxious, too, if it makes you feel any better." He turned and motioned them toward the house.

Beau stepped close to Sabine and took her hand in his, giving it a squeeze. She looked over at him, grateful for the strength his presence gave her. She took the first step following the attorney. Then another. And before she knew it they entered the mansion through a set of hand-carved doors.

Sabine tried not to gawk as they stepped inside, but the interior of the home was even more impressive than its exterior. She didn't know much about art and antiques, but one look at the paintings hanging in perfectly placed picture frame molding and the decorative tables nestled in front of them with beautiful ornate vases and crystal bowls screamed rare and expensive. The ceiling in this front room was vaulted all the way to the second floor and had an enormous crystal chandelier hanging in the center. Huge staircases spiraled on each side of the room, forming a balcony on the far wall.

"They're in the library," the attorney said and motioned to the hallway on the left.

Sabine followed slowly, trying to clear her mind, focus on the event she'd been wanting for over twenty years. She felt like she was in a dream and any minute she'd wake up back in her apartment, just as frustrated and alone as she'd always been. Her feet connected with the wood floor, her heels resounding on the hand-scraped wood, but she didn't feel the connection at all. It was almost as if she were gliding, floating in a forward motion. Surreal, that was the word for it.

The attorney opened a door at the end of the hallway and motioned for her to enter. She felt Beau give her hand one last squeeze. Then she took a deep breath and stepped through the doorway and looked at her family for the first time. A regal woman with silver hair stood next to the fireplace, holding a glass of wine. Her cream linen suit was obviously custom tailored and the diamonds surrounding her neck sparkled in the bright light. A man in a gray smoking jacket and black slacks stood beside her and Sabine stared, her breath catching in her throat. He was a perfectly aged re-creation of the image Helena had produced. Any shred of doubt she had that maybe Beau had made a mistake, that this wasn't her family, disappeared in an instant.

A woman sitting at the long table in the center of the room gasped. She had the same eyes and bone structure of the silver-haired woman, but that was where the similarities ended. The woman was probably in her fifties but the lines on her face belied the opulence surrounding them. Maybe living in such a state of presumed grace wasn't everything it was cut out to be. The woman rose from her chair and walked over to stand in front of Sabine. She reached up with one hand and touched Sabine's face, an amazed and somewhat fearful look on her face. The flat gray of her suit made her skin seem sallow. Her eyes were dull and lifeless.

"You look just like him," she whispered. "I didn't want to believe, but it's true."

Sabine froze, not certain what to do. The woman stared at her without blinking and somewhere deep in her gaze, Sabine saw something that didn't look right . . . didn't look stable.

The older woman stepped over to them and gently removed the younger woman. "You have to excuse Frances. She's a bit overwhelmed with all of this. She was very close to Adam when they were children, as twins often are."

Sabine snapped her attention to the older woman she presumed was her grandmother. "They were twins?" Surely that wasn't right. Sabine's father was only eighteen when he died. That would make him forty-six now. Frances looked at least ten years older than that.

"Yes," the older woman said. "A difficult birth but a blessed one as I got a boy and girl in one shot. Twins run in the family. It's something to keep in mind when you decide to start a family yourself." She smiled at Sabine. "I'm your grandmother, Catherine."

Sabine smiled back, but it felt weak. This was all so much more overwhelming than she'd ever imagined. Her vision blurred and she saw a distorted Catherine staring at her.

"Sit," Catherine said and guided her into a chair. "Hand me that glass of water," she directed Alford.

"Sabine?" She could hear Beau's voice next to her but couldn't force herself to turn and look.

"Poor dear," Catherine said, "this has all been a shock to you, too, hasn't it?" She placed a glass in Sabine's hands and helped guide it to her lips.

Sabine took a sip, then a deep breath in and out. Her vision sharpened and she looked over at Catherine and nodded. "I guess it has been a shock. I didn't realize . . ."

"I should have," Beau said and squeezed her arm. "Do you want to finish this another time?"

"No," Sabine said. "I'll be fine." She looked at Catherine, her grandmother. "I'm sorry about that. I promise to behave myself from now on." She smiled.

Catherine smiled back. "Well, since you're not going to hit the deck on us, I'd like you to meet your grandfather, William." She motioned to the silver-haired man who had been hovering at the end of the table. He stepped forward, and Sabine rose to greet him.

He studied her for a minute, almost making her uncomfortable with his scrutiny, then extended his hand. "You're the spitting image of your father." He smiled. "A bit prettier, though."

Sabine took his hand in hers and smiled back. "Thank you." Sabine looked over at the attorney. "And Mr. Alford? Is he family, too?"

"Not officially," Catherine said, "but he's here so often that it was either make him an honorary member or catalog him with the furniture." She smiled at her joke. Alford didn't look nearly as amused.

Sabine turned and gestured to Beau. "This is Beau Villeneuve. He's the private detective who solved the mystery."

William shook hands with Beau. "Guess we owe you a huge thanks. We never knew what happened to Adam and had no idea that he had a baby. We're sad to hear of his death, although after all these years we really didn't expect anything different. But Sabine is a surprise, and a good one at that."

"I'm glad I could help," Beau said.

"Why didn't you know?" Sabine asked, unable to hold back the question that had been stuck in her mind ever since Beau had told her that her family was in Louisiana and very well off. "Why did he leave? And why didn't you look for him?"

Catherine shot a look at William, then looked back at Sabine. "We didn't exactly approve of the relationship between him and your mother. Adam had plans to go to medical school. When we realized how much time he was spending with her, we were afraid he'd do something foolish and jeopardize his future. I'm afraid we forbade them to see each other, which looking back was foolish on our part, as it only made them more determined to be together."

"We did look," William said. "I don't want you to think we didn't, but it was if he'd vanished."

"And my mother's family?" Sabine asked.

Catherine shook her head. "She lived back in the bayou. We tried to locate her family, but no one back there would talk to us. We don't even know if she had any here."

William placed one hand on Catherine's arm. "It was a hard time," he said. "The police couldn't assist us, as Adam was an adult and had left on his own volition. We hired private detectives but with nothing to go on, we finally gave up after six months of futility. We honestly believed that he'd contact us again. And when he didn't, well, we were afraid the worst had happened."

Catherine nodded. "For years, every time the doorbell rang, my heart leapt in my throat with fear that the police were there to tell me he was gone." She sniffed and touched her nose with the back of her finger. "We didn't even know about you, Sabine. If we'd had any idea that your mother was pregnant when we forbid Adam to see her, we wouldn't have handled things that way. You're our granddaughter. We would have changed our plans to ensure you had a proper home and upbringing."

Sabine took all this in and nodded. "It must have been quite a shock when Mr. Alford told you about me."

"Oh, well, at first, certainly," Catherine said, "but then we were so excited, so happy that there was a piece of Adam in this world. We made a horrible mistake with our son, Sabine, and it cost us, him, you, and Mother. We're going to do everything we can to make up for that now. That is, if you'll allow us to."

Sabine studied Catherine's face, the anxiety, the sadness. "I'm certainly willing to try."

Catherine sniffed again, then nodded. "Well, now that the uncomfortable part is taken care of, what do you say we move into the living room and have coffee and some of Adelaide's great cookies? I happen to know she made a new batch this morning. We have so much to talk about and there's no point in being parched or uncomfortable while doing it."

Sabine and Beau rose and followed the family into a sprawling room filled with soft, plump leather furniture in beautifully blended earth tones. Sabine and Beau walked toward a chocolate-brown loveseat placed next to a beautiful stone fireplace, but before they could sit, an old Creole woman entered the room with a tray of cookies, a young Creole woman close behind her with coffee.

The old woman stopped short when she caught sight of Sabine, her mouth forming an "o." For a moment, Sabine was afraid she might dump the entire tray on what was most certainly a ridiculously expensive leather rug, but she steadied herself and placed the tray on a coffee table in front of the couch. She hurried over to Sabine and gathered her in a crushing hug.

Sabine was momentarily surprised at such an emotional response, especially since her family had been much more reserved, but she wrapped her arms around the woman and squeezed. When the woman pulled back, Sabine could see unshed tears in her eyes.

"Child," the woman said, "You are so beautiful. It's an omen that you come now. I feel it in my bones. Good's gonna come from this."

"Oh, Adelaide," Catherine said, waving a hand in dismissal. "Don't start with that voodoo nonsense of yours. I'm sure Sabine doesn't believe it any more than the rest of us." Catherine frowned at Adelaide, and then her expression shifted once more to her standard regal, bored look. "Adelaide has been with the family for all of her seventy-eight years. Her mother worked for my great-grandmother." Catherine gave the woman an indulgent but somewhat frustrated look. "You have to excuse her. She still holds to the old beliefs of her family."

"I have no problem with those beliefs," Sabine said and gave Adelaide a smile. "And I certainly hope this is a good omen. Thank you."

Catherine narrowed her eyes at Sabine. "You don't believe in that sort of thing, do you?"

Sabine shrugged. "I believe there are far more things in this world that can't be explained than can."

Frances gasped. "But surely you're a Christian. You *do* believe in God, don't you?"

"Yes," Sabine said, "but I don't limit His creations to only those I can understand."

Frances relaxed a bit but still seemed far more stressed than the comment deserved. "Well, I suppose you could have a point."

Adelaide laughed. "Oh child, it's gonna be so good having you home."

Sabine smiled back, comfortable that at least one person was truly happy to meet her and hopefully lacked a hidden agenda. "Well, it's not exactly my home. I already have a home in Mudbug . . . and a business, for that matter. But I hope to visit."

"You own a business?" Catherine asked and shot the attorney a questioning look "What kind of business is it?"

Sabine groaned inwardly. Apparently Alford had judiciously elected to leave out any information about her profession, not that she was surprised. After her exchange with Frances, she was afraid the answer to that question might push the family into scheduling a full-fledged exorcism. "It's a retail shop of sorts," she said, hoping that would distract them for a couple of days.

Catherine perked up a bit. "Clothing? I couldn't help but notice your shoes. They're very . . . interesting. I thought maybe one of those shops that carries old, unique items."

Sabine looked down at her pumps. They were white with different varieties of multi-colored flowers covering them. The five-inch heel was dark redwood. Interesting? Unique? Catherine uttered those words like she was wearing fuzzy, bunny house slippers. "Actually, I got these at Macy's."

Catherine glanced down at the shoes again and frowned. "Really? I've never seen anything like them before."

Sabine stared at Catherine, starting to feel a little irritated at their stiff-minded beliefs. *Might as well lay it all out now.* "I love the unique. I'm a psychic, and I own a paranormal shop in downtown Mudbug. I sell different magical items, herbs for spells, candles, that sort of thing. And I do tarot readings as well as channel dead relatives for those who are interested in talking to the other side."

The room went completely silent. Everyone was staring at her, with the exception of the lawyer, who looked irritated with the entire mess. The expressions ranged everywhere from confused (Catherine), to excited (Adelaide), and horrified (Frances).

Frances removed the hand that was covering her mouth. "You sell pagan items for profit?"

Sabine nodded. "I haven't ever heard it put quite that way, but yeah, I guess I do."

Frances stared at her, her eyes wide with fear, "You don't . . . I mean . . . I've heard that some people sacrifice chickens."

Catherine frowned. "You've been reading the newspaper again, Frances." She shot a look at Adelaide, who looked down at the floor. "You know reading the paper gets you upset."

"That's okay," Sabine said. "It's a common enough question." *From fools.* "I don't do anything like that in my shop. It's really more about fun than anything else."

Adelaide started to laugh. "Just what this family needed—something to shake the foundations."

William frowned at Adelaide. "Our foundations are fine, Adelaide. Don't you have something to take care of in the kitchen?"

"Certainly, Mr. Fortescue," Adelaide said. "I'll just leave you folks to sort out the rest of Sabine's life for her." She gave Sabine a wink and headed to the kitchen.

"Well," Catherine said, "this is certainly unexpected but nothing so dire as can't be fixed. You're a Fortescue now. I'd be more than happy to give you the money to start another enterprise . . . perhaps clothing, as we talked about before?"

"But I—"

Catherine gestured to Sabine to take a seat. "We have plenty of time to talk business. Now, it's time to talk family. Frances helped me pull all the photo albums from when she and Adam were children. I thought you might like to see those first."

Sabine sat on the couch and looked over at Beau. He was trying to appear nonchalant, but Sabine felt the tension coming off him. He looked around the room, barely glancing at the people, and for some inexplicable reason, she knew he got more in that glance than most would in a bio. He was sizing them up, reading them like he would a newspaper, then systematically calculating the inherent risks and consequences.

Sabine took in a deep breath and tried to concentrate on the album Catherine had placed on the table in front of her. Tried to squelch the bad feeling that she had just stepped into the eye of a hurricane.

It was long after dinnertime when Sabine and Beau drove through the giant iron gates on their way back to Mudbug. Sabine had been silent during the long drive down the winding road back to the highway, and Beau fought the urge to ask for her thoughts. But eventually he couldn't stand the silence any longer. "So . . . that was something."

Sabine looked over at him and smirked. "Don't you mean it was 'interesting'?"

Beau laughed. "Good Lord, woman. Remind me to never, ever comment on your shoes unless I think they're fabulous."

"It wasn't just the shoes, although the general holier-and-better-than-thou attitude got on my nerves." She frowned. "It was something else . . . just a feeling, but, oh heck, I don't know."

"A feeling like everyone in the room was performing a dance and you were the only one who didn't have the choreography?"

Sabine stared at him. "Wow. That's it exactly. You have an excellent way of describing things."

Beau shrugged. "I've seen that dance a time or two before."

"With the FBI?"

"With the FBI, in my private work, and unfortunately, in my own family."

Sabine studied him and Beau knew she wanted to ask about the reference to his family, but she apparently decided it was either rude or not the time. "So was that what you were expecting, given what you already knew about them?"

Beau considered this a minute. "You never know exactly what to expect from people, no matter how much you read about them on paper. But to some extent, it was what I was expecting."

"What part?"

"Everyone lies, Sabine. What you have to figure out is whether the lies are important."

Sabine stared out the windshield, her expression thoughtful. "Everyone lies. You really believe that?"

"Yeah. I do."

"I guess I do, too," Sabine said. "Although some are little white lies and some are told to keep someone from being hurt and others are told to avoid embarrassment."

"That's where the 'important' part comes in."

"I lied to you," she confessed. "Well, not exactly a lie, but I didn't tell you the entire truth."

Beau's hands tightened on the steering wheel, certain Sabine was about to tell him *the* secret. The one she'd kept even from Mildred. "The truth about what?"

"I'm not psychic. Not even a little. In college, I majored in business but had no idea what I was going to do when I graduated. Then one day I walked into a tarot shop in New Orleans as a last resort to find out anything about my family and met Raissa. Her shop was amazing. All those cool candles and powders and books. And the people who came in were so happy to see her." She sighed. "I guess I thought if I could recreate that for myself, I might find the answers I was looking for. Stupid, huh?"

Beau knew Sabine would be hurt if he showed her an honest reaction, but he couldn't stop the wave of relief that washed over him. Sabine was normal, kinda. At least far more normal that he'd thought she was just minutes before. But there was no way this was what she'd been keeping from Mildred. The hotel owner would have known that from the beginning.

Sabine shifted in her seat and Beau realized he had never said anything about her revelation. The anxious look on her face said it all. "It's not stupid," he said. "Creative, inventive, perhaps a shade of desperate, but not stupid at all."

Sabine smiled. "Thanks."

"No problem. So . . . Raissa, is she just in it for the pretty candles, too?"

"Oh, no! Raissa is the real deal. Her predictions are scary accurate. Makes Nostradamus look like he was smoking weed."

Beau laughed. "So you believe in it, but you can't do it?"

"Pretty much."

"Well, being open-minded rarely leads to surprises. At least, that's my opinion. So have you ever seen anything supernatural?"

Sabine smiled. "Once, I saw a ghost."

"Were you scared?"

"I was horrified, but that was because of her outfit."

"Ah, then maybe those people *are* your family."

Sabine grinned. "Touché."

"The drawing that Raissa did . . . was it really from a vision?"

Sabine's expression grew serious. "Yes."

Beau felt his curiosity rise. He hadn't believed for a moment that the psychic had gotten a drawing that accurate from a vision, but for the life of him, he hadn't been able to locate anything in Raissa's life that could have connected her with the Fortescues any way other than through Sabine. "But how did she see it? In a dream?"

"No. A ghost channeled it so that she could draw it for me."

Beau looked over at Sabine. "And you believe that?"

"I have to believe it. I saw it."

Beau immediately felt it—that twinge that Sabine wasn't exactly telling him the whole truth, but about what, he had no idea. Especially as she seemed completely sincere and adamant about the ghostly vision part of her story. "Well, now that you've met your family, there are some things I need to tell you about them and I don't think we should put it off very long."

Sabine nodded. "I know. I appreciate you respecting my wishes to meet them unbiased by the facts. But now that I've met them, I want to know what you found out."

"Of course. When do you want to do this?"

"I'm free tonight." Sabine looked over at him. "That is, unless you have plans already."

"No plans except taking care of my client."

A light flush crept up Sabine's neck and she lowered her eyes. "You're sure . . . I mean, it's not exactly a short drive back into New Orleans and I don't want to put you out, especially if you have things to do tomorrow."

"Not a thing but dirty laundry, and I'm pretty sure it won't care if I sleep in." Beau felt his jaw flex with the lie, but he didn't want Sabine to know he was staying across the street in the hotel. Not yet. Not until he had a damned good reason, and a gut feeling usually didn't qualify as a damned good reason for spying on a woman. Not to the woman, anyway.

"Well, I have leftover pot roast, chips, and sugar cookies. I can offer you a great sandwich and we won't have to worry about being overheard. Is that all right by you?"

Beau felt his pulse quicken. Alone with Sabine in her apartment. That was far more than all right. "That's fine," he said, hoping his voice sounded normal.

Chapter Nine

Sabine took a second bite out of her sandwich and tried to chew, but the roast beef that had been so juicy and filled with flavor the night before now tasted like cardboard. What the hell had she been thinking? Inviting Beau into her apartment? Feeding him roast beef? She should have suggested the restaurant. It was usually loud, and there would have been little chance of being overheard. No, instead she had to play happy hostess, serving home-cooked food just mere feet from the bedroom in her tiny apartment.

Like she didn't have enough trouble already. She should have told Beau no when he'd asked if she'd like him to accompany her to meet her family, although his offer had sounded more like an order now that she thought about it. Regardless, she couldn't afford to keep putting herself in this position. She was already horribly attracted to him, and spending time in such close proximity to wine and beds and the sexy lingerie in her dresser drawer wasn't the smartest thing to do.

But he's open-minded.

She held in a sigh. The men she'd dated in the past couldn't be bothered to hear anything about her job, her shop, her beliefs. They liked her but didn't buy into anything they couldn't prove. Which shouldn't have bothered her since, technically, Maryse had never believed either until Helena showed up. But Maryse had never had that smirk on her face when Sabine talked about the paranormal. Her friend had always respected her beliefs even if she hadn't been able to match them with her own.

And now this super sexy, kind, intelligent, single former FBI agent had actually listened to what she had to say about supernatural occurrences and considered the facts as seriously as he would have a fingerprint or a smoking gun. Sabine wasn't going to fool herself with thinking he believed everything she'd said, but he hadn't discounted it either. Which meant he was a rare individual.

"I hope I haven't scared you with all this," Beau said.

Sabine snapped back to the present. "Not exactly, although I must admit it's a little strange." Beau had been telling her dirty family secrets over the sandwiches and now she struggled to make some sense of it all.

She pulled a pad of paper over in front of her and began to write. After a minute, she pushed the pad over to Beau. "Is that right?"

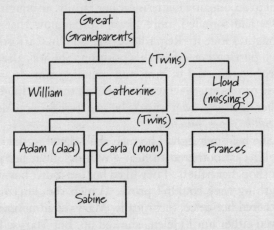

"Looks good to me."

Sabine looked at the family tree for a minute. "So the long and short of it is that my grandfather had a twin brother, Lloyd, who disappeared during Vietnam and was wanted for treason. The family is filthy rich and has spent almost a hundred years answering to essentially no one."

Beau nodded. "The FBI questioned them repeatedly about Lloyd and had them under surveillance for several years, but no one has seen hide nor hair of him since the Vietnam War."

"Any chance the family helped him hide?"

Beau shrugged. "Anything's possible, but the government tracked their funds for a long time. No money left their bank accounts that wasn't reasonable and explainable. And nothing was transferred to other countries."

"So most likely he died in Vietnam and his body was never recovered."

"Most likely."

"Well," Sabine said finally, "I'm glad you were so thorough. I would hate to start asking questions about the family twin legacy. Those people are so uptight, they'd probably have me removed from the property and banned for life."

"It does seem they're a little touchy about appearance," Beau agreed. "Based on the local gossip, at one time the family was a huge force in local charities, politics, and church, but ever since Vietnam they've become more reserved. Catherine still hosts several charitable events for the church during the year, but otherwise, she rarely interacts with the locals, and Frances is almost never seen out of the house except for church."

"Small wonder there," Sabine said. "I thought her head was going to spin around when she thought I killed chickens for a living."

Beau laughed. "I'd say Aunt Frances is definitely missing a step or two upstairs."

Sabine shook her head. "Hiding yourself away is counterproductive, really. Then people only assume you have something to hide, and let's face it, you probably do."

"Probably."

Sabine sighed. "I guess you're right. A family that old is bound to have secrets. What about William?"

"William seems to be the biggest disappointment locally. Apparently, before he left for the war he was always involved in a bunch of community service. He worked with underprivileged children at the local library, teaching them to read. He co-chaired several fundraisers to buy medical equipment for the clinic in town and was key in the development of a senior network that provided drop-in care for limited mobility seniors living alone, and all of that while he was still in high school."

"Wow, he sounds great."

"Past tense, I'm afraid. The William who came back from Vietnam isn't the same man as before. The only charity he attends to now is the local bar, and from what I hear, he's a big contributor."

Sabine shook her head. "Post-traumatic stress?"

Beau shrugged. "There's really no telling. Lots of men come back from war changed forever."

Sabine's mind went back to the scene in the living room when she'd described her business. "So what's the story on crazy Aunt Frances?"

Beau crinkled his brow. "You know, that's one thing I was never able to get much of a line on. Both kids attended the private Catholic school in town, but some of the older residents seemed to remember your father. He did some volunteer work down at the clinic, most particularly for a Dr. Grey, but the doctor died several years ago so I wasn't able to get any more than that."

"Makes sense with the family saying he was going to be a doctor."

"Yeah. Even wealthy families usually don't frown upon working for a living if you're a doctor."

"But the locals didn't really know Frances?"

"Not really. She attended private school until she was seventeen and was homeschooled after that with a private tutor from another parish. He's dead now, so that led nowhere. Other than that, she's never seen outside of the house, except attending church, always at her mother's hip and never speaking a word to anyone."

"Agoraphobic?"

Beau shrugged. "I don't know, and I seriously doubt you'll ever get them to admit it if that's the case. Whatever those people are hiding, they've been doing it successfully for a long time. That's why I thought you needed what little facts I had before you had any more interaction with them . . . assuming you want to, of course."

Sabine looked out the window and across Main Street. At the moment, she would honestly have to admit she didn't want any further interaction with them. The entire meeting had been like the tiny pop of a firecracker when she'd been setting up for a dynamite experience all these years. But then what choice did she have? "I . . . guess I do. I mean, I don't really know them yet and they don't know me. I suppose things could get better."

"I suppose."

Sabine smiled and looked over at Beau. "This is what you were warning me about, wasn't it? You and Maryse are cut from the same cloth in certain ways."

"Really? How's that?"

"Oh, Maryse has always supported my search for my family, even though I believe that for the most part, she's thought it was a waste of time. She thinks the relationships you choose to make are far more important than the ones that are forced on you. She's always saying 'you have to love your family, but you don't have to like them, or want to spend time with them.'"

Beau grinned. "You're right. We *are* cut from the same cloth. So what's up with Maryse's family that she doesn't have to like them?"

"Oh, nothing at all with her blood family. Her mom and dad are both dead and there's no other siblings. I think she's referring to her ex-husband and his mother when she makes that statement."

"That bad, huh?"

Sabine grimaced. "You have no idea. Helena Henry as a mother-in-law is enough to drive a girl to the convent."

"I read about Helena's death in the paper, then all the excitement that followed. That wasn't that long ago."

"Yeah, the funeral was last month."

"Well, then it looks like Maryse is free and clear again." He smiled at Sabine.

Sabine tried to smile but wasn't sure she managed it convincingly. "Seems like she should be," she hedged.

Beau glanced down at his watch and rose from the table. "It's late. I need to take off and let you get some rest. I'm sure you're exhausted."

Sabine rose from the table and walked with Beau to the door. "I am a little tired. I think I'm going to take a long, hot bath, then climb directly into bed."

Beau froze when she mentioned a bath and bed, and she stepped far too close to him for her own comfort, and probably his. He studied her for a moment, the desire in his eyes apparent. Even though she knew she should step away, open the door, and send him on his way, she didn't. No, she inched even closer . . . and tilted her head toward his.

His breath caught. She knew he was waiting for her to turn tail and run like she had at the café. When she held her ground, he lowered his head, his lips barely brushing hers. Her lips started to tingle and the tiny shock of pleasure radiated all the way down to her toes. He paused for just a second, but then moved in for a deeper kiss, his lips locked on hers.

She leaned into the kiss, her body perfectly molding into his. He wrapped his arms around her, and she felt the hard lines of his chest press into her. She parted her mouth, and he deepened the kiss before pulling away from her lips and trailing kisses down her neck. She sighed with pleasure, her skin jumping alive with every touch of his lips. She opened her eyes just a tiny bit, wanting to see his face, the desire that she knew would be there—and saw something move in the kitchen.

Somehow, she managed to keep herself in check, but as she opened her eyes completely, it was clear that they weren't alone. The refrigerator door stood wide open and a huge hunk of rapidly disappearing roast beef dangled just outside of the door. Instantly, Sabine's mind jerked back into reality. What the hell was she doing?

She broke away from Beau, her quick retreat leaving him with a confused expression. "I-I'm sorry . . . I can't . . ." She stepped to the side, praying he didn't turn his head or Beau Villeneuve was going to get a crash course in the "I want to believe" games.

Beau's expression hardened. "That's all right. I understand. You won't have to remind me again." He opened the door and stepped through it.

"Wait," Sabine called after him, but he hurried down the stairs, never once looking back.

Sabine waited until the door slammed shut, then trudged downstairs to lock the door. She peeked out the front window, but Beau's truck was already gone. Frustrated with herself, she went back up to her apartment.

The roast beef was still floating, but now a jar of mayonnaise was suspended along with it, the roast beef seeming to dip itself in the jar then disappear in pieces. "I don't care if you're dead—this is still breaking and entering, not to mention theft. And at the very least, it's just plain rude, even for you."

The sandwich stopped moving and hung in midair. "Oh, please," Helena said, "You were so wrapped up in that detective, I could have slaughtered a cow and started a barbeque right on your kitchen table and you wouldn't have noticed."

"Oh really? So why is it that I sent him packing as soon as I saw you?"

"Hmmmm, guess I didn't exactly put that together."

"How could you? You were too busy robbing me of my leftovers."

"Next time I'll be less obvious."

"Ha!" Sabine laughed. "You're about as unobtrusive as a freight train running through here. Besides, I don't want you sneaking, either."

"I can see why, if you're going to act like a hooker at your front door. Although, there's a huge advantage to you not being able to see me. That Beau is damned good looking . . . almost as good looking as Maryse's man, but she always catches me. With you, I have a really good shot at seeing some prime male behind before I leave this earth."

An image of making love with Beau flashed through Sabine's mind. Helena was right—his behind was grade-A prime beef. And the image would have been perfect, except for the floating buffet at the end of the bed. Sabine shuddered. *No way.* "From now on, you will announce yourself before you walk through the walls, do you understand me, Helena? I can still do that exorcism."

"Yeah, yeah. Jeez, you and Maryse are such bores. It's a wonder men are interested in you at all."

Sabine thought about the look Beau had flashed her just before he practically ran out of her apartment. "I don't think that's something I have to consider any longer."

"Oh, I wouldn't write him off just yet . . . not with the way I've seen him look at you." The roast beef began its journey into the mayonnaise again. "Damn! This is some of the best roast beef I've ever eaten. If you gave him some of this, he'll definitely be back."

Sabine sighed and sank into a chair at the kitchen table. "What if I don't want him to come back?"

The sandwich stopped moving again and just hung there. Finally, it moved forward along with the mayonnaise jar and then they both came to rest on the kitchen table. The chair across from her slid backwards and the cushion flattened.

"You're afraid," Helena said. "You're afraid of letting him close to you because of the cancer."

"Maybe. Yes. Well, wouldn't you be?"

"Probably. The question is, are you scared for him or yourself?"

Sabine buried her head in her hands, her heartbeat pounding in her temples. "I wish I knew."

"I know my opinion probably doesn't count for anything, but I'm going to tell you like I told Maryse. Don't make the same mistakes I did. I lived a pretty damned long life of nothing, hiding myself from people, afraid to make connections because I might get hurt. I married a man I knew I could never love, had a child that I never could connect with, and died without a single friend to my name."

Sabine looked across the table at the empty space, wishing she could actually see the woman who was speaking. "You think the risk is worth it? To admit your feelings for someone who might not feel the same way? To share your darkest secret knowing it could be the one thing that drives them away? Or even worse, to have them stay and love you and in the end, lose it all to a dreadful disease?"

"But you'll never ask yourself what if."

Tears began to form in Sabine's eyes. "I hate it when you're right." She wiped at her eyes with the back of her hand, silently willing the unshed tears to disappear. "I met my family today."

Her comment was met with dead silence and for a moment, Sabine wondered if Helena had left, but the seat cushion was still flattened. Finally, Helena spoke. "I didn't realize. So what happened? I mean, if you feel like telling me that is . . . wow, I can't even imagine . . . almost thirty years of not knowing, right?"

"Just about. They're . . . different, I guess would be the polite way to describe them. Wealthy. Hey, maybe you could help me understand things along that line. I know people with money have a different set of rules, but I'm having trouble getting a handle on it. The meeting today was, well, I guess the best word is 'weird.'"

"Wealth often comes with conditions. Most people don't realize it because the wealthy keep everything hidden. But family structure is paramount. Keeping appearances is the second priority, right after keeping the money. It's definitely a different world. And not often a pleasant one for children."

"Yeah, I'm kinda getting that."

"So who is the family? Anyone I would know of?"

"Maybe. They're not that far from here. The family name is Fortescue."

"Holy shit! The Fortescues? Jesus, no wonder you said they were weird. Hell, weird is polite. Nuts is a better description."

Sabine felt her pulse quicken. "You know them?"

"As well as one half-ass recluse can know another. I never had much interaction with the whole family, but I did deal with Catherine before she married William. The family pretty much dropped out of sight during

Vietnam and never really emerged again except church events, and I always tried to avoid church events. My hypocrisy only extended to writing checks, not actually attending. The rumor mill was always running on about them though."

"Really? About what, exactly?"

"Some said Frances went crazy, and that's why they didn't come out, but that never made sense to me. Frances was only a baby during Vietnam and attended the Catholic school in town for some time. Some said Catherine was the crazy one and she made Frances that way, since she dropped out of school her senior year. Some said William was never right after the war. No matter, most everyone assumed someone— or everyone—in the family was crazy. Then the son disappeared when he was a teenager—hey, that must have been your father. Damn, this is getting interesting. And seeing as how William's brother had disappeared years before, everyone wondered what religion exactly was being practiced in that house. Last I checked, Christians didn't make people disappear, but that family had more than their share of missing relatives and no answers for it, according to the local police."

"So what did people think happened?"

"There was speculation that the family was hiding the wanted brother, Lloyd, during and after Vietnam, which is why they pulled back so much from society. But I figure there was probably all sorts of government agencies just itching to find Lloyd, so there was little chance they could have hidden him all those years, even in that monstrous house of theirs. More likely he died in Vietnam and was never recovered."

Sabine nodded. "That seems to be the most likely.

And my father? Did you know anything of him besides his disappearance?"

"Seems the townspeople knew your father pretty well. Apparently he didn't stick to the rest of his family's rules about associating with the lower class. There was always rumors that he'd taken up with someone the family didn't or wouldn't approve of. Most thought he'd simply run away with the girl, even though he was giving up a fortune in inheritance to do it."

"And when no one saw him again?"

"I don't know. People speculated for a while, but I think they finally decided that the family must have given him some money to keep their secrets and stay away. After a while, no one spoke of him at all."

Sabine considered this for a moment. "But if anyone knew anything, or even thought they knew anything, they might be willing to tell me now, right?"

"Possibly, but I wouldn't swear to it. Some think the past is better left buried. Some just don't want to get involved in other people's business . . . not the serious kind anyway. General gossip over extramarital affairs and plastic surgery is one thing, speculating about the possibilities of bribery and murder is entirely different. And with Catherine and William still alive, it might not be the smartest thing to go speculating on."

"But it's possible someone would be willing to?"

Helena sighed. "You're not going to let this go, are you? I suppose I could come up with a name or two for you to start with, but you have to promise me to be careful. Hell, Maryse got caught up in all that mess just by doing her job. You asking questions about things people might want to keep buried is a lot more risky."

"I want the truth, Helena, but you're right. I promise to be careful, and if it starts to look dangerous at all, I'll stop. Okay?"

"It's already dangerous. The wealthy don't like their secrets in the public eye, even if everyone else wouldn't blink twice at them. Everything's a possible embarrassment to them. Everything's a possible slur to the family name. Whole lot of bullshit if you ask me, but then, I didn't exactly play by the rules of money. Probably why I never got invited to those fancy parties. Ha."

"If I didn't know any better, I'd guess that part was intentional."

"You've been hanging around me too long."

"That is an overstatement." Sabine rose from the table. "I'm going to take a hot bath and crawl in bed with a glass of wine."

"Hmmmm, wine sounds good. Hey, I wonder if I can get drunk. What do you think?"

"I think we're not going to try. Good night, Helena."

"Wait a minute. If you have a phone book, I can probably jot down a couple of names for you. My memory's not what it used to be, but the phone book should bring it back."

Sabine pulled a thin local phone book from her kitchen drawer. She placed the directory, a pad of paper, and a pen on the table in front of Helena's chair, then headed off to start her bath.

Twenty minutes later, she emerged from the steamy water feeling much more relaxed. Especially for someone whose life was falling apart at every end. She pulled on her pink cotton pajamas and headed into the kitchen to see what Helena had found. The ghost hadn't made a noise the entire time Sabine was in the bath, which meant she was either engrossed in her studies or all that food had put her in carb overload and she was asleep on the kitchen table.

"I came up with three names," Helena said as Sabine entered the kitchen, "but I think one of them died a couple of years ago, so maybe only two. Hell, to be quite honest, the other two might be dead by now, too. These women were closer to my mom's age than mine."

Sabine leaned over and took a look at the list, but the names weren't familiar to her. "Do they live in Mudbug?"

"No. The dead one was from Rabbit Island and the other two were up around Bayou Thibodeaux."

"That's close to my family, right?"

"Yeah, a couple of miles up the bayou from town, but they could be anywhere now. Still, if anyone's going to know the local gossip, it would be these two. If they're still alive."

Sabine nodded. "I'll check tomorrow." She stepped into the kitchen, pulled a brand-new bottle of wine from her refrigerator, removed the cork, and poured herself a generous glass. Then she took a couple of sugar cookies from the cookie tin, since apparently Helena had helped herself to the ones on the table, and headed to the bedroom. "I'm off to bed, Helena. Turn off the kitchen light when you're done, all right?"

"No problem," Helena replied.

Sabine placed the glass of wine and cookies on her nightstand next to the latest thriller she was reading and climbed into bed. Between the hot bath, the wine, the sugar, and the book, she ought to be out like a light in no time. She took a nice, slow sip of the wine, a huge bite of a cookie, and opened the book to her marker.

She'd barely read the first two sentences when she realized something was wrong.

Her breathing constricted, like a whooping asthma attack, and she could feel her heart beating double-time in her chest. She tried to sit up straight, hoping to expand her lungs a bit, but she seemed rooted in place, her limbs not responding at all. She tried to yell, but it came out not much more than a whisper. "Helena. Helena, help."

She strained to hear something . . . anything moving in her apartment, but only the ticking of the kitchen clock met her ears. *This is it. I'm going to die.* Frantic, she struggled with her lifeless body, but couldn't move her hand more than an inch. "Help. Helena, help."

"What the hell are you whispering for?" Helena's voice boomed next to her. "Speak up if you want something."

Sabine opened her mouth, at least she thought she did, but no sound emerged. She looked at the side of the bed where she'd heard Helena's voice, frightened beyond belief. Helena was her only chance. If the ghost couldn't figure out what was going on, she was going to die right here in her bed.

"Holy shit!" Helena said, apparently realizing something was very wrong. "Just hang in there. I'll dial 911."

Sabine saw the cordless phone rise from her dresser and heard the numbers being depressed. Then the phone glided across the room and stopped with the mouthpiece at her lips. The operator answered and Sabine struggled to get out a word. "Help." Her voice was so faint, she didn't know if the operator had heard her at all. "Help," she said again and slipped into unconsciousness.

Chapter Ten

Beau tossed Sabine's file on the dresser with his gun and wallet and plopped back onto the worn-out recliner with a sigh. Another hour of reading over the same information and still he had nothing. He reached for the remote and turned on the television. He needed a distraction—one that didn't have coal-black hair and a body that was an art form. He shook his head. *Stupid. That woman is nothing but trouble, yet you insist on humiliating yourself over her. Real smart, Villeneuve.* He jumped up from the chair and paced the length of the room, all three steps of it, then turned and paced it again. *The job is officially over, and it's not your business to play bodyguard. Get back to New Orleans and forget your ever met Sabine LeVeche.*

He sat on the end of the bed with a sigh. If only it was that easy.

It should have been easy. It should have been a piece of cake. It wasn't like Sabine was the first woman he had ever been attracted to. But this woman . . . this woman with strange beliefs and a huge can of worms for a family had stopped him cold in his tracks.

It just didn't make sense.

Sabine LeVeche was everything he didn't want in his life. Her beliefs defied logic and science. She was smack in the middle of a huge family drama, and her family was a nightmare of old-school beliefs and even older money. God only knew what they had been hiding behind those stone walls for all these years, and Beau didn't want to know. But Sabine would, and that's where his dilemma came in. Sabine LeVeche would look for answers until there were no questions left.

Beau knew all too well that those questions just might unleash a nightmare.

The family had been polite enough and had seemed as if they were glad to learn of Sabine, but they were still guarded in the information they dispensed. He wasn't even going to launch into the weirdness factor. It went without saying. If Sabine veered off into the wrong line of questioning, they'd close ranks in a second, complete with the attorney to back them up. The attorney had hovered over the group the entire afternoon. Always standing and studying the room like he was getting ready for a major coup. If Beau had been a lesser man, he might have found it unnerving. Instead, he'd just found it annoying.

And none of it is your problem.

Mind made up, Beau leaned over to untie his tennis shoe. He was going to get a good night's sleep and first thing in the morning he was going to head back to New Orleans, send an itemized bill to Sabine, and try to forget everything he knew about this case. He couldn't afford to get involved on a personal level. Already the dreams were starting to return. It had taken him years to get a good night's sleep again. He wasn't about to jeopardize that for a stranger who'd repeatedly made it clear she had no interest in getting to know him better.

He pulled one shoe off and had just started on the second when he heard the sirens. His heart leapt to his throat and the completely irrational feeling that something bad had happened to Sabine washed over him like rain. He jumped up from the bed and peered out the hotel window. The ambulance exited the highway and raced into town, sirens screaming. He hadn't taken a breath since he'd leapt off the bed, but when the ambulance screeched to a stop in front of Sabine's store, the air all came out in a whoosh. He didn't even stop to grab his other shoe before he tore out of the hotel, almost knocking down the hotel owner as he ran across the street.

The paramedics had already burst in through the front door of the shop and Beau ran past the policeman standing at the door without bothering to identify himself. He dashed up the stairs, the policeman close behind him, yelling for him to stop. He ran into the apartment and, finding the front rooms empty, dashed into the bedroom. What he saw brought him up short.

The paramedics wheeled Sabine out on a gurney, an oxygen mask strapped to her pale face. She looked unconscious. "What's wrong with her? What happened? Damn it, someone answer me!"

"We don't know. You have to move, sir!" one of the paramedics yelled as they rushed past him with the gurney.

"Where are you taking her?" he called after them.

"Mudbug General," the paramedic called back as they hurried down the stairs as fast as they could go.

Beau started to follow, but the policeman who had chased him upstairs hitched his pants up with one hand and put his other on Beau's chest. "Buddy, you ain't going nowhere until you tell me who the hell you are and how you know Sabine."

Mildred, who had followed close on the heels of the

officer, rolled her eyes at Barney Fife, then fixed a hard stared on Beau. "I'd like an answer to that question myself."

Beau reached into his pocket, then remembered he'd dashed out of the hotel without one of his shoes, much less his wallet. This wasn't going to go near as quickly as he'd like. So far, he was as unimpressed with the Mudbug police as Sabine was, but he'd bet money that the hotel owner could take him down if he failed to satisfy the two of them. "I'm a private detective, former FBI. I was hired by Ms. LeVeche to find her family. I'm staying at the hotel across the street and ran over here when I saw the paramedics enter Sabine's building. My wallet is in my hotel room."

"I'll be needing to see that before you can leave town." The officer stared at him for a moment. "So I can assume that when Ms. LeVeche is able, she'll verify your story?"

"Of course. Jesus, I just had dinner with her here, in this apartment. I only left a little over an hour ago, max. What the hell happened? Why did the paramedics come?"

"There was a 911 call from the phone here, but no one spoke. When that happens, the rulebook says we have to assume a crime is happening or someone's croaking, so the police and the ambulance have to pay a visit."

"And since there was no sign of forced entry, you assumed a medical emergency and the paramedics entered," Beau said.

The officer narrowed his eyes. "I didn't have time to check for 'forced entry,' as you call it. Damned medics had broke the door down before I got here."

Mildred looked at the cop in disgust. "For Christ's sake, Leroy, you're a block away and the hospital is ten miles up the highway. If you'd stop wasting taxpayer money looking at internet porn, you might be able to do your job. Although I still have my doubts."

Beau's opinion of the hotel owner went up a notch.

"I'll check out your story, Mr. Villeneuve. And assuming Ms. Mildred will vouch for you staying at her hotel, I guess I'll let you drop by with that identification. In the meantime, I'd prefer it if you stuck around Mudbug. At least until Sabine can verify what you've said."

"I'm only going as far as the hospital, as soon as someone tells me where it is exactly," Beau assured the man, who gave him a brief nod and left.

"Good," Mildred said, giving Beau a shrewd look. "I'll give you directions and you can give me a ride. And since I'm 'vouching' for you, you can explain on the way why you're staying in my hotel and requested a room that faced Sabine's store. Sabine told me her family was located days ago, so why all this bull about having business with her now?"

Beau sighed and motioned Mildred down the stairs. "I'll tell you, but you're probably not going to believe me."

"Try me," Mildred said and headed down the stairs and out the door.

Beau made the fifteen-mile drive to Mudbug General in ten minutes flat, hoping like hell that the policeman was back at the station checking on his story or looking at some of that internet porn Mildred had mentioned and not pulling over speeders headed out of town. Mildred had left a message for someone, probably Maryse, as soon as they got in the truck, then demanded he give her the details of his surveillance. He filled her in on the basic points of the situation and had just wrapped up when they reached the hospital. He tore into the parking lot and screeched to a halt in the closest parking space he could find to the emergency room. He jumped out of his truck and ran to the hospital. Mildred was hot on his heels, surprising him by how fast the large woman could move.

A nurse at the front desk gave them a dirty look when they burst into the lobby, but her expression shifted to concern when they asked for Sabine. "The doctors are working on her, but she's stabilized," the woman said. "I haven't heard any details yet, but Dr. Mitchell will be out as soon as there's something to tell." She gave Mildred a sympathetic look. "I'm sure we'll know more about your daughter soon. Is there anything I can get you while you wait?"

"No, thank you," Mildred said, "we'll just wait over here if that's okay." She pointed to a couple of chairs in the corner of the room with a clear view of the hallway to the emergency room.

"That's fine," the nurse said.

"Guess there's nothing left but the waiting." Mildred sat on the edge of one of the chairs, her hands clenched together in her lap.

Beau studied her for a moment. "You didn't correct the nurse when she assumed you were Sabine's mother."

"No cause to correct the facts, is there?"

"I thought her aunt raised her."

Mildred nodded. "She did, as best she could anyway. Margaret was no spring chicken when the state gave her custody of Sabine, and she didn't get any younger. Then Sabine met Maryse in elementary school and they were tied at the hip ever since. So you might say I got a double blessing."

Beau stared at Mildred in surprise. "You're Maryse's mother? I thought Sabine told me her parents were dead."

"They are. Her mother died shortly after Maryse's birth and her father a couple of years ago. I helped with the baby after her mother died, and eventually her father and I started seeing each other on a personal basis. Did right up until the day he died."

Beau nodded in understanding. "So you *are* their mother. In all the ways that count anyway."

Mildred sniffed and looked down at the floor. "I like to think so. Those girls mean the world to me. All that business with Maryse last month damned near gave me a heart attack, and now this. You told me on the way over here that you stayed in the hotel to look out for Sabine because you had a bad feeling but no evidence. What is going on with my girls, Beau? You gave me the facts, but that doesn't tell me anything. Tell me what you think—I don't care if you can prove it or not."

Beau took a deep breath and slowly blew it out. "I didn't know anything about Maryse's situation until Sabine mentioned it. Then I read up on it and I think it might have damned near given me a heart attack, too. She's very lucky to be alive. But the man who was after her is dead, right? Probate is over and the father-in-law is setting up residence in a New Orleans jail awaiting trial." He shook his head. "I can't see where that has anything to do with whatever is going on with Sabine."

"Just because we don't see it doesn't mean it's not there."

"You're right, of course. I'm just a little surprised to hear someone else try to make two and two equal five like I do."

Mildred waved a hand in dismissal. "Oh heck, I've been doing the hotel accounting long enough to know that two and two equals whatever you want it to be. It's simply a matter of perception and misdirection."

Beau smiled. "Okay. So let's say there's a common factor, but we don't know what it is. We also don't know if the common factor is the cause of the problem or not. It could be something as simple as them being friends, or Maryse inheriting money, or it could be nothing at all."

Mildred gave Beau a shrewd look. "Maryse isn't the only one set to come into money now, right?"

"Yeah . . . I started worrying about that all of about two seconds after I found out who Sabine's family was. Unless they're putting up an awful good front, the Fortescues have more money than any family I've ever met."

"I was gonna have breakfast with Sabine tomorrow morning and hear all about the meeting. Guess that might have to wait now. So did the Fortescues accept what you told them about her?"

"They seemed to take it all in stride. I'm sure when it comes down to the details, someone, most likely the attorney, will insist on a DNA test."

"But you have no doubts?"

Beau shook his head. "No. Sabine is the spitting image of her father, and the grandfather, for that matter. If you could have seen those pictures of when he was young . . . it was mighty convincing. By my estimate, Sabine is poised to inherit a fortune."

"You really think they'll just hand over a buttload of money to someone who is still essentially a stranger, DNA or no?"

Beau nodded. "Yeah, I do. Once word gets out that Adam had a daughter and she was found, the family will do everything they can to make up for lost time. Remember, appearances are the most important thing to the Fortescues. And what would people think if they didn't bring Sabine into the fold and treat her as the grandchild she is?"

"And you think that might make someone un-happy?"

"Maybe. There's only the aunt left in the house with the grandparents and they don't associate with any extended family, but assuming no aunt and no Sabine, there's any number of estranged cousins and such who would probably come into a tidy sum when the grandparents were gone. The aunt didn't strike me as all that healthy looking, so she probably isn't a huge concern. She seems emotionally unstable and it might be that she couldn't even withstand her parents' death."

"Which leaves Sabine."

"Exactly."

Mildred sighed. "Does it strike you that all these problems seem to center on money, even though Maryse's situation ultimately wasn't about the money, per se?"

"Oh, yeah. If there's one thing I learned in the FBI, it was that money is the greatest motivator of all. We had a saying there—'there's three things you don't mess with, a man's money, his wife, or his children—in that order.'"

Mildred gave him a knowing look. "Some days, it just pays to be poor, single, and childless."

Sabine awoke with a series of wires attached to various parts of her body. She blinked, trying to clear her blurry vision, then blinked again. Her eyes were still watery, but she could make out a small hospital room, like the equipment hadn't given that away. No separate bathroom, so she must be in the emergency room. Helena must have been able to make the call. Thank God. The last thing she remembered was calling to the ghost for help.

"Sabine, can you hear me?"

Sabine looked across the room but didn't see anyone. "Helena? Is that you?"

"Yeah. I'm standing next to your bed."

Sabine turned to the side, expecting to find nothing but air, and sucked in a breath when she saw Helena, clear as day, standing next to her bed. "Holy shit! I really am dead this time."

Helena peered down at her, her eyes hidden behind a pair of polarized sunglasses. "You can see me again?"

"Of course I can see you. For some god-awful reason, you're dressed like John Lennon. Why wouldn't I be able to see you? We're both dead and apparently stuck here."

"Uh, I hate to point out the obvious, but hospitals as a general rule do not attach heart monitors to dead people. And even if they did, I'm fairly certain dead people wouldn't have a pulse."

Sabine twisted around to get a good look at the monitor behind her and felt relief wash over her. Sure enough, her heart was beating. Albeit, it was probably beating a good bit faster now than it had before, but that was fixable. Dead wasn't.

"What happened?"

"I don't know, but I don't think you'll have to wait long for an answer. In a minute, they'll let Mildred and that hunky investigator in here."

"Hunky investigator? What's he still doing here?" She shook her head. "Never mind that. Have you been here the whole time? Have the doctors said anything?"

"Yeah, they've said plenty, but not a damn thing I understood. They're moving you to a room, though, so I guess that's good news. I'm really glad, Sabine. I know I am a real annoyance to you and Maryse, but I don't want to see anything bad happen to either of you." She sighed. "Sometimes, I wish—"

Before Helena could finish her sentence, the door burst open. Mildred went straight to Sabine's side, walking through Helena, and clutched Sabine's hand in her own. "My God, Sabine, you've scared the life right out of me." Beau was right behind her.

Sabine squeezed Mildred's hand and watched as Helena strolled through the hospital wall. "Looks like I came closer to scaring it out of myself. What happened? Have you talked to the doctor?"

Mildred shook her head. "They're coming in a minute, but I insisted on seeing you now."

Sabine smiled. "I bet you did. Maryse?"

"I got her voice mail, but I left a message."

"I thought you'd be halfway back to New Orleans by now," Sabine said to Beau.

"You didn't tell her you were staying in the hotel?" Mildred asked.

"You're staying at the hotel?" Sabine repeated. "Since when?"

Beau paused for a moment before answering. "I checked in three days ago."

Sabine frowned at Mildred. "You knew this and didn't tell me?"

Mildred raised her hands in protest. "I didn't know who he was until tonight. Darn near ran me over getting to your apartment when he heard the sirens. You know I wouldn't keep something like that from you, Sabine." Mildred shot a dirty look at Beau. "You didn't tell me you were lying to her."

"I wasn't lying, exactly." He stepped next to the bed and looked down at Sabine. "That break-in at your place worried me. I just didn't like the sound of it, but then I've been accused of being paranoid, so I didn't want to get you riled up in case it turned out to be nothing."

"So you thought you'd spy on me for a couple of days, then let me know if you thought I was in danger . . . something I might have needed to know before tonight. Where the hell is that doctor?" Sabine flashed an angry glance at the door to her room, agitated that they were keeping her waiting.

Beau ran one hand through his hair. "I swear, Sabine. If I'd thought . . . I didn't know . . ."

"Stop," Sabine said. "I'll decide how I feel about all this after I find out what happened to me. For all we know, this might be nothing."

"Nothing?" Mildred said. "You were unconscious. It's a miracle you dialed 911 before you passed out. That can't be nothing."

"She's right," a voice sounded from the doorway.

They all turned to look at the young doctor who had entered the room. "I'm Dr. Mitchell. I just started here last week. I would say it's a pleasure to meet you all, but I'm certain we'd all rather it be under different circumstances." He smiled at Sabine. "You are one lucky lady. The paramedics are amazed you managed to dial for help given the state you were in when they arrived. And since I'm assuming none of us would like a repeat performance, we're going to have to rethink your dinner choices."

Sabine stared at the doctor. "What are you talking about? I had a roast beef sandwich, same as yesterday."

The doctor studied her. "Any dessert? Cookies, perhaps? A brownie?"

"I took a glass of wine and some sugar cookies to bed."

"We had cookies at the Fortescues', too," Beau reminded her.

"*You* had cookies. I moved two of mine onto your plate so no one would think I was being rude when I didn't eat them."

Beau gave her a surprised look. "I didn't even notice."

Sabine rolled her eyes. "Some detective."

The doctor narrowed his eyes at her. "You're certain. You've had nothing else to eat or drink since lunch but your sugar cookies and wine?"

"Of course I'm certain. What is this about? You're starting to worry me."

"You had an allergic reaction," the doctor replied. "The kind of reaction that can kill people."

"Peanuts? You're saying peanuts caused this?" She shook her head. "I know I'm allergic to peanuts—have known forever and I promise you I avoid them like the plague. Why do you think I didn't eat the cookies when they were served? I don't take any chances. There is no way I ate a peanut, not even accidentally. I cooked the roast beef myself yesterday and have eaten three meals from it now. The bottle of wine was brand new. I opened it last night."

"And the cookies?" the doctor asked.

"I made them," Mildred said. "A couple of days ago, and I assure you they didn't contain peanut oil. I'm allergic to peanuts myself and I've been eating those cookies ever since I baked them."

Sabine stared at the doctor. "You must be mistaken."

"I was with her from midafternoon until last night through supper," Beau added. "She only had the roast beef and a bottled water for supper."

"And the wine," the doctor asked Beau. "Did you drink any as well?"

"No," Beau said and looked a little embarrassed. "I left before Ms. LeVeche retired for the night."

"Where did you get the wine, Ms. LeVeche, and is it a brand you drink regularly?"

"Yes, it's my favorite zinfandel, and Mildred gave it to me day before yesterday. Mildred, Maryse, and I like the same brand, but it's not sold here in Mudbug, so anyone who's going to New Orleans usually picks up a bottle or two when they're there."

The doctor turned to Mildred. "Do you remember where you bought the wine?"

Mildred nodded. "Sure. At Bayou Beverages just on the highway before you get to the city. Why? Is that important?"

"It could be if someone else reports a problem." The doctor made a note in his file. "Who else knows about your allergy?"

"Everyone," Sabine replied. "Everyone in Mudbug, anyway. The restaurants are very careful with my food preparation and no one ever brings me Christmas goodies with nuts. I figured keeping something like that a secret was bound to be trouble."

Dr. Mitchell nodded. "And usually it is, but I wonder if this time it didn't work against you."

Sabine felt a wave of cold wash over her. She wasn't sure what he was getting at, but she was certain she wasn't going to like it. "Surely, you're wrong, Dr. Mitchell," Sabine said, trying to clutch onto a reasonable explanation. "Maybe something else . . . a spider bite or something simple like an anxiety attack?"

The doctor shook his head. "I'm not mistaken. The symptoms are textbook and the tests showed peanut oil in your stomach." He looked at Beau and Mildred, then back at Sabine, obviously nervous. "Ms. LeVeche, I don't know how to say this any other way, but since you and your friend are certain of your dietary intake, I think you need to contact the police. They're going to want to search your apartment and test that bottle of wine and the food."

Sabine stared at the doctor in shock. "The police? Test my food?"

The doctor nodded. "There is a chance the wine was somehow tainted before the sale, but I honestly can't imagine peanut oil being any part of the process for wine-making, so it's a real long shot. And you need to start considering who might have the access and the desire to do something like this. Any new business associates, friends, a slighted customer . . . the police are going to want to know."

Sabine tried to answer, but her voice caught in her throat. The only new things in her life were Beau and her family. Surely Beau had no reason at all to harm her; in fact, he'd been trying to tell her that digging up the past might not be a good idea. But her family? They barely knew her, so it was highly unlikely they knew about her allergies. Besides, she wasn't asking them for anything and didn't want anything, except to gain a better knowledge of her parents. Hell, Catherine had been the one suggesting the Fortescues fund a new business for Sabine that was apparently more "worthy" of the grand family name.

Sabine took a drink of water and tried to keep her hand from shaking. "I . . . I don't really know what to say."

"The doctor's right," Beau said. "If you ingested peanuts, it probably wasn't an accident. I'll call the police and get them over to your apartment and have them send someone here to get all the information from you. Tell them to talk to me afterward. I can provide all the details on the new people in your life."

Sabine shook her head. "I'm not about to let the police tromp around my apartment, digging through my drawers, taking inventory of my stuff. And not for nothing, but the Mudbug police still haven't come up with anything on the break-in or the lurker I kicked. I seriously doubt they'd have any idea what to do about a poisoning." Especially since the small matter of Helena Henry's poisoning had seemed to fly right past both the police and the doctors. Sabine's odds did not look good with the "experts" of Mudbug on the case.

"Now, Sabine," Mildred said, "I think you ought to listen to the doctor, and to Beau."

"Fine," Sabine said. "If the hospital will release me, I'll take care of everything with the police."

Dr. Mitchell shook his head. "I'm sorry, Ms. LeVeche, but I can't do that. We really need to monitor you overnight to ensure nothing else is wrong. I'm not trying to scare you, but you had a major attack. Quite frankly, you're lucky to be alive. If the paramedics had been just a couple of minutes later . . ."

"I'll contact the police and meet them at your apartment," Beau offered. "I'll oversee everything. Make sure they do a thorough job. I have connections in New Orleans. I'll make sure anything that needs to be tested is sent to a lab there."

Sabine sighed, feeling her independence slipping away.

Beau held one hand up. "I promise I won't go through your panty drawer."

Mildred shook her head. "She doesn't have a panty drawer. What her and Maryse have against covering their rear, I simply don't know."

Sabine groaned and pulled the sheet up over her head, but not before seeing the embarrassment on the doctor's face and the grin on Beau's. "Get out of here, all of you, before I just go ahead and die to escape it all." It was bad enough that all the medical personnel of Mudbug General already had a good idea of her feelings about undergarments.

She heard Beau laugh and Mildred said, "I'll go with Beau and let them into your apartment. I'll be back as soon as we're done with the police. Don't worry about a thing. You just work on getting better."

Sabine waited until she heard the door close, then pulled the sheet down and thought over everything that had happened that day. "What the hell is going on?" she asked out loud.

"I don't know," Helena answered, making her jump.

"Jesus," Sabine said, sucking in a breath. "I didn't know you were still here."

"Can you still see me?"

Sabine nodded. "The John Lennon thing still isn't working for me. Why did you come back?"

"I thought maybe someone ought to keep an eye on you and since the others all left . . ."

"What could possibly happen in the hospital?"

"Hmmmm, well, although I started to feel weird after I drank that brandy, technically, I was in the hospital when I died," Helena said.

Sabine stared at the wall. "Shit."

"But having an overnight stay here does give us all sorts of other possibilities."

"Like what?" Sabine didn't like the sound of that at all.

"Oh, I was thinking that taking a peek at the medical records of the Fortescues might be a good idea. Obviously someone's out of their damned mind because I can't think of anyone else who'd want to kill you. Maybe if we read their medical records, we can see if there's any history of mental illness."

"Oh, no. Maryse already did that breaking-and-entering medical-records search with you and it wasn't exactly an overwhelming success."

"Yeah, but this time there's no breaking or entering. That's over half the battle. Besides, don't tell me you're not just a little interested in getting a peek at those records. You're still looking for a match, right? You might just get two possible answers with one small, unobtrusive trip down the hall."

Sabine bit her lower lip. Any other time, she would never, ever agree with what Helena was saying, but the ghost did have a point. If someone had tried to poison her, the medical records might indeed give her the clue she needed to identify who it was. And it certainly wouldn't hurt to look for their blood types while she was at it. A matching blood type didn't mean a bone marrow match, but it was a good start.

Shit.

"Okay," she said before she could change her mind. "We'll do this tonight."

"If you don't want to risk it, I understand. I can get the files myself and bring them to you."

"Oh, no! I am not going to have a repeat of the New Orleans police department on my hands. There aren't any hotdog stands in the hospital to cover up your exit, and hospital carts do not move themselves down the hallways, especially on level ground."

"Fine, if you're going to get all picky and geographical on me. You're still going to need a key, though. The lock on that door is a deadbolt and doesn't open from the inside."

Sabine threw her hands in the air in frustration. "Then what are we even talking about this for? I don't have the keys and wouldn't know the first thing about picking a lock."

"Oh, I can get them."

Sabine groaned, knowing from the sound of her voice that Helena's offer would come with strings attached. "Out with it, Helena. What do you want?"

"Well, I just figured that while we were in the records room you might be able to get a copy of my autopsy report."

Sabine narrowed her eyes. "Is that all?"

"Scout's honor." Helena worked up her best sincere look.

Sabine frowned. It sounded so simple. Copy a couple of sheets of paper in exchange for a set of keys. Unfortunately, she already knew that anything involving Helena was never easy or without consequences.

Helena or the Mudbug police. Her two options for solving a crime.

Sabine sighed. "What time should we do this?"

Chapter Eleven

It was two more long hours and after three a.m. before Sabine was transferred to a private room. The entire time, Helena had been champing at the bit—and a bag of beef jerky from the vending machine. Watching the ghost inhale the dried meat, Sabine couldn't help thinking people should be very, very careful what they wished for.

All her life she'd wanted to see a ghost, and she'd gotten Helena.

All her life she'd wanted to find her family, and now it looked like it might have been better—and safer—if she hadn't.

All her life she'd wanted to find "the" guy. The guy who made her heart skip a beat, who made her skin tingle with the slightest touch, who made her palms sweat when he looked at her. And in he'd walked, just after she'd been given a potential death sentence by cancer, and a much more probable one by poisoning unless they got a grip, and fast, on what the hell was going on.

Sabine pushed herself out of the wheelchair and slid into her new hospital bed with a sigh. The nurse gave her a critical eye for a couple of seconds, then went about the business of checking her blood pressure for the hundredth time since she'd been brought to the hospital. She'd been too critical of Maryse, Sabine decided. She'd accused her friend of avoiding life, of avoiding relationships, especially when Luc had come on the scene. It wasn't like her accusations were untrue, but now that Sabine found herself in a frighteningly similar position—her world upside down, everything she'd known as fact now in question, her life in danger, and a veritable Adonis just waiting for the word—she regretted having ever pushed her friend.

The overload to her emotional and mental systems was staggering, and although she'd thought it was as high as possible, Sabine's respect for Maryse shot up even another notch. As soon as she saw her friend, she was going to give her a huge hug, a high five, and an apology. Then she was going to demand her secret. How the hell had she handled all this pressure without exploding?

The nurse removed the cuff and made some notes on her file. "I'll be back in a couple of hours. Try to get some sleep." She pulled the covers up on the bed, flipped out the lights, and left the room.

"Thanffkt Godfft," Helena said, her mouth full of jerky. She paused for a minute and swallowed. "I thought she'd never leave. Are you ready?"

"No, but that's totally irrelevant, isn't it? Do you have the key?"

Helena nodded. "Swiped it from the front desk." She tugged at the key ring wedged in the front pocket of her entirely too-tight blue jeans and finally managed to wrench it loose while pushing up the bottom of her spandex tank top by two inches and at least three stomach rolls. "I should probably change into something loose and comfortable for the mission, right?"

"You should probably change into something loose and comfortable because I can *see* you."

Helena glared at Sabine. "You skinny broads are all the same. You don't think fat people should dress fashionably."

"No. I don't think fat people should show their fat. There are plenty of fashionable tops that don't let your stomach hang out."

Helena stuck out her tongue, complete with partially-chewed jerky. "Anorexic."

"Glutton."

Helena grinned. "You got me there, but damn, do you realize I've eaten over six thousand calories a day for the past week and haven't gained a pound? How many people get that opportunity?"

"You could also jump off the roof of the hospital and not die, but I don't see you racing up the stairs to try that."

"Where the hell's the fun in that? I'm just doing things I would have liked to do while I was alive. I don't recall ever wanting to jump off a building, although I would have probably pushed a person or two." Helena frowned for a moment, and then her face brightened. "Hey, what do you think the odds are I could find a way to have sex? I didn't do hardly any of that while I was alive. And now I wouldn't have to worry about getting one of those CDs or anything."

Sabine closed her eyes and counted to five. "STDs, and no, I am not about to start an escort service for the dead. It would be fraught with misery and no profit at all." Sabine went to the door and peeked outside. "It's clear. Let's just get this over with."

She stepped out into the hall, and a second later Helena strolled through the wall to join her. Sabine took one look at the ghost's new wardrobe creation and almost choked. Helena glared and went off down the hall, the full nun's habit she wore giving her the appearance of gliding. Sabine stared after her in dismay. The fat rolls were covered, sure, but somewhere in the heavens, Jesus was surely crying.

Sabine made the sign of the cross and followed Helena down the hall.

Since Sabine had been placed on the second floor, they opted for the stairs over the elevator, figuring it was the safest option to avoid detection. At the end of the hall, Helena motioned for Sabine to stop while she stepped around. "It's clear," Helena said and waved her on. "The records room is at the end of this hall. I hope this time goes better than last."

Sabine's mind raced with arguments against what she was about to do, but her feet continued to move, one in front of the other, until finally she was at the end of the hall, standing behind the largest penguin she'd ever seen and watching her struggle with the ancient lock.

"Finally," Helena said when the lock turned at last. She pushed the door open and slipped inside, Sabine close behind. "The Dead records are on the last row. Guess that's sorta fitting. All the living assholes are on the first three. You start there and get some dirt on the Fortescues. I'm going to find my autopsy report."

Sabine cringed. *Dead records.* That was rude.

Sabine slipped to the front row and looked down the rows of shelves until she'd located the F's. Field . . . Fontaine . . . Fox. She looked beyond Fox but the Fu's had started. She looked more closely, pulled each file out a little from the shelf. At the spot where the Fortescues' files should have been, assuming there were any at this hospital, there was a single sheet of bright orange paper. Sabine pulled the paper from the shelf and saw that it contained a list of every member of the Fortescue family, alive and dead, and some she'd never heard of. Cousins, she supposed.

But where were the records? There must have been files at some time. Otherwise, why have a sheet of paper marking this spot? Sabine could understand medical personnel pulling a single file in order to treat a patient, but an entire family? That was just weird.

A sudden thought flashed through her mind and she moved to the next row. Landry . . . Lattimer . . . LeVeche. She pulled her file from the stack and opened it. She frowned at the results of her biopsy, but as she flipped through the file, everything seemed in order. Maybe the Fortescue files had been checked out for review.

She stepped over to the medical records manager's desk and went through the files stacked on top. Nothing. She was just about to give up when she saw a sliver of orange peeking out from under a stack of paper in the In box. Sabine pulled the orange paper from the box and began to read, her heart beating faster as she read. It was an inventory of files stolen during the hospital break-in. There were a bunch of names on the list, but the ones that stood out to Sabine all ended in Fortescue. Everyone in Mudbug had assumed it was junkies that had broken into the hospital; only Sabine didn't see any drugs on the list of missing items. Just medical records.

It wasn't possible. The hospital break-in happened before she knew about the Fortescues, before Beau knew, before he'd even been hired. Something was very, very wrong with all of this. It couldn't possibly be random.

"Hey." Helena's voice caused her to jump. "I need your help here." Helena shoved a file in Sabine's face. "The autopsy report is there, but I don't understand all that medical mumbo jumbo. Can you take a look and jot down the important things? That way if you don't understand it either, we'll have something to show to Maryse."

Sabine nodded, trying to get a grip on the situation. The last thing she wanted to do was let Helena in on more than she already knew. And Sabine needed to make some sense of everything before she could formulate an opinion, much less a plan. She took the file from Helena and sat down at the desk, pulling a legal pad and pen toward her.

She read the first line of the autopsy report and sucked in a breath.

"What's wrong?" Helena asked. "What does it say? I don't understand, Sabine. What killed me?"

Sabine continued to read down on the report, growing more surprised with every word. "I've got to write this down. Maryse will understand it better than I do."

Helena stared at her. "But you know something. I saw that look on your face. There's something in that file you didn't expect to see. Why won't you tell me what it is?"

Sabine shook her head and wrote furiously. "I can't be sure. I think I'm confusing my terminology and I don't want to tell you the wrong thing. Let's just get it all down and talk to Maryse. Okay?" Helena didn't look the least bit convinced, but she didn't argue either.

Sabine continued to write, word for word, everything in the report. Maybe by the time she talked to Maryse she'd have come up with a way to tell Helena that the autopsy had found no sign of foul play.

And that Helena had been dying of cancer.

Sabine stood at the hospital room window. The sun was just beginning to rise, casting an orange glow over the marsh. She'd barely slept, only managing ten-minute increments, and was positive she looked as bad as she felt. The nurse had already been in to check on her and promised to bring breakfast in directly. Sabine could hardly wait. Hospital food was so tasty. She'd just decided that a shower might not be a bad idea when Helena came huffing into the room, still wearing the habit, and threw a stack of files behind a recliner in the corner. Before Sabine could get a word out of her mouth, the nurse bustled in with Sabine's breakfast. Sabine glanced over at Helena, who'd collapsed in the recliner wheezing like she'd just run the New York marathon, and tried not to even think about what Helena had tossed behind the chair.

Sabine excused herself to the bathroom, hoping it would hurry the cheerful, chatty nurse along. It probably took all of a minute before she heard the door close, but it felt like hours. Sabine stepped out of the bathroom to find Helena sitting up in her bed, a half-eaten pancake dangling from the plastic fork.

"You know," Helena said as she shoved the other half of the pancake in her mouth. "Hospital food isn't near as bad as I remember." She stabbed a half-cooked sausage with the fork and wolfed it down.

"You have a serious problem. This is just so not normal."

Helena rolled her eyes and poked at the scrambled eggs. It lifted in one big blob. "The fake psychic is telling me this isn't normal. Hell, you think I hadn't already figured that out?"

"I don't mean this as in everything, I mean this"—she pointed to the empty plate—"is not normal. Dead people do not need to eat. Dead people shouldn't even want to eat. Ghosts should not develop addictions, Helena."

Helena gulped down the coffee, then belched. "Guess ghosts shouldn't lose their manners either, huh? But what the hell. You're the only one who can hear me."

Sabine closed her eyes and counted to ten, trying to keep herself from wishing that she or Maryse had strangled Helena when she was alive. At least then they could have said they deserved having Helena haunt them from beyond.

Sabine peeked behind the recliner. Just as she'd feared, there was a stack of files that look suspiciously like those she'd seen in the records room the night before. "What did you do, Helena?"

Helena, who had been licking residual syrup off the breakfast plate, placed the now spotless plastic dish on the table. "Just some files I thought we'd need." She swirled her finger around the inside of the coffee cup, then licked it.

Sabine felt her jaw clench involuntarily. "What files? Damn it, Helena! I wrote down everything we needed last night. Why would you take more? They'll send me to jail if they find those files in here. What were you thinking? And why aren't you saying anything?"

The ghost had gone strangely silent and it took a second for Sabine to realize that she was glancing at the doorway. Sabine whirled around, fully expecting to find the chatty nurse calling for a straitjacket and police backup, and let out a breath of relief when she saw Raissa standing in the doorway, a curious expression on her face.

"Raissa, thank God!" Sabine collapsed into the recliner, what little was remaining of her energy completely drained. "I thought for sure I was on my way to a padded room or jail, whichever one had available space. What are you doing here?"

Raissa stepped into the room and closed the door behind her. "Maryse called me. She got held up at the airport in Houston and thought you might need to hear a voice of reason since Mildred called yelling at her twice last night."

"Mildred yelled at Maryse?" Sabine stared at Raissa. "What in the world for?"

Raissa smiled. "Apparently this attempt on your life is all Maryse's fault because she went and tried to get killed first and you always want to do everything Maryse does."

Sabine groaned. "I wanted to do everything Maryse did in second grade. I haven't wanted to since. Well, except that one time I saw Luc walk out of the shower wearing nothing but a towel. I have to admit that Maryse definitely got that one right."

Raissa laughed. "I confess to a lingering bit of jealousy myself. Not only is the man hot, but he's so obviously over the moon for Maryse. Makes you want one of your own."

"Only for a moment. Once they put their clothes on, then there's bills to pay and work to do and in-laws to deal with, and we all know how that in-law thing worked out for Maryse the first time." Sabine glared at Helena.

Raissa followed Sabine's gaze and studied the hospital bed. "I take it the ghost is here? Either that or you are on some really good drugs and your bed is incredibly lumpy."

"Oh yeah," Sabine said. "She's here in all her glory—every should-be-expanding pound of her."

Helena jumped off the bed. "I don't have to take this abuse." She stalked out of the room.

Sabine gave a silent prayer of thanks and reported Helena's exit to Raissa.

"Well, since I'm pretty sure you're not going to be arrested for having someone else eat your hospital food, do you want to tell me what she stole?" Raissa said.

"Hospital records." Sabine pointed over her head and behind the recliner. "She threw them behind the chair when the nurse came in. I am going straight to jail if they catch me with these files in my room."

Helena stuck her head in through the wall. "Please," she said. "Like you wouldn't have been in trouble if we'd got caught in the records room last night. You weren't whining when it was about you."

"Breaking into the records room is not the same as stealing the records," Sabine shot back, but she seriously doubted her voice carried the same conviction as her words. "Don't you have a buffet to conquer?"

Helena gave her the finger and popped back out the wall.

"And take off that habit," Sabine yelled after her. "It's sacrilegious."

Raissa raised her eyebrows, and Sabine remembered the psychic could only hear one side of the conversation. "We sorta helped ourselves to the medical records room last night."

"And it required wearing habits?" Raissa shook her head. "Never mind. I don't think I want to know. What were you looking for exactly? Or is this answer going to be as bad as the habit one?"

"I wanted to check the files on my family."

"You were hoping to find one with a 'psychotic killer' notation on it?" Raissa asked.

"No. I mean, I was kinda hoping for some indication of instability or something. I thought that might narrow things down a bit."

"And you're certain your family is the problem?"

"Yes, no . . . I don't know. All I know is my family is the only thing new in my life, well, except Helena, so I figured it has to have something to do with them. And they'd have to be crazy to want to kill me, because I'm not asking for anything . . . yet, and even if I get around to it, it's not going to be money. I've already turned down a business loan from Catherine."

"Sounds reasonable—in the sort of reason you and Maryse have taken to since Helena appeared. So what did you find?"

Sabine frowned. "Nothing."

"No crazy people?"

"No. No records."

Raissa stared at her. "The only doctors in the town have their offices here, right? Are there any in the Fortescues' town?"

"Not anymore," Sabine said. "The last doctor retired years ago and has never been replaced."

"Then their records should have been transferred here. Unless you think they went all the way to New Orleans to see the doctor."

Sabine shook her head. "Their records were apparently here at one time. But on the shelf where all the Fortescue files should have been was this orange piece of paper with a list of their names."

"So someone checked them out?"

"That's what I thought at first, but when I shuffled through the manager's desk, I found a sheet of paper listing all the files that were stolen in the hospital break-in a couple of weeks ago." Sabine felt a chill run through her. "There were other people's names on the list, but they didn't appear related. Except for the Fortescues. But Raissa, no one knew we were related then—not me, you, them—you hadn't even hired Beau when the break-in happened."

Raissa narrowed her eyes. "You're right. That's very strange."

"It can't be a coincidence. Not after this."

Raissa shook her head, her expression thoughtful. "No, I don't believe it's a coincidence, but I can't put the pieces together, either. I'll do a reading this afternoon and let you know if I come up with something."

"Thanks."

"So . . . if your family files were missing, what did Helena steal?"

Sabine groaned. "I don't even know. She ran into the room just ahead of the nurse. It's a miracle the nurse didn't see a floating file display. How in the world would

I have explained that one?" Sabine rose from the chair and reached for the files.

Raissa smiled. "And just think—you're supposed to be equipped to deal with the dead."

"No one could be prepared for Helena," Sabine said as she stood back up, files in hand. "The Spartans couldn't have prepared for Helena. You know, I'm not really sure she didn't pass over. I'm starting to think Satan couldn't handle her either so he sent her back."

Raissa laughed. "Well, the next time you or Helena need to procure some illegal data, let me know and I'll loan you my scanner."

"Scanner?"

"Yeah, a scanner," Raissa said. "Mine is small—just big enough for a sheet of paper, and really thin and portable. You could scan all the documents Helena stole onto a USB, then review them at your leisure on your home computer. No hand cramps, floating file scares, or habits required."

"I never even thought about something like that. You constantly amaze me with your grip on technology."

"Hey, the spirits don't help with filing and I don't want to rent storage. Digital file cabinets are the way to go." Raissa walked over to Sabine and gave her a hug. "I'm going to clear out. I want to talk to Beau before I head back to New Orleans and open the shop. You let me know if you need anything. Promise?"

Sabine nodded. "Promise."

Raissa gave her a wave and left the room. Sabine looked down at the files, then frowned when she saw who the records belonged to—Helena's family. Why in the world would Helena want those? Her parents were long dead—they couldn't possibly have killed her.

Sabine shoved the files in her overnight bag and zipped it shut. Helena wouldn't be able to return them until nighttime. Which would give Sabine plenty of time to ask the ghost what the hell was going on.

Chapter Twelve

It was past sunrise before Beau finished up with the Mudbug police, locked up Sabine's apartment, and loaded the evidence bagged for testing in his truck. Logic told him that Sabine had to have been poisoned in her apartment and most likely by something she consumed that night, but for the life of him, Beau couldn't figure out how anyone had gotten inside. There was no sign of forced entry on any of the doors or windows, and since the property manager had gotten approval to replace the locks after the break-in on both the front and back doors, anyone who'd previously had a key was out of luck.

Someone could have jimmied the lock, but the new technology would have been extremely difficult for anyone but a professional. There was always the locksmith to consider, but the company the property manager used was based out of New Orleans and had been in business forever. Still, Beau supposed he would talk to someone there after he finished at the lab.

He was just climbing in the truck when he heard Mildred yelling from across the street. The hotel owner came running toward him, clutching a stack of white Styrofoam boxes. "I was hoping to catch you before you left for the hospital. Can you give me a ride?"

"Sure," Beau said and motioned her into the truck,

"but I thought you were driving Sabine home after they released her."

"I was," Mildred said, her face flushed with the exertion. "Doggone battery on my car is dead again. It's happened four times now in the past two weeks, but I haven't had time to get another. I don't need the car that often, so I've been borrowing Sabine's, but in all the excitement, I've misplaced my spare key."

"Do you need some help?" Beau pointed to the stack of boxes, about to topple as Mildred struggled with the seat belt.

"What—oh, no, thank you." She clicked the belt into place and righted the boxes. "I got breakfast for all of us over at the café. I figured you haven't had time to get anything, same as me, and I know my Sabine. She's not going to eat any of that hospital food."

"I don't blame her," Beau said as he started down the highway to the hospital. "So do you need me to give the two of you a ride home?"

"No. You've got much more important business to take care of in New Orleans. I'll get Sabine's keys from her and have one of my friends give me a lift home. Then I'll come back for Sabine."

"You sure you have time? I can't imagine Sabine is going to sit in that hospital one minute longer than required, even if it means walking home."

Mildred laughed. "You got my girl pegged, all right. But not to worry. They won't release her before noon. Dr. Breaux doesn't make rounds as early as he used to and even though that Dr. Mitchell seemed sharp, Dr. Breaux's probably going to want to see Sabine himself."

"Dr. Breaux's the local?"

"Yes. In his seventies and still kicking." She shifted in her seat to stare at Beau. "So are you planning on taking care of my girl?"

Beau gave a start and glanced over at Mildred. "Depends on what you mean by taking care of. I'm going to find out who's trying to hurt her, and I'm going to do my damndest to see that whoever it is doesn't get another shot."

Mildred sighed. "Why do you young people make everything so difficult? I've seen the way you look at her. You darn near ran me over trying to get to her apartment last night, and the way you were shouting questions at those paramedics . . . all I'm saying is it looked like a lot more than concern for a client to me."

Beau groaned inwardly. Was his attraction to Sabine really that apparent, or was the hotel owner just fishing and hoping? Either way, Beau wasn't about to accommodate her. Sabine's rejection was embarrassing enough kept between the two of them. He wasn't about to share it with anyone else.

"I look at her like a cop does a potential victim. I was FBI, remember? And I'm not about to lose a client . . . not on my watch. I'm going to protect Sabine, but once I know what's going on here and the guilty party is in jail, then my job is done."

Mildred studied him for a moment. "Your job, huh? Okay then."

Beau glanced over at her as he pulled in to the hospital parking lot and knew he hadn't fooled her for a minute. But at least she'd stopped pressing the issue. For the moment.

Sabine was sitting cross-legged on the end of her hospital bed watching television when they walked into her room. Beau took one look at her and felt his heart leap. Never before had he wanted to gather someone in his arms and hide them away from the world to protect them. He'd known he was lying to Mildred when he'd told her that Sabine was another victim he was trying to protect, but he hadn't realized quite how much he was lying.

He swore the room got brighter when she smiled at them. He blinked once, certain he was seeing things, but reality was perched on the end of the bed, so obviously happy to see them. Beau managed a weak hello as Mildred dropped her breakfast box on the table and gathered Sabine for a hug. Beau placed the boxes on the tray next to the bed and tried to get a grip.

It simply wasn't fair, he decided. No one should look that good, ever. Much less after being poisoned, almost dying, and spending the night in a hospital, which contrary to what it should be was never restful. No makeup, a drab green hospital gown, her hair tied in some strange-looking knot on top of her head, and she was still gorgeous. Why couldn't Raissa have been friends with a sixty-year-old retired librarian or something?

Mildred finally released Sabine and pointed to an empty hospital food tray on a small table next to a recliner. "Don't tell me you ate that garbage?"

Sabine looked momentarily guilty. "Not a chance. I dumped it down the toilet. Didn't want the nurse to make a fuss. Besides, I knew you wouldn't let me starve."

"Darn straight," Mildred said and pulled a couple of sodas out of her handbag. "Pancakes and sausage for everyone. You two go ahead and start. I'm going to check with the nurse and see what time they'll be releasing you." She handed Beau a box and gave him a wink.

"Oh, and Sabine," Mildred said as she paused at the door. "I must have dislodged your gown when I hugged you. Your heinie is showing." She grinned and left the room.

It was an involuntary reaction, and God knows he should have figured out some way to stop it, but Beau couldn't help looking at Sabine's butt. Her face blushed ten shades of red as she grabbed the hospital gown and tugged it together in the back, but not before he saw the silky smooth curve of her bottom peeking out.

Sabine groaned. "She'll use this forever as a reason I should wear underwear."

Beau grinned. "Hard to argue with her at the moment. Not that I'm agreeing, mind you."

Sabine looked over at Beau and shook her head. "You know, normally I would have gone into hiding over something like this. The fact that flashing a man with my bare butt is the least of my problems is a real testament to just how screwed up my life is at the moment."

"A butt like that should never be hidden away. Statues should be erected in its honor."

Sabine's lips quivered with amusement. "Maybe I won't die of embarrassment today, then. So are you hungry?"

"Starved." He just wasn't saying for what.

She patted the bed. "You can sit on the bed with me if you'd like," Sabine suggested as she uncrossed her legs and turned to the side. "The table is long enough for both of us to use it."

Beau swallowed when Sabine said the word "bed" but took a seat next to her and pulled the table in front of them. "How are you feeling?"

"How do I look? I mean the rest of me, not just my butt."

He choked on his soda and set the can on the table. "Great. You look great."

"For an almost dead woman, you mean?"

To hell with it. Beau looked directly at Sabine. "You're beautiful. A little paler, perhaps, a little tired around the eyes, but otherwise just as beautiful as you were yesterday and the day before."

Sabine's eyes widened and for a couple of seconds said absolutely nothing. The room was so quiet that Beau could hear the ticking of his watch. *Shit, shit, shit, shit . . .* it seemed to echo in his mind.

Finally, she gave him a shy smile. "That's the nicest thing anyone has ever said to me. Thank you."

Beau shook his head. "I wasn't saying it to make you feel better. Damn it, Sabine, you're a beautiful, desirable woman, and any man who doesn't see that is stupid or blind. I'm neither."

"No," she agreed. "You're definitely not the stupid one in this equation." She sighed. "Before Mildred gets back and more importantly, before I say something I'll regret, I need to tell you about something I did last night."

Beau felt a momentary wave of disappointment, but it was quickly gone. As much as he would love to hear Sabine say something she'd regret, the fact that she'd apparently done something the night before that she didn't want the hotel owner to know about had him intrigued. "Okay. Shoot."

Sabine took a breath. "I snuck into the medical records room last night, hoping to get some background information on my family."

Of all the things she could have said, this wasn't even on the list. "You broke into the medical records room?"

"No, it was unlocked," Sabine said, but the look on her face immediately told him that she wasn't being completely honest.

"Okaaay," Beau said, deciding it was easier to let however she'd gained access to the room slide. "And did you find out anything?"

Sabine told him about the missing files and the corresponding list.

"Wow." Beau shook his head, trying to wrap his mind around the information Sabine had given him and the repercussions it had on his investigation. "I don't even know what to think."

"Me either."

"I don't like it." Beau turned to face Sabine. "You've been looking for your family for years. Even if someone has always known you're related to the Fortescues, why go after their medical records right before you hired me? I could understand if this had happened after I started poking around, but this makes no sense at all."

"I wish I knew, but I've run through every possible scenario and there's simply nothing I've done recently or in the past to warrant this kind of action. Unless it was a past life." She gave Beau a shaky smile.

"You're not safe in your apartment," Beau said. "Until we figure out what's going on, I don't think you should stay there."

"It's my home, Beau. I have to stay there."

Beau shook his head, ready to argue. "I couldn't find a single sign of forced entry. That means whoever got in had a key. Even if I installed deadbolts only on the inside of the doors, I still wouldn't think it was safe. Someone is too close . . . their access is far too free." He took in a breath and before he could change his mind said, "Let me stay with you. I can sleep on the couch."

Sabine instantly shook her head. "No way!"

"I promise I won't do anything to make you uncomfortable. I won't even tell you you're beautiful."

"I can't. I can't have you in my space that way. My apartment is tiny. There's no way I could feel comfortable staying there with you even if you were a mute. This isn't about you, Beau, it's about me. You scare me." She ran one hand across the top of her head. "Not like the someone trying to kill me scares me. The way you make me feel scares me. I'm afraid if I cross that line with you, there's no return, and a future between the two of us is filled with impossibilities, most of which you don't even know about."

"So explain them to me."

"No. There are certain things I can't talk to you about."

"Can't or won't?"

"Doesn't matter. You're going to have to take my word for it."

Beau struggled to hold in his frustration. Why was she making things so hard? She felt the same pull that he did. Why was she struggling so hard against it? *And why are* you *pushing so hard for it?* "Fine. Then at least consider staying at the hotel until this is settled. That way you can have your own private space, but Mildred and I are close by to keep watch."

Sabine was silent for a moment, then nodded. "I'd feel better knowing you and Mildred were close."

"Just not too close and only me."

Sabine looked down at the bed. "No," she said, her voice barely a whisper.

Beau rose from the bed. "Then I guess since we got all that decided, I'll take off. I've got to drop off the stuff for testing at a lab in New Orleans, and then there's a couple of other things I want to look into before I come back. I'll see you sometime this evening, okay?"

Sabine looked up at him and nodded. "Thanks, Beau. For everything."

"You're welcome," he said and left the room before he did something even more stupid than telling her how beautiful she was. Like kiss her.

Again.

It was after noon before Sabine was ensconced in a room at the hotel. It had been a relief to find that Beau had kept the Mudbug police's destruction of her apartment to a minimum, but it was still going to take hours to get everything back where she wanted it. Since she wouldn't be living there anyway for the time being, she supposed it shouldn't matter. She'd endured almost an hour of Mildred's puttering around the hotel room, bringing her some soup and crackers for lunch, fluffing her pillows, and generally treating her like an invalid, but Sabine understood that Mildred wouldn't feel good unless she thought she was doing something to help.

Finally, Mildred had gone downstairs to balance the books, and Sabine was left in the peace and quiet she'd been waiting for. She grabbed one of the four tote bags she'd packed and pulled out the hospital files that Helena had stolen. Raissa had gladly agreed to loan her the scanner and would meet Beau somewhere in New Orleans so that he could bring it back with him that afternoon or evening, whenever he managed to finish up and return to Mudbug. Sabine figured as long as the files were already stolen she might as well get a copy of everything. If nothing else, it would save the trouble of ever having to break into the hospital records room again.

Sabine already knew what Maryse was going to say. Maryse had warned her nine ways to Sunday about Helena and her shenanigans, and Sabine was just starting to get a clear view of the problem. Helena was definitely a pro. She came out with these outlandish requests when she knew you were at a personal low and somehow made them seem completely logical and necessary. Then when the dust had settled, you were left wondering how you'd gone temporarily insane.

Sabine opened Helena's folder and started to read the autopsy report again. She hadn't been mistaken—Helena definitely had cancer, and it was very advanced. In fact, Sabine doubted the woman would have had more than six months to live. She flipped past the autopsy report and through the other papers in Helena's file. This file only contained the last ten years, but it was a revealing ten years. Helena had asthma and her blood pressure was borderline, but otherwise, she'd been deemed healthy at every checkup. If she'd been sick with colds or the flu or the occasional virus, she hadn't been to the doctor for them.

And there was absolutely no other note about the cancer other than the autopsy.

Which made no sense. Helena should have had some symptoms—dizziness, lethargy, pain. If the cancer had been caught soon enough, she most likely would have been given a round of chemo, then progressed to the radiation treatments. If that didn't work, she would have been a candidate for a marrow transplant, like Sabine. But apparently, no one had known.

Sabine closed the file and bit her lower lip. Could Helena really have ignored the symptoms that easily? Or even stranger—could she have really lived with cancer advanced to the stage it had and had no symptoms at all? Was that possible? She was just about to open Hank's file when Maryse burst into the room.

"Are you all right? What did the doctor say? What did the police say? Where's that investigator and what the hell is he doing about all this?"

"Whoa," Sabine said and laughed. "One question at a time or my brain might explode."

Maryse grimaced and sat down on the end of the bed. "I know the feeling. Start talking, woman."

Sabine spent the next fifteen minutes filling Maryse in on everything that had transpired, including her newfound ability to see Helena and their break-in at the hospital. Maryse listened closely, occasionally interjecting an "oh no," "good Lord," or "shit."

When Sabine was finished, Maryse blew out a breath and stared at her for a moment. "You've got some nerve, Sabine LeVeche, trying to one-up me on this. Wasn't one attempted murder enough?"

Sabine smiled. "Raissa told me Mildred yelled at you."

"Yelling would have been polite. That woman scalded my eardrum over the phone. I snuck in the back door of the hotel to come see you. I'm not sure I can take another round."

Sabine laughed. "I think that was stress and temporary insanity on her part. Mildred knows you didn't have anything to do with this. If I hadn't insisted on finding my family, none of this would be happening. I should have let this go years ago."

"A week ago, I would have agreed. But things are

different now. We need to find a donor and your family is the best possibility. Besides, the break-in at your house and the hospital happened before you found your family. Maybe the two aren't related."

"Someone stole all of my family's medical records and you think that's not related?"

"Okay, so maybe it's related. But you still have no idea who did it or why. You say the Fortescues seemed surprised . . . what if there was a third party trying to connect the dots? A reporter or something. It will be a huge story. 'Missing daughter of heir to millions finally found.' I can just see the headline already."

"Maybe, but it's a stretch."

"I think you should ask Beau to check into it. He might have connections that can get information we can't. We can't even ask without admitting we know what was stolen."

"You're right. I should probably ask Beau." Sabine stared out the hotel window for a moment and sighed.

Maryse narrowed her eyes at Sabine. "You make that sound like such a chore."

"I don't want to talk about it."

"I do. I mean, I did before you protested, but now I'm dying to. C'mon, Sabine. Luc's been gone for days. Please tell me that one of us is getting some action."

"I am *not* getting any action. I'm surprised at you. You know I don't play fast and loose, and with everything else going on, the last thing on my mind is getting some action."

Maryse raised her eyebrows. "Methinks she doth protest too much. Granted you have a lot on your plate, but I still don't think sex is the *last* thing on your mind. Remember, I've seen the guy, and I know from experience that even attempted murder does not squelch the desire for a hot man—especially if the hot man is interested in you."

"You don't know he's interested in me." Sabine struggled to direct the conversation away from her. "He's just doing his job."

Maryse laughed. "I saw the way he looked at you in the café, and I've seen that look before. Thank God, I stayed alive long enough to see that look on a regular basis."

"He kissed me," Sabine blurted.

Maryse stared. "And . . ."

"And what? That's it. He kissed me and I asked him to leave." Sabine felt a flush start to creep up her neck.

"Oh boy!" Maryse bounced up and down on the bed like a child. "I remember the first time Luc kissed me. My whole body was on fire and I thought my head was going to pop off my shoulders and into outer space. I went stomping out of the office, mad, flattered, sexually charged, and scared to death."

Sabine felt all her resolve crumble. "God help me, Maryse. I *am* scared to death. I've never felt this way about someone. I mean, I hardly know him. How can he have this effect on me?"

Maryse reached over and took her friend's hand. "I don't have an answer for you, even now that I've lived it myself. You were always the one that believed everything had intent and purpose—bad and good. Maybe people are linked before this life and if they find each other again, that link overrides everything lived this lifetime."

"I don't know that I believe in past lives," Sabine said.

"Okay, so what if your souls were hanging out in the same office before they were assigned a mother? Whatever you want to believe. I just know that when I met Luc, I felt things I hadn't felt before, and I'm not just talking about the sexual attraction—although certainly that was part of it." She blew out a breath. "As a scientist, I want to think maybe it's pheromones or some other biological draw that happens to fit Luc and I together better than I'd fit with others. Maybe he's the first man I've met with the same biological imperative that matches mine."

Sabine studied her friend. "You don't believe that for a minute, do you?"

"No. I believe it's love."

Sabine squeezed Maryse's hand, so profoundly happy for her friend and yet scared to take the same gamble herself.

"There's no scientific explanation for love, Sabine, but we can't deny its existence."

"I barely know him," Sabine argued.

"Yet you're drawn to him."

"It might just be lust."

"What's the downside if it is?"

Sabine stared down at the bed. "What if I die?" she whispered.

Maryse hugged her. "What if you don't?"

Chapter Thirteen

Sabine shoved the medical files Helena stole into a backpack for Maryse and played lookout since her friend insisted on sneaking out the hotel's back way to avoid Mildred. Sabine had barely made it back to her room before her cell phone rang. It was a number she didn't recognize and she was surprised and pleased to hear Beau's voice when she answered.

"I'm at the lab in New Orleans. Raissa dropped the scanner off here, so I'm heading back that way in a few minutes, but something else has come up."

Sabine felt her pulse quicken. "With the tests?"

"No. It will be a while before we know something for certain on that end. I got a call from the Fortescues' attorney. He wants to talk to you at his office this afternoon. I started to say no because of everything that happened last night, but I didn't want to tip our hand on the poisoning. If he hears through the grapevine, that's one thing, but I thought we'd better keep it quiet as long as we can."

"Definitely. No, you did the right thing. So did you tell him I'd be there?"

"I told him I'd check with you. He got a little agitated and asked for your cell number, which I refused to give him."

"What do you think he wants?"

"I don't know, but my guess is the Fortescues are putting some pressure on him about something. I don't think he'll be put off forever. More likely if you don't show up there, he'll show up in Mudbug."

Sabine stepped to the window and looked out across Main Street at her shop. "You think I should go?"

"I think . . . oh hell, I don't know what I think. I'm in a bad position here, Sabine. Professionally, my mind is screaming for you to go because whatever he wants might give us some insight into all the other things going on. Personally, my mind is screaming at me to drag you to New Orleans and put you in a safe house."

Sabine thought about her upcoming radiation treatment. "That's not an option. I have something important to do next week."

"Something worth risking your life for?"

Sabine pressed her fingers to her temple. The irony was overwhelming. "In this case, yes."

"Care to tell what it is?"

"No. There are certain aspects of my life that I intend to keep private. This has nothing to do with the other situation, I assure you."

"Fine." His voice was short and Sabine could tell he was frustrated with her.

"Do you have the attorney's number so that I can schedule the appointment?"

"I'll do it. Is four-thirty okay?"

Sabine glanced down at her watch. Two and a half hours from now. "I'm sure it will be fine. I just need to check with Maryse about driving me there. Mildred is hellbent on me not driving and won't give me back my car keys."

"Don't worry about it. I plan on going with you. I want to see what Mr. Alford has to say."

"That's not necessary."

"Yes, it is. I have a lot of experience at reading people and probably know more about the law than you do. I want to make sure this attorney isn't trying to pull something off for those nuts."

"Fine, but there's someone else I want to try to see while we're there, if she'll meet with me, that is."

"Who?"

"Someone who might have known the Fortescues back when my father was a kid. Unless you think it's a bad idea."

"No . . . no, I think it's a really good one as long as her memory is sound. I'll pick you up around three-thirty, okay?"

It was just shy of four-thirty when Beau and Sabine pulled up in front of Martin Alford's office. It was a beautiful antebellum home just off the main street in town. What was once most likely a carriage house had been converted into his place of business, a small, tasteful sign identifying his estate law practice. They walked up the beautifully landscaped path to the office entrance and Beau rang the buzzer at the side of the door. Sabine looked around nervously and plucked a New Orleans newspaper from the top of the bush beside the door. She twirled the loose end of the plastic wrapper around on her finger, every possible scenario imaginable running through her mind. The attorney opened the door a minute later and motioned them inside.

They took a seat in two overstuffed taupe leather chairs placed in front of an ornate redwood writing desk, and Sabine handed the attorney his newspaper.

Alford thanked her and took a seat behind the desk, his expression almost one of embarrassment. "I'm so sorry to ask you here on such short notice, but we've had a situation arise."

Sabine sat up straight in her chair. "What kind of situation?"

"Catherine asked the domestic staff to keep your identity confidential, at least until all the particulars could be worked out, but apparently Adelaide has been talking at the grocery store, and news is starting to spread."

"Why would she deliberately disobey Catherine?"

Alford shrugged. "I don't think she was trying to cause trouble. Adelaide's mind simply isn't what it used to be. Dementia, Alzheimer's, or maybe just old age. Either way, her reliability isn't, well, reliable."

Sabine glanced over at Beau, wondering where this was going, but he looked as confused as she felt. "What does all this have to do with me, Mr. Alford?"

"I need to ask you to have a DNA test. I'm sorry to move straight to the legal aspects of this so soon after your reunion, but I'm left with little choice now."

Sabine suddenly understood. "The family wants to make sure I'm the real deal before Adelaide spreads any more tales."

Alford jumped up from his chair, an agitated expression on his face. "No, I'm sorry, that's not it at all. I don't mean to imply that the family doesn't trust you because nothing could be further from the truth. The family is certain you're Adam's daughter and so am I. You look exactly like him, and the dates and facts surrounding your birth coincide with the things we know from our end."

Sabine stared at him. "Mr. Alford, I have no issue with providing a sample for a DNA test. In fact, I fully expected to be asked to. I guess what I'm not understanding is why the urgency now if not for the family's protection?"

"It's not for the family's protection. It's for your own." The attorney sank back into his chair. "Over the years scam artists who found out about Adam showed up pretending to be a long-lost granddaughter or grandson. They've always proved to be frauds, but not before they've stolen from the house or managed to get money out of Frances—she's very gullible."

"The family is worried that everyone will think I'm another scam artist."

"Yes. They don't want this to cause any trouble for you, and the reality is, without medical proof of your claim, you will probably endure a certain level of animosity from the townsfolk."

"I see," Sabine said, although she didn't really buy his explanation for a moment. More likely the Fortescues didn't want to cause any more embarrassment for the family, but Sabine saw no benefit to pointing out the obvious to the one man who probably knew that to begin with.

He gave her an apologetic look. "I am so sorry about this, Ms. LeVeche. We were hoping to explain this situation and take care of these things over time. No one wanted to make you prove yourself as soon as you walked in the door. The Fortescues are a lot of things, but ill-mannered is certainly not one of them."

Sabine held in a smile. Only the most proper—and mentally imbalanced—of people would consider a

DNA test rude when there were millions at stake. "Is there a facility I need to go to?"

Alford shook his head and pulled a bag from his desk drawer. "All I need is a hair sample and I can send this off. Again, I apologize for this, Ms. LeVeche. I also lost both my parents when I was very young. I know how important family is. The Fortescues wanted to give both sides time to get to know each other before making it public. No one wanted things to get out this way."

"There is no need to apologize, Mr. Alford. No harm has been done but a little tongue-wagging. I assure you, tongues have wagged about me a time or two in the past. I'm a psychic, remember?"

Alford looked relieved. "Yes, of course. I'm just so used to dealing with the family, and they're so . . . I guess *particular* is the best word." He gave Sabine a small smile. "I sometimes forget that the rest of society is not as stringent. The family has arranged for a rush on the tests. They should be notified with the results by tomorrow morning and will contact me immediately following. If you'll give me a way to reach you, I'll let you know as soon as I've spoken with the family."

"No problem," Sabine said and jotted her cell number down on the back of one of her business cards. "I also have a question for you, Mr. Alford. I wondered if I could get a copy of my father's medical records, after the DNA results are back, of course. I've had a couple of minor medical issues come up in the past, and that information would be nice to have."

"Certainly," the attorney said, but Sabine could tell the question has flustered him. Was the attorney aware that her father's records had been stolen, or was he just hesitant to agree to provide any personal information about the family?

When the DNA results were back, she had every intention of pressing him again.

Ruth Boudreaux's home was a spacious Victorian, just a couple of blocks from Alford's office. Sabine had called several times that afternoon but had been unable to get a hold of anyone. She asked Beau to stop by the house just in case Mrs. Boudreaux was home now and would agree to speak to her.

The woman who answered the door clearly wasn't Ruth Boudreaux. For one thing, she was at least forty years younger, and her accent was northern. "May I help you?" she asked politely.

"I hope so," Sabine said. "My name is Sabine LeVeche. I've been trying to get in touch with Mrs. Boudreaux. I've been doing some family research and I think she might know some of my relatives."

"My name is Anna. I'm Mrs. Boudreaux's nurse." She motioned them inside to a formal living room. "If you tried to reach her today, we were probably at church at the time. Mrs. Boudreaux insists on praying daily and lighting a candle for two of her brothers. She lost them in Vietnam."

"Do you think she will speak to me?"

"Oh, certainly. Mrs. Boudreaux enjoys having visitors. It's just that, well, her memory's not quite what it used to be."

"Alzheimer's?"

"Yes. Not horribly progressed yet, but there was an incident with the stove and the family felt it best if she had someone with her full time."

"Of course," Sabine said, trying to hide her disappointment. "Well, I suppose it can't hurt then. Anything she can remember is more than I know now, and there aren't so many alive any longer who were around at that time."

"Oh," the nurse brightened. "You want to ask her about the past? You might be in luck, then. On a good day, her memory of years past is very vivid. It's more recent events that she can't seem to recall." She motioned them down a hallway. "If you'll come with me. She's sitting in the sunroom. The light is good for her and she often spends evenings in there."

Feeling a bit more hopeful, Sabine followed the nurse down the hall and into a huge sunroom at the back of the house, Beau close behind. The room was on the west side of the house and the late afternoon sun cast a warm glow over the multitude of blooming plants, causing a burst of color throughout the room. A thin, silver-haired lady sat in a rocking chair at the far corner, gazing out the window at a group of birds playing in a fountain in the backyard. She looked up when they entered the room.

"Mrs. Boudreaux," the nurse said. "This lady is doing some research on her family and would like to speak to you about them."

Mrs. Boudreaux looked up at Sabine and squinted. "Do I know you, dear?"

"No, ma'am," Sabine replied. "I don't think we've ever met before. But I think you know my family."

"Who's your family?"

"The Fortescues."

Mrs. Boudreaux's face cleared and she smiled. "Why, of course. That's why you seemed so familiar. You're the spitting image of your father. Why don't you and your husband pull up a seat, and I'll see what I can do to help you."

Sabine momentarily cringed at the woman's assumption that Beau was her husband, but it wasn't worth correcting. She and Beau pulled two wicker chairs closer to Mrs. Boudreaux and took a seat. "So you knew my father?" Sabine asked.

"Of course I did. We attended twelve years of school together, and goodness knows how many times we shared a pew in church. Why, William was almost a brother to me."

Sabine immediately understood. Mrs. Boudreaux didn't remember Sabine's father, Adam. She remembered her grandfather. "That's nice, Mrs. Boudreaux."

The woman studied her for a couple of seconds. "Something I don't understand . . . why don't you just talk to William if you have questions?"

Sabine was prepared for this very question. "I've been estranged from the family for quite a while. We've just recently come together again and I don't want to say anything that might upset the relationship. I understand that people of certain social status don't like to be reminded of or discuss things that might cause embarrassment or sadness. I don't want to inadvertently upset someone if I can prevent it."

Mrs. Boudreaux looked pleased. "Very proper of you to remember the family status in your reconciliation. And I suppose since you are family and your purpose is honorable, God won't consider my talking to you gossip."

"I'm certain He wouldn't, Mrs. Boudreaux, or I wouldn't even have asked."

Mrs. Boudreaux gave her a single nod of approval.

"Well, I can honestly say that the only scandal I'm aware of concerning the Fortescues would have been that business during the war concerning William's brother, Lloyd. He always was the disreputable one of the family. You would never have known those two boys were raised in the same household, much less born identical."

"So I take it their looks were where the similarities ended?"

"Heavens, yes. William was a true gentleman, as far back as I can remember. Even in grade school he was always protecting the smaller children from bullies or helping young ladies up the steps." She smiled. "Our skirts were much longer in those days, and sometimes a steady hand on your elbow helped when you were balancing books in one hand and clutching a large portion of your skirt in the other."

Sabine smiled at the image of her grandfather helping a young, and likely beautiful, Mrs. Boudreaux into the schoolhouse. "But Lloyd wasn't a gentleman?"

"Absolutely not. Lloyd was one of the bullies, always stealing lunch money from the younger children when William wasn't looking. He'd sooner push girls down the steps than help them up, and he was always playing pranks on the teachers, many of them cruel."

"I imagine once you were older, all the girls chased William."

Mrs. Boudreaux blushed. "Well, of course, we weren't so forward back then as children are now. Why sometimes I just cringe at the way they dress and behave in church, and it's even worse at the market. I have to wonder what kind of future this country has with them as adults. But yes, William had his share of admirers."

"Anyone special?"

"Not that I ever knew, but I always wondered. Sometimes there would be parties or other events in the school gymnasium. We were mostly chaperoned, but I'd see William sneak out sometimes and not see him again for hours."

"So where did you think he was going?"

Mrs. Boudreaux shrugged. "I always assumed he was seeing someone the family wouldn't have approved of. Once at church, I was certain I saw him slip a piece of paper to one of the girls in the back pews. The poorer families sat toward the back of the church then."

"Do you remember the girl's name?"

"Heavens, no. I'm not even certain I knew it then, but she was a good Catholic, always at Mass. Not that it would have mattered to his parents. William's inheritance depended on his making a good marital match. The Fortescues would have insisted. And besides, they'd already picked Catherine for William. The Fortescues had political aspirations for William, and Catherine's family had the right connections."

"And that's who he married, so I guess the family was happy."

"I suppose they were."

"You don't sound convinced."

Mrs. Boudreaux waved a hand in dismissal. "Oh, it's probably nothing. We were all children at the time, and I guess if one is going to be foolish, that's the time to do it."

"You did something foolish?"

"Not me, dear. Catherine. I had a silly fight with my best friend at a dance one night and decided to walk down the hall and regain my composure. At the end of the hall, I saw Catherine kissing someone in the stairwell. I thought it was William, but when he looked up and saw me, he winked, and I realized it wasn't William at all, but Lloyd."

Sabine considered this. "So Catherine fancied Lloyd, and William fancied someone unsuitable, but they still married."

"Well, yes, dear. Wealth comes with duty, and a marriage between Catherine and William merged two of the most powerful families in southern Louisiana. The elder Fortescues died in a car crash soon after William and Lloyd left to begin their military service. William was firstborn and the estate, its staff, and the largest portion of the family's assets became his responsibility upon his parents' death."

"So he did his duty and married Catherine."

"You make it sound like such a sacrifice. William and Catherine began seeing each other before he left for the war. All that other nonsense happened in high school, and besides, there were the children to consider."

"What children?"

"No one really spoke of such things back then, it wasn't proper, but everyone close to her knew Catherine was pregnant when she and William married. The brothers had been home on leave just a couple of months before, which made the timing possible."

She wrinkled her brow. "And then there was the wedding itself. A rushed affair. Just the minister in the Fortescues living room and hardly the event that a family of that status would normally have hosted. But then, William was given only a brief leave to make arrangements for his inheritance and attend his parents' funeral, and Lloyd was already missing in Vietnam and wanted by the military police and the FBI. With his parents' death, Catherine's pregnancy, and all the investigation surrounding Lloyd's disappearance, it's no wonder the family kept the wedding so private."

Sabine glanced over at Beau, who nodded. She pressed forward. "Then after his military service, William came home and he and Catherine raised the children. Did everything go well then?"

Mrs. Boudreaux smiled at Sabine. "You were such a beautiful little girl, Frances. Always so full of life and energy. And the questions you would ask. You wanted to know the answers to everything. Precocious is the word, I think. But then I'm not telling you anything you don't already know."

Thoughts raced through Sabine's mind. The elderly woman was obviously confused, but would it do any harm to pretend to be Frances? It took only a moment for her to make up her mind. "Actually, Mrs. Boudreaux, I don't remember much from my childhood. I wasn't . . . well for some time."

Mrs. Boudreaux continued, "You were just beginning your senior year of high school when I started to notice the change. Before, you'd always been so sweet, so outgoing, but over time you became more and more withdrawn. You barely spoke to people in town and when you did your voice was clipped and filled with anger. Your teachers were at their wits' end. You were their best student, but your marks had slipped so low they were afraid you wouldn't even graduate. Then you got meningitis and after a prolonged recovery, Catherine insisted on private tutors for the rest of your education. Why, we hardly saw you again in town after that."

"And that's when my parents shut themselves away, also?"

"Well, Catherine was always busy with her church charities and such, but William was never the same after Vietnam." She frowned. "Such a shame what that kind of tragedy can do to a man. A real shame."

"Yes, it is," Sabine agreed.

Mrs. Boudreaux leaned forward in her rocker and patted Sabine's leg. "I'm so glad you got well, Frances. It's been so nice talking to you, but if you young people don't mind, I'm going to take a nap before dinner."

"Of course," Sabine said and rose from her chair. "Thank you so much for taking the time to talk to me, Mrs. Boudreaux. It's been a pleasure meeting you."

Mrs. Boudreaux nodded once, then dropped off to sleep. Sabine and Beau quietly left the room and let the nurse know they were leaving. They had no sooner turned onto the freeway when Sabine's cell phone rang.

"Maryse," Sabine said. "What's up?"

"Something went wrong with the car. Mildred's been in an accident," Maryse said, her voice shaky. "I'm at Mudbug General."

"I'll be there in thirty minutes," Sabine said. "Call me as soon as you hear anything." Sabine closed her phone and looked over at Beau, panic already sweeping over her. "We have to get to Mudbug General. Mildred's been in a car accident."

"Don't start worrying until we know the score,"

Beau said. "I'm sure she's going to be fine. Maryse is with her, right?"

Sabine shook her head. "You don't understand."

"Understand what?"

"She was driving *my* car."

Chapter Fourteen

Beau tried to get control of his emotions as he raced into the hospital parking lot. Until he had more information, he needed to remain calm, objective. One thing he knew for certain, though: he'd paid far too many trips to the hospital in the last couple of days. They rushed into the emergency room and found Maryse waiting for them right inside the door.

"How is she?" Sabine asked.

"The doctors say she's going to be fine. Her foot is broken and there's some burns on her hands and arms, but they can't find anything else."

"Burns!" Sabine cried. "Oh my God. What happened?"

Maryse shook her head. "I'm still not quite sure. All I know is Mildred was on her way back from an errand in New Orleans and drove off the road and into the ditch. I don't know if the car caught on fire before or after she ran off the road. She was only half conscious when they brought her in and all I could make out was her saying 'Tell Sabine it was the car.' Then the doctors took her away and now she's out for the count."

Beau felt his jaw clench. Cars did not arbitrarily catch fire. "Do you know where they took the car?"

Maryse nodded and pulled a business card from her pocket. "One of the state troopers gave me his card.

He wrote down a number on the back for the shop they towed the car to."

Beau took the card from Maryse and looked over at Sabine. "I'll need you to call the garage and give them permission to talk to me about the car."

Sabine nodded, her face pale. "You don't think it was an accident, do you?"

"No, and neither do you. You didn't from the moment Maryse called."

Beau pulled out his cell phone and stored the number to the garage, then gave the card to Sabine. "I'm going to the garage now, so give them a call before I get there. If you need to leave the hospital before I get back, do *not* go alone." He looked over at Maryse. "I want someone with her at all times."

Maryse nodded. "I know the drill."

Beau studied her for a moment. "Yeah, I guess you do. The safest place is the hotel, so if you leave before I get back, go straight there. Eat at the hospital, or get something here to go, but don't under any circumstances have anything delivered or eat any food Mildred or Sabine have on hand."

"No problem," Maryse agreed.

Sabine's eyes were full of fear. Fighting the overwhelming urge to pull her into his arms, he squeezed her arm instead. "I'll be back as soon as I can. We're going to get to the bottom of this. I promise you."

Sabine threw her arms around him in a crushing hug. Surprised, Beau circled his arms around her, trying not to dwell on how their bodies molded together in a perfect fit, or how his heart leapt at the warmth of her body. He buried his head in her neck, breathing in the sweet smell of her hair.

"Thank you," she whispered, giving him a final squeeze before she dropped her arms and took a step back.

"You're going to be fine," he promised her.

Maryse placed a hand on Sabine's shoulder. "Of course she is," Maryse said, then grinned at Beau.

Beau gave his new ally a wave and headed out of the hospital. Mudbug didn't have a shop large enough for the kind of damage he imagined was done to Sabine's car, so he figured it had been towed to New Orleans. A quick phone call verified his hunch and provided him with the location of the shop and the technician who was looking at her car.

He made the drive in just under an hour and hurried into the service garage. Sabine's car was in the first stall and what he saw brought him up short. The entire front of the car was scorched black, the remnants of the fire almost glowing against the pale silver of her car. The black extended past the front seat and halfway into the back.

Beau said a silent prayer of thanks that Mildred had made it out of this wreck with as few injuries as she had, then gave a second thanks that Maryse and Sabine hadn't seen the car. They would probably have had heart attacks. He was just about to step inside and ask the receptionist to locate the manager when he saw a stocky, middle-aged man walking his way.

"You must be Mr. Villeneuve," the man said and extended his hand. "I'm Russell Benoit, the manager here."

Beau shook the man's hand. "Please, call me Beau."

The manager nodded and pointed to the car. "Ms. LeVeche said you were a friend and I should tell you everything I knew about her car." He blew out a breath. "I gotta be honest with you . . . this is a matter for the police, not a friend. I called them about twenty minutes ago."

Beau nodded. "I figured as much. I'm also a private investigator, former FBI. Go ahead and tell me what you've found. You're not going to surprise me."

The manager's eyes widened. "Well, that makes this a bit easier, that's for sure." He motioned Beau over to the car and wrenched open the hood. Some of the engine had already been removed, probably as they looked for the cause of the fire, and the manager pointed to a hole on the right side. "Look down through there. You see that little piece of metal on the bottom that's a bit shinier than the rest, right there next to what's left of the fuel line?"

Beau peered through the hole and located the shiny piece of metal. "Yeah. It doesn't belong there, right?"

"Not even close."

Beau straightened. "So, what, someone shoved it in the fuel line?"

The manager shook his head, a concerned look on his face. "I don't think you understand. A cut fuel line can't cause a fire, not by itself."

Beau stared at the manager. "Okay, so then what caused the fire?"

The manager ran a hand through his hair. "A bomb."

It was a little over an hour before Sabine and Maryse were allowed to see Mildred. Sabine teared up at the sight of her "mother," hands and forearms bandaged and her foot in a cast. She felt Maryse's hand on hers and gave it a squeeze. Together they stepped close to the bed and looked down at the woman who had raised them. "She's going to be okay, right?" Maryse asked the nurse, even though they'd just spoken to the doctor in the waiting room.

"Yes," the nurse said, reassuring them. "It looks much worse than it is. She's a strong woman and I imagine she'll be up and around in no time."

Mildred opened her eyes and looked around the room. "Damned hospitals. I hate hospitals."

The nurse gave them a sympathetic nod. "She's receiving a bit of painkiller through her IV. You can visit for a few minutes, but I wouldn't expect her to make much sense."

Sabine thanked the nurse and she left the room. "Mildred," Sabine said and leaned over the bed. "Can you hear me?"

"Of course I can hear you, Mom," Mildred said. "I'm hurt, not deaf."

Sabine looked over at Maryse, who raised her eyebrows. Apparently there were some *really* good drugs in that IV. "Mildred, it's Sabine and Maryse."

Mildred blinked once and stared at them. "Well, of course it is. Who did you think you were?"

Maryse placed her hand over her mouth, but Sabine still heard the giggle. Not that she could blame her. It was kinda funny, in a someone-tried-to-kill-you-because-they-thought-you-were-me kind of way. Mildred closed her eyes and let out a snore. Sabine was just about to suggest they leave and let Mildred rest when Helena Henry walked through the outside wall and into the room.

The ghost scrunched her brow in confusion. "What

are you doing back here, Sabine? I've been looking for you everywhere. I was sure they released you hours ago."

"I *was* released hours ago," Sabine said and gestured to the bed. "Mildred had a car wreck."

Helena stepped between Sabine and Maryse and peered over at Mildred. "Oh, man, that looks bad. Is she going to be all right?"

"The doctor says she will be. She's got some burns and a broken foot, but otherwise, she's okay."

Helena shook her head. "Damn woman is too cheap. Don't tell me she doesn't make enough money at that hotel to buy a decent car."

"She wasn't driving her car," Sabine said. "She was driving mine."

Helena jerked around and looked directly at Sabine. "You don't think . . ."

"I don't know what to think yet. Beau's at the garage talking to the mechanic. But Maryse said when they brought her in that Mildred was saying something was wrong with the car."

"Shit." Helena looked back at Mildred, who was awake again and squinting at them.

"Sabine," Mildred said, "who's your friend?"

"That's Maryse, Mildred." Sabine whispered to Helena, "She's on drugs."

"Well, heck," Mildred said, "I know who Maryse is. I mean the one next to you."

Sabine felt her blood run cold. She heard a sharp intake of breath but couldn't be sure whether it had been Maryse or Helena. *She's hallucinating. That's got to be it. Please God, let her be hallucinating.* "I don't have another friend here, Mildred." It wasn't exactly a lie. Sabine hadn't yet gotten to the point of considering Helena a friend, and the jury was still out on if she ever would.

Mildred gave her an exasperated look and pointed directly at Helena. "Then who is the fat woman with the pompadour hairdo?"

Helena straightened up and glared at Mildred. "Who the hell is she calling fat? And that do of hers has looked like a hat helmet since the 1960s."

Sabine looked over at Maryse, but it was clear her friend was going to be no help. Her expression wavered between needing to pray and wanting to cry. Sabine took a deep breath. *Calm down. Obviously she can't hear Helena or she would have made a comment back to her. That just means she can see her.* Which meant . . . what? Sabine rubbed her fingers on her temples, certain that at any minute, her head was going to explode.

Before she could form a plan of action, or arrange for a mass burial, the nurse walked back in. "I'm sorry," the nurse said, "but I'm going to have to ask you to leave for the time being. We'll transfer Ms. Mildred to a room in a couple of hours. Dr. Breaux wants to keep her overnight for observation, but assuming everything goes well, she should be able to go home in a couple of days."

Sabine nodded at Maryse, then narrowed her eyes at Helena. Helena glared back but stomped out of the room after them. "Well, that was rude," Helena bitched as soon as they stepped into the hall and closed the door behind them.

"What was that?" Maryse asked, her eyes wide. "We've already had this discussion about what happens when someone sees Helena."

Helena looked at Maryse. "What happens? You never told me anything."

"Death, Helena," Sabine said. "Maryse has this theory that you're only visible to people who are close to death."

Helena shot Maryse a dirty look. "That's just as rude as Mildred calling me fat."

"And just as accurate," Sabine shot back. "Name me one person who's seen you whose life hasn't been in danger."

"Well, that's hardly fair since I'm mostly trapped in Mudbug. Maybe if I ventured out some, more people might see me and prove your theory wrong. Besides, Luc can see me."

"*Could* see you," Maryse corrected. "And you're not the first ghost he's seen."

Helena spun around to look at Maryse. "Luc can't see me anymore?"

"You didn't notice that when you sat down at breakfast and he never said a word?"

Helena shrugged. "I just thought he was ignoring me. So what does it mean that Mildred can see me? I mean I know she was in danger from the car wreck, but it was Sabine's car, so that doesn't add up at all."

Sabine shook her head. "I don't know. Maybe it has something to do with the drugs, and being in an altered state of consciousness. Maybe it allows people to see things they couldn't otherwise. Remember, the first time I saw you was when I'd given myself a concussion in the attic."

Maryse nodded, obviously happy to grasp any explanation that didn't involve death. "That makes sense. I mean, as much as any of this does."

"Maybe," Sabine said, but she still wasn't convinced. "Let's get out of here. I feel like locking myself in my hotel room and not coming out again for a week."

"I know the feeling," Maryse said and gave her a sympathetic look. "Do you want to grab something to eat before we head out?"

Sabine shook her head. "I really don't have much of an appetite. If I'm hungry later, I'll ask Beau to get me something. Unless you're hungry."

Maryse shook her head. "Not a chance. I can't eat when I'm stressed. I've lost twelve pounds over the last five weeks. And I didn't really have them to lose."

"I could eat something," Helena interjected.

"No," Sabine said. "I'm positive you won't starve."

"Fine," Helena pouted. "Will you at least give me a ride to Mudbug? I stashed some books in the hedges outside of my house. I thought you might want to see them, Sabine. We can pick them up on the way to the hotel."

Sabine narrowed her eyes at Helena. "Please tell me you did not steal anything else."

"How the hell can I steal my own things? The books have pictures and newspaper clippings from years ago. They belong to me. I cut out the clippings. I pasted them in the books."

"You donated your house and everything in it to the Mudbug Historical Society," Sabine reminded her.

"I'm sure if they could understand any of this and take a vote, they'd all agree that you not being murdered is worth my borrowing my own books for a couple of days. You're going to have to stop being so uptight, Sabine. Killers don't play by the rules. If you want to get ahead of him, you're going to have to ignore them, too."

Sabine sighed and started down the hall and out of the hospital. She really, really hated it when Helena was right.

* * *

"Pull over here," Helena instructed and pointed to a huge hedge that stretched the length of her former residence. Maryse pulled over on the shoulder of the road in front of the stretch of bushes. Helena hopped out of the car and ran through the hedge.

Sabine shook her head. "Thank God she's a ghost. Otherwise those bushes wouldn't have survived."

Maryse nodded in agreement.

A couple of seconds later, Helena emerged from the hedge carrying a stack of albums that had managed to make it through the hedge-passing with only some scratches. She tossed the albums onto the backseat through the window, then slipped into the car. "Now, pull up in the next drive where that magnolia tree is," Helena instructed.

"Why?" Sabine asked. "We've got the books."

"I forgot something," Helena said. "What does it matter? Remember that whole 'rule' discussion we had?"

Sabine sighed and motioned for Maryse to pull into the drive. Maryse shook her head and muttered, "This feels way too familiar."

Helena rolled her eyes and jumped out of the car as soon as Maryse stopped. "Back in a minute," she said as she started off across the lawn to the huge home next to her own estate.

Sabine sat us straight in her seat. "Where's she going? That's not her house, or her garage, or her boat house."

"You think I don't know this?" Maryse shot back. "That's Lois Cormier's house."

"What could Helena possibly want there?"

"I don't know but I'm positive it's not going to be good."

Ten minutes later, Helena still hadn't emerged from the house. Sabine looked over at Maryse, who was alternating between looking at the house and checking her mirrors for visitors. "I think we should leave," Sabine said. "We have the books and Helena can find her own way to the hotel."

"You're right," Maryse agreed and started the car.

"Wait!" Sabine said before Maryse could put the car in gear. "I think the front door's opening."

"Oh, no," Maryse whispered. "I hope the alarm isn't on."

"Get out of here. Now!"

Maryse put the car in reverse just as the front door of the house flew open and Helena came running out dragging an enormous garbage bag, stuffed to the brim. "Hurry up!" Helena yelled. "That alarm is going to go off any second."

"Crap, crap, crap," Maryse said as she threw the car in drive and floored it. "I thought I was done with this nonsense."

"Just leave her," Sabine said as she scanned the neighborhood, hoping to God no one had seen them yet.

"That will only make things worse, trust me," Maryse said as she screeched to a stop next to Helena. The ghost yanked open the car door and lifted the bag just high enough to get it onto the floorboard before she jumped in herself, slammed the door, and collapsed on the backseat. Maryse floored the car and they were pulling out of the driveway before the alarm went off.

Sabine glanced over at Maryse, who was slumped as far down in the driver's seat as she could be and still see over the steering wheel. If dealing with Helena wasn't so aggravating, it might have been funny. Maryse had been driving the same rental car ever since she and her truck had taken an unexpected dip in the bayou weeks before. Everyone in Mudbug knew it was her just by seeing the car, so unless she was planning on reporting it stolen, hiding while driving wasn't really going to get her anywhere.

They pulled onto the highway and were a good mile down the road before a cop car came racing past in the opposite direction. Maryse let out a huge breath that she'd probably been holding for the last two miles and sat up a little straighter in her seat.

"Helena!" Sabine yelled at the ghost, who was laid out on the back seat like she was having a heart attack. "What in the world was so important that you risked getting us arrested? And it better be good."

"It's a surprise," Helena said, but the guilty look on her face gave her away.

Sabine reached over the seat and grabbed the trash bag, which was surprisingly heavy. She yanked the bag over the car seat, its contents clanking and rattling. "What did you steal? Their silver?" She opened the bag and looked inside, then groaned.

"I'm afraid to ask," Maryse said.

"It's food! She broke into someone's house to raid their pantry." Sabine looked back at Helena. "This is low, even for you. How could you justify stealing food when you don't even need to eat?"

Helena sat up in the seat. "Lois is on a cruise for the next two weeks. The food would have gone bad and been thrown away. What's the big deal?"

Sabine reached into the bag and pulled out a can of sweet potatoes. "This expires two years from now."

"Oh, sorry. I must have accidentally picked up that can."

"Bull, Helena. You went through that woman's pantry and took whatever you wanted. You have an eating disorder and need to get help." Sabine clutched her head with both hands. "Oh, God, I cannot believe I just said that to a dead person."

"I can," Maryse said. "I gave up on logic weeks ago."

Helena glared at Sabine. "Have you seen Lois Cormier's ass? Trust me, I'm doing her a favor."

Sabine threw her hands in the air and turned back around in her seat. "I give up. You know, I thought a time or two that if you weren't already dead, I would take on the job. Now, I'm just wondering if it's not safer and a heck of a lot more peaceful if whoever's trying to kill me is successful. Whatever afterlife there is has to be less aggravating than this."

Maryse shook her head. "I thought that, too, but then I was afraid if the killer was successful but didn't get caught, that I'd just be stuck in limbo with Helena."

Sabine shuddered. "Oh, God, you're right."

"Maybe you should just leave town," Maryse suggested.

"For how long?" Sabine shook her head. "We have no idea why someone is after me. Leaving will most likely only postpone the inevitable."

Maryse sighed. "You're right. I know you're right." She looked over at Sabine. "Well, look at the bright side—at least we've got plenty to snack on while we try to sort all this out."

"That's what I was thinking," Helena said. "And I figured while we were having a snack, Maryse could tell me what she figured out from my family's medical files. You've looked at them, right?"

Maryse looked at Sabine, waiting for a cue, and Sabine nodded. Now was as good a time as any to deliver the news. "Okay," Maryse said. "We'll talk as soon as we get back to the hotel."

Fifteen minutes later they were ensconced in Sabine's hotel room, Sabine perched on the dresser, Maryse pacing all five steps that was the length of the room, and Helena sitting on the end of the bed, stuffing her face with truffles and apparently completely oblivious to Maryse's discomfort.

"So shoot," Helena said. "Let me have it."

Maryse stopped pacing and looked down at Helena. "I don't know how to tell you this any other way, Helena, so I'm just going to put it all out there."

"Go for it."

"You had cancer, Helena, advanced. Even if someone hadn't murdered you, I don't think you could have made it a year."

Helena dropped her truffle and stared. "But . . . how . . . I didn't feel . . . I mean, I was a little more tired than usual, but I was getting old, so I thought . . . but that's not what killed me?"

"No," Maryse said, "but unfortunately, the autopsy didn't find anything, either."

"What?" Helena shook her head. "I'm not crazy. There's no way my death was natural. I was there . . . I ought to know."

"No one's giving up on this, Helena. Sabine and I want you to know that."

Helena sighed. "I know you are doing your best, and I appreciate it all. Cancer, huh? I guess that gives me something else to think on." Helena rose from the bed. "I'm going to take a walk and sort this out, okay, guys? I'll check in later."

"We understand," Sabine said and watched Helena leave through the wall. When she was certain the ghost was gone, she looked over at Maryse. "You left something out. I can tell by your face."

"I know, but she was already struggling with the other stuff. I guess I figured we should give her a little time to adjust before we hit her with the rest."

"What else is there?" Sabine asked.

Maryse looked at Sabine, a pained expression on her face. "Based on the medical files, there's no way Hank is Helena's son."

It was almost eight o'clock before Beau made it back to Mudbug. After his conversation with the garage manager, he'd called a buddy who knew something about explosives and had agreed to come immediately and take a look at the car. His friend verified the manager's assessment of the situation, but poking around the engine for a while and studying some of the pieces recovered from the blast, he concluded that whoever had constructed the bomb was no expert.

Damn internet.

All you needed was an ISP and Google and information of all sorts was at your fingertips. Beau parked in front of the hotel and rushed inside. He knew Maryse had been with Sabine the entire time, but ever since he'd found out about the bomb, he'd been counting the seconds until he could see Sabine with his own two eyes. The peanut oil had been clever and could have been deemed an accident, but strapping a bomb to someone's car was an act of desperation, and that wasn't a good sign at all.

Beau hurried up the stairs and knocked on Sabine's door. Maryse gave him a brief quiz, then unlocked the door and let him into the room. He paused for a moment as he stepped inside, not sure what to think of the display. There was food everywhere—canned goods, boxes of crackers, chips, a loaf of bread, peanut butter, three different varieties of cookies, and he couldn't even count how many pieces of chocolate candies.

Sabine sat cross-legged on the bed, a stack of photo albums and discarded chocolate candy wrappers in front of her. She looked up at him and smiled.

"Please tell me this did not come from either of your houses," he said.

"No," Sabine reassured him. "It was a, uh, well-meaning friend."

Beau glanced around at the grocery store display. "She kinda overdid it, huh?"

Sabine grimaced. "She tends to overdo everything."

"Did you find out anything about the car?" Maryse asked.

Beau paused, not wanting to tell them about the bomb until he knew more about the device used and who had the ability to design it. His buddy had promised him that information as soon as possible. "Something caused the fuel line to catch fire," he said finally, "but the manager's still looking into it. We should know more by tomorrow."

Maryse rose from the chair in the corner and picked up a stack of papers sitting on top of the scanner Raissa had loaned Sabine. "Looks like my shift is over." Sabine rose from the bed and Maryse gave her a hug.

"I've got to go feed the cat, and I'll take a look at all of this tonight." She looked at Beau. "Unless you need me to stay here tonight."

"No," Beau said. "I moved to the room with the adjoining door. That way Sabine can still have her space and I can indulge my paranoid, overprotective tendencies."

Maryse grinned. "It's not paranoia if they're really out to get you." She stepped out of room and gave Sabine a wave. "Don't do anything I wouldn't do," she said and closed the door before Sabine could even formulate a reply.

"I should really get new friends," Sabine said.

Beau laughed. "I like her. The way she goes after life full speed, she probably doesn't have a lot of regrets."

"Ha. Before you start heralding all her living-life-with-gusto qualities, I'm going to inform you that prior to drawing the short end of the someone's-trying-to-murder-me stick, Maryse was one of the worst introverts ever."

"No way. Really?"

"She used to live in this two-room cabin on the bayou. You couldn't even get to it without a boat, unless you wanted to swim with the gators. If she ran out of food, she'd go fishing before she'd drive into town to the general store. It was nothing for me to go a month without seeing her, unless Mildred and I ganged up on her."

Beau stared at Sabine. "I never would have guessed any of that. What changed?"

"Well, someone trying to kill you tends to force you to take a closer look at your life, although I never really understood how much until now. And there was Luc."

"So the handsome hero clinched the deal." Beau reached over to the dresser and grabbed a bottle of water, looking for any distraction from the fact that he was in a hotel, with Sabine, alone.

Sabine smiled. "A storybook ending."

Beau nodded. "Not bad considering it was a horror story."

Sabine sobered. "Speaking of which, I know I'm working on a sequel, so why don't you go ahead and tell me what you didn't want to say in front of Maryse."

Beau struggled to maintain his composure. "What makes you think I'm hiding anything?"

Sabine shrugged. "I just know."

"So now you're psychic?"

"No," Sabine said and frowned. "I just know you weren't giving us the whole story. As much as I've been trying to avoid it, I'm drawn to you in a way I've never felt before and can't explain given the length of our relationship. It's like we're connected on some different level." She laughed. "I know that's probably all too woo-woo for you, but if I had a more scientific explanation, I'd give it to you."

Beau couldn't put his feelings into words, either. "I know exactly what you're talking about, and I don't have an explanation either, scientific or otherwise."

"So you're going to tell me about the car."

Seeing no other way around it, Beau nodded. "It was a bomb."

Sabine's eyes grew round and she sucked in a breath. "A bomb. Oh my God. I mean, I was expecting something, but a bomb is so . . . evil. I know that sounds melodramatic—"

"No," Beau cut her off. "It doesn't. I believe evil is

alive and well and flourishing in a society that wants to excuse away abhorrent behaviors. I sometimes think some people are just born bad."

Sabine moved closer to Beau and placed her hand on his arm. "I'm glad you're here with me. There's an inner peace I have when I'm with you that I don't otherwise."

"You just feel safe."

"No. It's more than that. I can't explain it."

"Then don't." Beau leaned forward and brushed his lips against Sabine's. He waited for her to pull away, and when she didn't, he moved closer to her and pressed his lips to hers.

Chapter Fifteen

The touch of Beau's lips on hers sent Sabine's body into overdrive. Her skin tingled as if she'd never been touched before, and in a way, it was true. Certainly, she'd never been touched before like *this*. Beau was different, special, and even though she knew the last thing in the world she should be doing is kissing him back, that's exactly what she did. As their kiss deepened, he pulled her body close to his.

He was hard and ready, and Sabine moaned as he pressed his hips into hers. He broke off their kiss and began trailing kisses down her neck until he was at the sensitive flesh just at the vee of her blouse. Sabine sucked in a breath, then gasped as he pulled her blouse aside and lowered her lacy bra just enough to take one hardened nipple into his mouth. He slowly swirled his tongue, sending her into fits of pleasure.

Knowing there was no going back now, Sabine slid her hand across the front of Beau's jeans, stroking the long, hard length of him through the denim. He paused for a moment, his breathing irregular. Then with one swift motion, he lifted her off the floor and gently laid her on the bed. He unbuttoned her blouse and expertly removed her bra, then lowered himself to continue his erotic assault of her breasts. As his mouth worked its magic, he unbuttoned her pants and slid one hand inside.

For the first time in weeks, Sabine thanked God she didn't wear underwear.

He found her sensitive spot and swirled his fingers around it, matching the pace of his tongue on her nipple. Sabine felt the pleasure building in her until she was afraid she would explode. She placed her hand over his and gasped. "Wait. I want it to be together."

Beau nodded and leaned down to kiss her deeply, his tongue dancing with hers. Then he rose from the bed and shrugged off his clothes. Sabine sucked in a breath when she looked at him, so hard and hot and so totally male. She reached out with one hand and circled the length of him, then ran her hand up and down, squeezing slightly every time she approached the tip. Beau closed his eyes and groaned, and she increased the pace.

Mere seconds later, he moved her hand away and rolled on protection, then rose over her on the bed. He leaned down to kiss her, then entered her in a single stroke. Sabine gasped with pleasure and clutched his back, digging her nails into his skin. She thrust her hips up to match his strokes. As they found their natural rhythm, she felt the pressure building in her.

"Now, Beau," she whispered, "I can't hold it any longer."

"Yes," Beau said as he moved with increased intensity. Suddenly his body stiffened. "Now."

The orgasm crashed over her like a tidal wave, every nerve ending in her body responding. They cried out at the same time and Sabine clutched his back, pulling him deep inside her as the pleasure rolled over her again and again.

* * *

Beau leaned back in the bed against the stack of pillows and Sabine lay against him. He wrapped his arms around her, trying to control his warring emotions. He couldn't lose her and knew his only chance was to convince her to give up her newfound family and anything that went along with them.

"Sabine," he said quietly, "there's something I need to tell you."

Sabine shifted a bit so that she could look up at him. "What is it?"

Beau took a breath, trying to decide how to begin, how to end, how to explain the horror, the heartache, the devastation. Finally, he decided to start at the beginning. "I was raised by a foster family. When I was two years old, my mother gave me to nuns at a church in New Orleans and left."

Sabine's eyes widened in surprise. "Why?"

"The nuns didn't know why. She'd only said she couldn't take care of me and asked them to give me to someone that could. Then she left. The nuns tried to locate her or my father, but she didn't give them any name. She didn't tell them where she was from or where she was going. She simply gave me to the nuns and disappeared."

"So the nuns raised you?"

"No, they gave me to a couple from the church who couldn't have children. They were thrilled to take me and were wonderful parents. I will always be grateful to them."

"But you wanted to know."

Beau nodded. "I had to know why a woman would raise a child for two years, then abandon him to strangers. Why she would never come back to get him. What kind of person could do that, and why? When I joined the FBI, I chose to specialize in missing persons. Every single day, I tried to find people who had vanished, and every night I applied my new skills to finding the answer to my own private mystery."

"And did you ever find them?"

"Yes. I won't go into all the details, except to say that it took six long years of digging before I caught a break. I'd found a man who might be my father." Beau ran one hand through his hair. "I was working in D.C. at the time, but I booked the first flight to New Orleans and drove a couple of hours to a small town north of the city. When the man opened his door, I knew at once that I'd found half of my answer. It was like looking into a mirror twenty years away."

Sabine shifted in the bed so that she could face him, her torso propped against his chest. "What did he say?"

"He didn't say anything for a while. Then finally he said, 'I guess your momma sent you.' I told him I didn't know my mother and that I'd been raised by a foster family. That I'd been looking for him and my mother for over six years. He invited me in and I thought that was it. I was about to get all the answers I'd been searching for. The puzzle would be complete."

"But you didn't?"

"No. He didn't know where my mother was. In fact, he hadn't seen her since that very day she'd left me with the nuns. She'd been going to visit her sister in Mississippi, or at least that's what she'd told him. He'd driven her to the bus station and bought her a ticket to Gulfport. Her sister called that night, wanting to know why we weren't on the bus. The ticket had been collected at the exchange in New Orleans and her luggage was on the bus when it reached Gulfport but there was no sign of my mother."

"So something happened to her between New Orleans and Gulfport."

"That's what everyone thought, which is why the police didn't even concentrate on New Orleans with their search. If there was an announcement on the news, the nuns wouldn't have seen it, and since my parents were poor, the only photos of me were as an infant and my mother from her high school yearbook. They didn't even have a wedding photo."

"So no one would have recognized you from the photos, even if they'd seen a news story."

"Not likely. The police searched every bus stop between New Orleans and Gulfport, but they never found a thing. She'd simply vanished. Finally, they assumed we'd been taken by a person or persons unknown and the file was shoved to the back of the cabinet in favor of others that had more evidence and might be possible to solve."

"So you had to give up?"

"No. I talked extensively to my father about my mother's behavior before that trip. Something could have happened to her, certainly, but her leaving me with the nuns was deliberate. My father spoke of her erratic behavior—drinking, paranoia, said she always felt like someone was watching her. It sounded like a mental breakdown to me. And I figured that's what she meant when she told the nuns she wasn't fit to take care of me. So I started looking at mental health facilities around Louisiana."

"Smart," Sabine said. "And the perfect explanation for why she never returned."

Beau nodded. "That's what I thought, too. It took

another two weeks before I came up with anything, but finally, I found a nurse that had worked at a facility in Monroe. She remembered a woman who'd come to the home at around the time I was asking about. The woman couldn't remember her name and had no identification. A full medical exam had revealed that she'd given birth, but when they asked her about the baby, she became confused and always insisted that she didn't have a child. Finally, they decided that the baby must have been stillborn and that perhaps that was what had sent her over the edge."

"She didn't remember. That's so sad."

"I thought so, too. The woman stayed at the home for three years. She never regained her memory. Finally, the state issued her new identification and the home assisted her with finding a job and a new place to live, as she was otherwise quite competent to take care of herself. She went to work at a local library and, as far as the nurse knew, was still working there. Only you would understand my excitement, the thrill of knowing that the thirty-year-old mystery of who I was would finally be solved."

Sabine nodded. "I understand."

"I couldn't find a listing for her in the local phone book, so I called the library and found that the woman I was sure was my mother would be at work that afternoon. Four more hours and I would have all my answers. Then I called my father with the news and he was elated. I waited for her in the parking lot of the library, certain I'd recognize her, and I did. She was older, of course, and her hair was starting to gray, but I could still clearly see the woman from that high school photograph."

Sabine put her hand over her mouth. "Oh, Beau, what a moment in time."

Beau grimaced. "Yeah. It was a moment all right. I started walking toward her and she looked at me. I could tell by the look on her face that she knew exactly who I was. She shook her head and said 'Please leave. Leave and pretend you never saw me.' I knew then she'd been pretending amnesia all those years. I opened my mouth to ask why. I deserved a reason. That's when a car squealed into the parking lot. It was my father. She looked at the car and her face went completely white, filled with fear."

Sabine sat upright and stared at him. "Oh no!"

"I immediately knew why she'd left—why she'd given me away, and why she'd stayed hidden all that time. My father jumped out of the car and took her out with a single shot to the head, then he turned the gun on himself."

Tears ran down Sabine's face and she wrapped her arms around him. Beau hugged her tightly, choked with emotion. "I've never told anyone all of that, until now."

Sabine pulled back a bit and looked at him. "Why did you tell me, Beau?"

"Because I need you to understand how family can hurt you. Biology doesn't make people care. Please, Sabine, I'm begging you, let this thing with your family go. Stop all contact with them. Have an attorney draw up papers stating that you relinquish any part of the estate you might be entitled to."

Sabine pulled away from him. "I can't," she whispered.

Beau rose from the bed, his heart breaking in two.

"What in the world could possibly be worth your life? Please explain to me why these people, these strangers, mean more to you than everyone who loves you?"

Sabine looked at the pain so clearly etched on Beau's face and her mind raced trying to find a way to erase it. Right now he must think her incredibly shallow, or greedy for the possible inheritance, because from his standpoint, there simply couldn't be a valid enough reason to keep oneself in such danger. She had to tell him the truth. Even if he was angrier at her than before. "My life," she began, "is worth so much to me that I'm willing to risk it in order to save it."

He stared at her for a moment. "That makes no sense."

Sabine sighed. "It does if you need a bone marrow transplant."

Beau's eyes widened in surprise, and Sabine knew that of all the things he'd expected she might say, that wasn't even on the list. He dropped back down on the bed next to her. "You have cancer?"

Sabine nodded. "Acute myeloid leukemia. I start treatment next week, but in the event that treatment isn't effective . . ."

"You'll need a bone marrow transplant," Beau finished. "And the best possible scenario is a blood relative." Beau wrapped his arms around her. "Oh, Jesus, Sabine, why didn't you tell me?"

Sabine's body responded instantly to the warmth of Beau's embrace, and her heart broke all over again for what she knew could never be. "I didn't even tell Mildred about it, Beau. If Maryse hadn't snitched, she still wouldn't know."

"And all that time Maryse spends in labs with scientists?"

Sabine nodded. "She's been looking for a cure for cancer for years, and all that stuff last month brought it to a head. She hasn't found a cure, but all the experts are fairly certain she's found a way to prevent ninety percent of the side effects from radiation treatment."

Beau's face cleared in understanding. "I thought it a bit strange that someone who obviously cared about you deeply was gone so often when important things were happening, but she's trying to push the test through to get you the drug."

"Actually," Sabine hedged, "she kinda already gave me a round of it. She's been prepping me for a couple of weeks before my first treatment. But she's pushing for the grants and the tests to make sure the formula is the best she can get. She lost her mother and father to cancer . . . it's pretty much been her lifelong pursuit to not lose anyone else."

"She must be frantic, and Mildred. She dated Maryse's dad forever, didn't she? That's why you didn't tell her."

"I didn't want Mildred to worry as much as I didn't want to drag you into my problems or guilt you into helping me do something you didn't think I should be doing."

Beau pushed back enough so that he could look at her. "But I helped you anyway."

Sabine nodded and brushed a tear from her cheek. "I know."

"So, in the beginning when you were pushing me away, was it that you really weren't interested or were you afraid to get involved because of the cancer?"

Sabine closed her eyes for a moment, trying to formulate the right response. The response that would let him know she cared without leading him on. "I still am afraid, Beau. I have feelings for you, and I'm not going to deny that, but I can't make you any promises when I don't know what the future holds for me. I'm not in a position to consider anyone else but myself right now, and it's not fair to you to keep you on hold."

Beau dropped his hands from her and stared at her for a moment. Finally, he sighed. "I think you're wrong, but I respect your wishes."

Sabine's relief warred with her guilt. She didn't deserve this man or his protection. She placed one hand on his arm. "I am so sorry that taking my case has opened wounds in you that were better off closed."

"It's probably time I put them to rest for good. But I've got to be honest with you. When this is over, I'm going to ask you to reconsider."

Sabine nodded, praying that when it was all over, she'd have any reason at all to gamble on a future with Beau. "I'll be waiting," she said.

Beau leaned over and brushed his lips gently against hers. "Let's get some rest. I know you're as exhausted as I am." He gathered her in his arms and they lay back on the bed. Minutes later, his breathing changed and Sabine knew he was asleep.

She lay there, enveloped in the warmth and caring of the most perfect man she'd ever met, and prayed that tonight wouldn't be the last time she ever felt this secure.

Sabine had no idea what time it was when she opened one eye and glanced at the dresser. The red light of her cell phone blinked off and on, seemingly magnified by the darkness. Beau was snoring beside her, so she eased out from under his arm and stepped over to the dresser to retrieve her cell phone. As she pressed the message button, she crossed the room and opened the drapes, surprised to see the sun already shining brightly. Maryse was going to kill her for sleeping so late with Mildred in the hospital. She was surprised her friend hadn't already stormed the hotel, but since Maryse was also hoping Sabine would get lucky, that probably explained everything. When she heard Martin Alford's voice, she stiffened, frozen in place as he gave her the results of the test.

It was official. Sabine was a Fortescue.

She sank down on the end of the bed and blew out a breath. This was it. It was exactly what she'd been looking for. Well, maybe not the weirdness and definitely not the threats on her life and Mildred getting caught in the crossfire, but she was one enormous step closer to finding a matching donor. Someone in the family might not want her around, but Sabine seriously doubted that every family member was conspiring to kill her.

If they could just find whoever was trying to kill her, everything could go back to some semblance of normal, and God willing, Sabine would have plenty of time left on this earth to enjoy the pure mundane. Beau stirred and looked up at her. The expression on her face must have worried him, because he immediately sat up.

"What's wrong?" he asked.

"Nothing. Alford called. I'm officially a Fortescue."

Beau ran one hand through his hair. "Well, that's a good thing, right? I mean, considering everything else.

Jesus, I never thought I'd be glad for you to be related to those nuts."

Sabine smiled. "Perspective is a real bitch sometimes."

"Definitely." Beau looked over at the window and frowned. "I can't believe we slept that late."

"I'd like to believe I wore you out," Sabine said and grinned, "but I'm guessing the murder games were probably a bigger exhaustion factor."

"Well," he said and looked her up and down, "since we're already starting late, what's another half hour?"

Sabine's body immediately responded to his suggestion. Her nipples hardened and she felt an ache in her core. The same ache that Beau had quenched the night before. She hesitated for a moment, knowing this was a really, really bad idea, but then the memory of incredible pleasure overrode all common sense and she took one step toward him.

And that's when someone banged on the motel room door.

"Sabine, Beau!" Raissa's voice sounded outside the door. "Are you there?"

Sabine froze for an instant, then went into overdrive, tossing Beau his clothes and tugging on her own. The oddity of calm-and-collected Raissa banging on her hotel door at a time when she'd normally be opening her shop had sent Sabine into a bit of a panic. Fortunately, Beau sensed her urgency and was dressed, of sorts, before Sabine yanked open the door. Raissa burst into the room, holding a folder and looked relieved when she saw Beau there as well. "I've been trying to reach you since last night," Raissa said. "Don't you people answer your cell phones?"

Sabine felt the heat rise up her neck and shot Beau a sideways look. He didn't look any more comfortable. At least neither of them planned on volunteering exactly why they had ignored their phones. "I overslept and was just checking messages," Sabine said. "I'm sorry we worried you. Did you drive all the way over here for that?"

Raissa shook her head. "I've got some information for you, but I'm not sure what to make of it." She opened the folder and stepped between Beau and Sabine so that they could both see the stack of papers inside. "That whole issue with the missing medical records concerned me, so I called in a favor. A lot of hospitals have started making digital backups of all their files, so I did some poking around to find out if Mudbug General had joined the wave of the future."

Sabine stared down at the first sheet of paper. "Holy crap, Raissa. This is my dad's file."

Beau raised his eyebrows and looked at Raissa. "People owe you favors that include hacking a hospital's database? I don't suppose you're going to tell me what you did for them?"

Raissa looked a bit flustered but waved one hand in dismissal. "I don't suppose I am. I expect you to use the information and pretend you have no idea how you got it. And don't, for any reason, let anyone see it. My friend broke at least a hundred different laws to get this."

Beau smiled. "Given the type of friends you have, Raissa, I'm not really interested in becoming one of your enemies. So I assume there's something interesting in here and not just your usual run of the flu and athlete's foot?"

"Anyone insane?" Sabine asked.

"Well," Raissa said. "There's nothing on Frances until she was seventeen and she was hospitalized for meningitis, but after that the rest of her file reads like something out of a Stephen King novel. That woman has some serious issues."

"What's wrong with her?" Sabine asked.

"Paranoid schizophrenic, according to this. Apparently they keep her fairly well-medicated so there's minimal outbursts, but it says in her file that the last time they hospitalized her, she swore someone was coming out of the ground to get her. It's no small wonder she's been kept in the house and drugged to a stupor."

"God, that's awful," Sabine said.

"Another interesting thing," Raissa continued, "is that all the Fortescues are allergic to peanuts. It's in all their records, except Catherine, but she's a Fortescue by marriage."

"So any of them could have guessed I had the same allergy, given that it was that prevalent in the family."

"Unfortunately, yes," Raissa said, "but that leads me to the really interesting part."

Sabine stared at her. "There's more?"

"Oh, yeah, and it's a doozy." Raissa flipped through a couple of sheets and pulled one from the middle of the stack. "This is part of your father's file, except, well, take a look at the test."

Sabine and Beau leaned over to read the line Raissa was pointing to. Sabine gasped. "He was impotent." She read the next line out loud. "'Impotency most likely as a result of scarlet fever as an infant.' But it's not possible."

Raissa stared at the paper, then looked at Sabine. "Maybe it's a huge coincidence that you favor them. Maybe you're a distant cousin—"

"No," Sabine interrupted. "Alford left a message this morning. The results of the DNA test were positive."

Beau and Raissa stared at her, then looked at each other, then back at her. No one seemed to have any idea what to say. "Maybe the test was wrong," Sabine suggested. "That can happen, right? I mean, men who have vasectomies sometimes still surprise their wives with a baby."

Raissa frowned. "I don't know that this is the same thing. Your father was working for a doctor at the time they ran these tests. It looks like he was taking part in some sort of medical trial, but the file doesn't state for what. I guess anything's possible . . ."

Beau shook his head. "But it's more likely that *if* you're really related, your father is a different Fortescue."

"My mother got pregnant by a different Fortescue?" Sabine sank onto the bed, her mind whirling with a million jumbled thoughts. "But even if that were the case, that wouldn't show up as a positive paternity, not if I were the child of some distant cousin, would it?"

"Not likely," Raissa said. "It would have to be an uncle, or a grandparent, I think, to register that closely."

Sabine covered her hand with her hands. "Oh, Lord, that's awful. My dad couldn't possibly have known, could he?"

"Don't go down that road just yet," Beau said. "There's always another explanation."

Sabine looked up at him. "Like what?"

"Well, the Fortecues could have lied about the results," Beau said.

"Why would they do that? What could they possibly have to gain by pretending I was Adam's daughter?"

Beau looked at Raissa, who frowned. "Maybe so you'd stop looking for your father," Raissa said.

Sabine stared at her for a moment. "Then that means they know the truth."

Raissa nodded. "I think they've always known."

Chapter Sixteen

The shrill ring of Sabine's cell phone cut into their conversation, and Sabine flipped it open, desperate for any possible distraction. Her mind was overloaded, her emotions overwhelmed. This was so much more confusing than she'd thought it would be. And so much more dangerous. She glanced at Beau and Raissa, who were studying her with matched looks of concern, and pressed the Talk button.

"Sabine?" Catherine Fortescue's voice was the absolute last one she expected to hear at the moment, and the last one she was prepared to speak to.

"Ye-yes." Sabine pointed to the phone and signaled to Beau and Raissa.

"Sabine, this is Catherine Fortescue. I hope I didn't call too early."

"No, Catherine," Sabine said, trying to keep her voice calm. "I've been up for a while."

"Good, then that means you've gotten the message from Mr. Alford about the test results. I can't tell you how pleased the family is to have Adam's child with us. I'm sorry we had to jump to legal proof so soon after our first meeting, but now all that unpleasantness is behind us."

"I understand," Sabine said, "and I told Mr. Alford that I'd expected to take the test. It wasn't an inconvenience, I assure you."

"Thank goodness. I was a little concerned. It's all so tacky, really. But the reason I called is that we'd like to meet with you to get to know you better and to start working on some of the more unfortunate legal work required to set up your trust fund."

"Oh no," Sabine protested, "I already told you I didn't want any money."

"The Fortescue estate is quite clear on the rules for heirs. You're the firstborn child of a firstborn child, and that comes with certain privileges, as well as obligations, I'm afraid. While I certainly have the utmost respect for your wishes, we really don't have much choice in the matter. Of course, you're free to do whatever you'd like with the money once the fund is established and transferred."

"Of course." No point arguing. She'd just deal with it later.

"If you're available, we'd love to have you over tonight for dinner."

Deciding the best possible decision at the moment was no decision, Sabine said finally, "I need to check my schedule at the shop first. If that's okay, can I give you a call in the next hour or so and let you know for sure?"

"That will be fine," Catherine replied. "And please feel free to bring your detective friend. Mr. Alford says he has a reputation for being quite a specialist at this sort of family dynamic. He might be able to lend some advice."

"Thank you. I'll let him know." Sabine said goodbye and closed the phone. Beau and Raissa were brimming with impatience. "Catherine wants me to go to dinner tonight to 'get to know me better and start the legal work for my trust fund.'" She looked at Beau. "You're invited."

Beau shook his head. "I don't like it."

"Nobody likes it," Raissa pointed out, "but it does present an opportunity for the two of you to get a closer look at the Fortescues in a somewhat manageable environment. The sooner you find out what they're hiding, the sooner Sabine's life might get back to normal."

Beau stared at Raissa as if she'd lost her mind. "How the hell is that manageable? Possibly confronting a killer on his own turf? Especially *that* turf—isolated doesn't even begin to describe the Fortescue estate. That's the quickest way to ensure a call to the coroner in my experience."

Raissa shrugged. "So go about your normal business and wonder if today is the day, or if it's going to happen in Sabine's apartment, or her shop, or this hotel. Since Sabine's poisoning never got out and Sabine herself hasn't mentioned it to the family, whoever took that shot at her probably thinks the entire thing was dismissed as accidental. Same with Mildred's accident in Sabine's car."

"Great," Beau said. "So he's not on the defensive. Instead, he's looking for another opportunity to strike."

Raissa shook her head. "If it is a Fortescue behind this, do you really think he will take a shot at Sabine while she's on the family estate? Talk about bringing down the house of cards, unless of course he *is* insane, but then it's not going to matter where you are or what you're doing, he's going to keep trying. And most likely get more desperate. This dinner might be an opportunity to do a little spy work. Especially if one of you could get out of the Fortescues' sight long enough to do a little snooping."

Beau blew out a breath and looked at Sabine. "I still don't like it, but Raissa's right. We can't lock you up in this hotel room and wait for another bomb escapade. And at least I was included in the invitation so you don't have to make up some excuse to bring me along. Not to mention that I'm guessing they won't be put off forever."

Sabine nodded and glanced over at Raissa. The psychic mouthed the word "Helena," and all of a sudden Sabine understood exactly why Raissa was suggesting this was a great opportunity to snoop. And what could possibly be a better weapon than the spy no one could hear or see?

It was inching toward evening and Helena Henry sat propped up on the bed in Sabine's hotel room, eating her third moon pie since arriving ten minutes before. Sabine wasn't sure whether she should be amazed or disgusted. However, a critical review of Helena's current outfit—some leather/spandex, studded combination reminiscent of eighties hair bands—gave Sabine pause. Despite eating the gross national product in carbs, fat, and sugar, the ghost was right. She hadn't gained a single pound.

Maybe jealousy was a more appropriate emotion, although Sabine wasn't quite ready to trade in her life for a permanent, calorie-free binge. She looked over at her half-eaten lunch of plain turkey sandwich on the dresser. Yet.

"So are you clear on what I need, Helena?"

"Yepfft . . . marphmellows sticking . . . wait." She

chewed a couple of seconds more, then swallowed twice and took a huge breath. "Man, that's good. I haven't eaten moon pies in forever."

Sabine narrowed her eyes at Helena. "Where exactly did you get . . . no, never mind. It's better if I don't know. Do you understand the plan?"

"I'm a bitch, not a moron. I hitch a ride with you and that sexy detective to the nutso house, then take a look around and see if I can find any skeletons in their closets." Helena straightened up. "Hey, do you think they really have a skeleton in the closet?"

"I hope not. But anything you find that looks suspect, you report immediately back to me. Just no yelling, and for God's sake, no eating while you're there."

Helena frowned. "No one said anything about not eating. Damn. Rich people always have fancy food when they have important company. What could be more important than a long-lost granddaughter? Maybe I could sneak a dessert or a dinner roll?" She gave Sabine an expectant look.

"Absolutely not! I am not going to play distract-people-from-the-floating-roll all evening. You will sneak and snoop and get dirt on these people as if you're searching for a bottomless pot of red beans and rice. I don't think I should have to remind you that this *is* a matter of life or death. And you of all people ought to know what an iffy thing death is."

Helena sighed. "Fine. You don't have to go all guilt trip on me. It's not like I want you stuck here with me. Now, that detective would be a whole other story." Helena's expression brightened. "Hey, I don't suppose there will be a little truck hanky-panky?"

"You don't suppose right," Sabine shot back, but the

disappointed look on Helena's face was too comical for her to maintain her stern stance. Finally, she smiled. "But if you're really good, I might see what I can do about a big pot of gumbo when we get back."

Helena clapped her hands. "Whoohoo! Can we have beer, too?"

"I don't know. Can you get drunk?"

"I can try."

Sabine grimaced. "That's what I was afraid of." She was about to follow that up with the no alcohol rule when Beau knocked on the connecting door and poked his head in.

"Are you ready?" he asked. "I thought you were talking to someone on the phone."

Sabine forced a smile. "Just hung up. Give me a sec and I'll meet you in the lobby."

"Everything okay with Mildred?" Beau asked.

Sabine nodded. "It's all settled. Maryse is going to stay with her tonight, for which I will officially owe her a trip to New Orleans for a manicure and pedicure because she has to sleep in the stinky hospital in a lumpy recliner."

"Not exactly a bad deal. I thought you women loved a pedicure."

"I love pedicures, and if I wasn't having one with Maryse it would be a good deal, but she takes picky to a whole new level. There was this incident a couple of years ago with a bottle of Purple Passion polish and the local police . . ." Sabine shook her head. "No, I don't even have time to explain. I'll be downstairs in a minute."

Beau grinned and closed the door behind him.

Sabine gave Helena a stern look. "You will be quiet on the ride over there. I'm not going to give him any reason to think the insanity is hereditary." Helena nodded and pulled another moon pie from the box. Sabine snatched the pie and the box from her hand. "And no food. It's not invisible like you, remember?"

Helena climbed off the bed and cast a wistful glance at the moon pie box. "You're such a grouch, Sabine. What is it about you and Maryse?"

Sabine grabbed her purse and tucked her cell phone in a side pocket. "Gee, I don't know. There's that whole someone's-trying-to-kill-me thing, or the I-can't-live-a-normal-life-in-my-own-house and my-friends-are-getting-caught-in-the-fallout thing, and hey, we could always throw in getting-haunted-by-the-constantly-bitching-and-eating-ghost-of-the-nastiest-person-I-knew-in-real-life part of the equation."

"Well, if you put it that way," Helena grumbled and headed out the door and down the steps to the lobby.

Sabine followed, praying that this whole thing didn't blow up in her face. Praying that she'd even be around tomorrow to pray.

The drive to the Fortescues was painfully long and silent. Sabine was afraid to say anything lest she give Helena a reason to start sounding off and blow their cover. Beau was suspiciously silent and appeared to be in deep thought. Over what, she had no idea. At this point, it could be anything—her situation with the Fortescues, her earlier cancer announcement, the new information Raissa had provided, their lovemaking the night before, this fall's football lineup.

She sighed and rested her head back on the seat.

Beau looked over at her. "Anything wrong?"

"Aside from the obvious, no. I was just thinking that a full night's sleep last night might have been a good idea given what we're doing now. My mind's all fuzzy."

"Whoohoo!" Helena sounded from the back of the car. "Why weren't you sleeping? Details, woman, I want details. You can start with the bottom half and work your way up."

Sabine closed her eyes again and clenched her jaw. *Do not respond. Do not even look at her.*

"I know what you mean," Beau said. "This whole thing was bizarre to begin with and it just keeps throwing angles at us that I didn't see coming and can't seem to fit to anything else. I wish it would all clear up. I have this overwhelming feeling that we're missing something, but I'll be damned if I can figure out what."

Sabine straightened in her seat as they pulled through the massive iron gates of the Fortescue estate. "Well, you've got a couple of minutes to figure it all out. Otherwise we're back to Plan B."

"There's a Plan B?"

Sabine looked at the opposing structure and felt a cold shiver rush across her. "Yeah, stay alive."

Two hours later, Sabine was mentally and emotionally drained as she'd never been before. Catherine and her ideas about "proper" behavior for a Fortescue, Frances's interruptions with scripture that didn't apply to anything they were speaking of, William's uninterested silence, and Alford's mild annoyance had gotten on her last nerve. In fact, it was more likely the last nerve was gone, too, and now they were eating away at bone.

Dinner had been an elaborate affair, served by the enthusiastic Adelaide, and while Sabine had to admit the food was fantastic, the atmosphere was so . . . oppressed, she guessed was the best word . . . that it made it difficult to enjoy the meal. Finally, the last dish was cleared away and they left the stiff, formal dining hall for the relative comfort of the living room. Alford excused himself, claiming he had some documents to review for a client meeting the following morning. Sabine didn't think he was telling the truth for a minute, but since contemplating the fuzz in her navel would be more interesting than hearing Catherine drone on any longer, she could hardly blame him for escaping. After all, he had to deal with the family far more than she did and had probably heard Catherine's opinions every week for the last twenty or thirty years.

A couple of times Helena had popped her head into the room, but only long enough to shake her head at Sabine and pop back out again. Sabine was growing dreadfully afraid that she was enduring this insult to her entire life for nothing.

They had just settled in the living room with coffee and Catherine was droning on about the high-end, dresses-only clothing store that Sabine should open when Adelaide hurried into the room, interrupting Catherine's monologue on "proper fashion for heiresses."

"Mrs. Fortescue, a storm is moving in something fierce and there's a leak around one of the library windows. It came up so sudden-like, I'm afraid we didn't even know until quite a bit of the floor was soaked."

Catherine frowned and left the room. She returned a minute later, a grim look on her face. "Adelaide is right. I can't see an inch beyond the hallway window. The living room is so well insulated we couldn't hear a thing." She looked at the housekeeper, her agitation obvious and unusual for the normally ultra-composed woman. "Have you checked the news? Where is the storm coming from?"

Adelaide shook her head. "Can't get any signal on the television. As soon as we realized it was raining, we tried. I got an old radio up in my room. You want me to get it?"

"Yes," Catherine said. "That would be very helpful." She looked at Sabine and Beau. "I'm so sorry about all of this. The storm must have shifted at the last minute. If you'll excuse William and me, there are some things we should tend to in case we lose power." Catherine nodded at her husband and they left the room through opposite doors, the quickness in their step belying the calm presentation.

Sabine shot a look at Beau. No power meant no lights. Shut up in this house with a possible killer and no lights wasn't an option Sabine hadn't considered, and she didn't like considering it now. As soon as Catherine left, Sabine crossed the room and retrieved her purse from the table in the corner. She opened it and ensured that her pistol was still safely tucked inside, then walked back across the room, purse in tow, and pulled a cough drop from a pocket inside. She sat the purse on a table within easy reach and looked over at Frances, who was sitting ramrod stiff, her face filled with fear.

"Frances?" Sabine asked. "Are you all right?"

Frances twisted the edge of her sweater with both hands. "I don't like the storm. I put them in the garden, but they came back. It was the water."

Adelaide came into the room and patted Frances on the arm. "Now, Frances, you didn't plant any flowers this spring and besides, William fixed the drainage years ago. Those plants aren't going anywhere." Adelaide helped Frances up from her chair. "Why don't you let me get you settled in your room before the worst of this comes? I'll bring you a cup of hot chocolate as soon as you're tucked down deep in them covers."

Frances looked at Adelaide with a blank stare for a couple of seconds, then nodded. "Hot chocolate does sound nice."

"Of course it does," Adelaide soothed. She turned to Sabine and Beau. "Give me a minute to see to Frances, and then I'll get you two some flashlights from the kitchen. Just in case." She guided Frances out of the room and into the hallway.

"It's the 'just in case' that worries me the most," Sabine whispered. "What are we supposed to do now?"

Beau crossed the room and checked up and down the halls at both entrances. "I don't know, but that storm is starting to worry me."

"Maybe we should start home before it gets any worse."

"Too late for that," Martin Alford's voice sounded from the front entrance, causing Sabine to jump. "The bridge is already under water, and the river was still rising. It will take hours after the rain subsides before the river will be low enough to cross."

Sabine stared at him. "Surely there's another way. A way around?"

"Not to speak of," Alford said, as he wiped at his dripping wet face with a tissue. "A long ways back there was a road that ran north of here and circled the river, but when the Fortescues acquired the land containing the road about thirty years back, they closed off the road and it's since grown over so you wouldn't really know it was there unless you knew where to look."

"Oh, I don't know that I'd like living here knowing that every time it rained I was cut off from the rest of the world. What if they have an emergency?"

Alford brushed wet hair off his forehead and reached for a tissue to wipe his brow. "If there's a serious situation, there's plenty of room to land a helicopter, and those pilots can fly in just about anything. Of course, you'd have to take one of the horses to actually get into town as the phones usually go right along with the power, but it's rarely necessary. The bridge usually doesn't go all the way under. It just happens when it rains hard and fast, a real downpour."

"Where did this come from?" Sabine asked. "Everyone thought the storms were headed east of here."

Alford nodded. "They are, but not far enough east for us to avoid a bit of the lashing. It was clear as a bell when I left and not five minutes later the bottom dropped out of the sky. I thought I'd get past the bridge before it went under, but with all the rain we've had lately, the river was already running high and this storm is really pouring it out."

"So what do we do?" Sabine asked. "I mean, if Mr. Alford is right and we won't be able to get over the bridge until tomorrow—" A huge clap of thunder boomed through the house, causing the walls to shake. The lights flickered once, then again, then went off completely, leaving the room pitch black.

"Holy shit!" Sabine passed her hand over the table until she found her purse, then lifted it up and pulled it on her shoulder.

"Just stay still," Beau advised and stepped closer to Sabine, finding her hand with his. "Adelaide said she'd be back with flashlights. She can't be much longer."

Sabine felt her pulse begin to increase and hoped Adelaide came before she was in cardiac arrest mode. She looked to the doorway that Adelaide had escorted Frances through and saw a faint flicker of light. She squinted, trying to make out the source, and as it grew closer, she realized it was an old-fashioned oil lantern. The lantern cast an eerie glow on Catherine's face as she walked into the room.

Catherine's gaze stopped on Alford. "Mr. Alford . . . I was afraid you might not make it out in time. I can only assume the bridge is underwater."

"Yes," Alford said. "I don't think it's going to be passable for quite a while after the storm stops."

"Then you'll all stay here," Catherine said and looked over at Sabine. "I'm so sorry about this inconvenience. If I'd had any idea the storm would hit here, we would have postponed dinner. Adelaide is finishing up with Frances. I'll have her make up three guest rooms on the same hall."

"Do you have any flashlights?" Beau asked. "Adelaide was going to bring some back with her."

"Yes," Catherine said. "We keep several in the kitchen for just this reason. I'll go get them. William is bringing in more lanterns from the garage, and there's the generator, of course, but it only produces enough power to light the kitchen. I'm afraid you're going to have to relive ancient history for a night—except for the indoor plumbing part, of course." She gave them a smile, then turned and walked toward the kitchen. Alford fell in step behind her.

"If you don't mind," he said, "I'd like to get one of those flashlights and check on my car. I think I left an interior light on."

"Of course," Catherine said and the two left the room through the entrance to the kitchen.

The light in the room faded with Catherine's lantern, and once again Sabine and Beau were cast into darkness. "I don't like it," Beau said, keeping his voice low. "It's not safe. I don't want you in that room alone. I'm staying with you."

"Catherine would never agree to that. It wouldn't be 'proper.'"

"Then I'll sneak in after she's gone."

"With all of us occupying the same hallway? If you use a light, Alford or Frances will see it and if you don't use a light, you'll take out one of the five thousand antiques they have lining every hall in this monstrosity."

"I'll take my chances."

Sabine opened her mouth to respond, but felt a jab in her side from Beau's elbow. She looked over at the entrance as Catherine walked back into the room, carrying two flashlights. A second look revealed Helena strolling behind her, a worried look on her face. Catherine handed them each a flashlight and said, "Adelaide has already started putting out the linens. It will only be a bit longer before the rooms are ready. I know it's a little early, but I figured it would be better to retire now than risk walking around with the lanterns. I worry about fire, especially in a house this old."

Sabine just nodded, trying not to look at Helena, but dying to know what the ghost had found out.

"I don't blame you," Beau said. "Just let us know when everything's ready. We're not going anywhere."

Catherine tried to smile at his attempt at a joke, but it came out more like a grimace. Whatever was bothering her seemed to intensify right along with the storm. She nodded and left the room.

Sabine watched as the light of the lantern faded away, then turned on her flashlight and faced Beau. "I know this wasn't in the plans and I'll admit this house and the people who live here give me the creeps, but this might also be the opportunity to get to the bottom of this."

Beau stared at her as if she'd lost her mind. "We are trapped in this mansion out of a horror novel and you think this is some sort of opportunity? An opportunity for what—a shallow grave?"

"An opportunity to catch the killer in the act."

"You're not exactly convincing me of anything here, Sabine."

"If I'm in a room alone, then the killer might take a shot at me."

Beau shook his head. "Which is exactly my problem with all of this. No way. I'm not letting you stay by yourself."

"But I have a plan—"

"Damn it, Sabine! You want me to sit in my room, and who knows how far away that is, and wait for someone to attack you? And what? Hope you can fight them off or yell loud enough for me to hear you and get there in time? That's a bullshit plan and you know it. And if you want to throw in the insanity angle then our number one suspect is Frances and her room is on the same hall."

"It's not like I'm unprotected, Beau—you've seen me shoot. I'll be fine. If they'd slipped anything into my food, I'd be laid out on the floor already, and I won't drink the hot chocolate. That way I can stay conscious."

"Really? And if the killer gets creative and pumps gas through a vent in your room—what then? You going to tell me you can shoot people in your sleep? Because if so, you should have warned me last night and I would have worn a bulletproof vest to bed."

"Whoohoo!" Helena hooted and danced a jig. "Sabine got lucky." Helena looked Beau up and down. "*Really* lucky. Damn."

Sabine felt her checks burning red and was glad the flashlight didn't give away her mortal embarrassment. Bad enough her roll with the sexy PI had been announced to Helena, but even worse, she'd had a vivid recall of just how good Beau Villeneuve looked in bed. She bit her lower lip, struggling with a way to let Beau in on her secret weapon, but there simply wasn't any way to lessen the blow. "You trust me, right?"

"This has nothing to do with me trusting you. It's about *not* trusting them."

"What if I told you I could ensure that even if something happened to me, you could be notified?"

Beau shook his head. "Our cell phones don't get a signal out this far. I've already checked. And even if they did normally, they wouldn't in this storm. Maybe if the rooms are right next to each other, but I seriously doubt prim and proper Catherine is going to go for that."

"What if I had a more elusive, albeit much more offensive, method of calling you for help?" She bit her lip, then pressed forward before she could change her mind. "I snuck someone into the estate with us."

"Where, in your handbag? Even if there wasn't a monsoon outside, there's no way into this fortress that isn't covered with iron bars or security cameras."

"She rode with us in the truck."

Beau blew out a breath of frustration. "I don't have time for games. We have to come up with a plan, and right now the best one I can think of involves walking out of here and swimming across that damned bayou of alligators. It's the safer of the two options."

"She's a ghost. Helena Henry's ghost, to be exact."

Beau stared. "What do you want from me, Sabine? Jesus, I've kept an open mind about everything, but telling me I taxied a ghost over here is way beyond my limit."

"Helena," Sabine said and pointed to a desk in the corner. "Get that pad of paper and pen and bring it over here so that you can answer some questions. And make it fast. We need to go from 'no way in hell' to 'I believe' in a minute or less."

Helena lifted the paper and pen from the desk and walked over to stand next to Beau. The look on his face was beyond comprehension, and Sabine could only imagine what thoughts must be racing through his mind. Helena began to write and Beau looked down at the paper in amazement.

I am Helena Henry. I was murdered and have been visible to Maryse since my death and more recently to Sabine. Sorry if this startles the shit out of you, but it's not a fucking picnic for me either. I've been here spying on these psychos for hours and haven't had a thing to eat. Deal with it and let's get this over with.

Chapter Seventeen

Sabine waited anxiously for Beau to react, worried that she'd thrown way too much at him at once, especially with everything else going on. He stared at the paper as if it were going to explode. Then he took one hand and slowly passed it through Helena. "It's colder. I swear, the air is colder where she's standing." He looked at Sabine. "I can't believe it, but it's real." His expression instantly shifted to one of immediate realization. "Holy mother of God, she's been following you around all this time. That's how you got into the medical records room."

Sabine nodded. "She's also the one who created the vision for Raissa to draw my parents from. Helena's been involved from the beginning, and she's going to see it to the end. I'm so sorry to spring it on you like this. I'd hoped you would never have to know."

"That might have been nice." He glanced at the paper once more then looked at Sabine, a pained expression on his face. "She wasn't in the room last night . . ."

"No! Maryse and I have a strict rule about unannounced visiting—especially bedroom visits."

The pen began moving again and Beau leaned over. A single word appeared.

Spoilsports.

Beau smiled. "She's kinda a handful, isn't she?"

"You have no idea. But she'll also do anything to help me. If anything happens to me while I'm alone in my room, Helena will alert you."

Beau stared at the wall for a couple of seconds, obviously lost in thought. Finally, he looked Sabine directly in the eyes. "It was Helena who called 911 that night in your apartment, wasn't it? That's why no one ever spoke. You were already passed out."

Sabine nodded.

Beau paced the length of the room twice, then stopped and looked at the pad of paper again. "You know this is insane, right?"

"Seems to be no shortage of crazy in this house. Why should we be any different?"

"I do have an idea. It's not very nice, but I think if you can pull it off it might get Adelaide's tongue loosened. I'd be willing to bet she knows everything that goes on in this house."

"What's the idea?"

Beau smiled. "Adelaide believes in spirits, the afterlife, right? Couldn't Helena create visions for her just like she did for Raissa? I figure if Adelaide is the one to settle you in your room, then you might have a chance to call up spirits via Helena, and get Adelaide to tell some family secrets."

Sabine frowned. "But if Adelaide's memory is going, like Alford said, is anything she says really dependable?"

"We only have Alford's word that Adelaide's mind is going, and he's getting that directly from the Fortescues. What better way to discount the ramblings of an old woman than to say she's losing her faculties?"

"You have a point." Sabine looked over at Helena.

"Do you think you can help me spook the house-keeper?"

Helena shrugged. "I could probably manage a vision or two . . . for a piece of that chocolate cake I saw y'all eating."

Sabine sighed. "I'll see what I can do, but it's going to have to wait. Now, before Catherine gets back, tell me what you've found, Helena. You had a strange look on your face when you entered the room."

"The first place I checked was Catherine and William's room. Catherine had this box of clippings on William with parts of the text highlighted—everything he'd ever done, looks like, from birth to the war. But after the war, there was nothing. I assumed at first that after she got married and had the kids, she was just too busy to keep up with it any longer, but then I started reading the highlighted text and it didn't make sense at all."

"Why not?"

"Well, like the article about William receiving a medal of bravery for being shot in the leg trying to help another soldier. You'd think she would have high-lighted his name and medal of bravery, right? But in-stead, she'd highlighted the text that mentioned the shot he took to the leg. They were all like that. I couldn't make any sense of the things she highlighted. I started to take them, but I figured it wasn't a good idea."

"No," Sabine agreed. "We don't want anyone to get suspicious. And be careful when you search and make sure you put everything back exactly as you found it, okay?"

"I'm being careful," Helena promised. "After that I took a trip to Frances's room and what a doozy that was. The woman has more crosses in that tiny space than the entire cathedral in Rome and a candle on every level surface. I figure either she's trying to repent for something major or believes in vampires. Then I found a newspaper stashed in between her mattresses."

Sabine nodded. "Catherine mentioned something about Frances reading the newspaper again. I got the impression they tried to keep it from her."

"Well, the odd part about this one is it was a month old. So I flipped through it and you'll never guess what I found—that photo of you at that breast cancer walk in New Orleans. Your picture was circled along with a comment in the article about you owning Read 'em and Reap."

Sabine sucked in a breath. "That's how she knew about me before Beau contacted Mr. Alford. She saw me in the paper and noticed my resemblance to her brother. Could it have been Frances who tried to break into my store?"

Helena nodded. "I wondered that myself, so I took off out of there and made my way through the garage and the carriage house. Sure enough, in the carriage house there was the white truck that I saw in the park the day of the break-in."

"You're sure it was the same?"

"It was the same make and model. I'm pretty sure there's another one or two in the world like it but it's too big of a coincidence to ignore, don't you think?"

"Yes," Sabine agreed, "and with Catherine busy with church things and William throwing them back at the bar, Frances would have had plenty of opportunities to take the truck and pay me a visit. But for what?" Sabine frowned and repeated everything Helena had said so far to Beau.

Beau shook his head. "Maybe she was going to talk

to you but when the shop was closed, she figured no one was there and she'd do some snooping. Lord only knows for what . . . a birth certificate, pictures? Either way, I don't think it's a coincidence that the truck is the same make and model as the one Helena saw."

Sabine frowned. "But what about the person I kicked that night outside of the general store? That couldn't have been Frances. A kick would have sent her sprawling."

"Not necessarily," Beau said. "Sometimes the insane can show remarkable strength if they're experiencing an adrenaline rush. It's documented all the time."

"And the poison . . . the bomb? Do you really think Frances is capable of those things?"

"No," Beau said, "but I think she's capable of getting someone else to do them, and I'm sure she's got the trust fund to back it up. But we also have to remember that anyone with access to the household could have used that truck. Frances might be winning the insanity wars, but we still don't know for sure it was her that tried to break into your store, or that attacked you on the street. And if it was, we don't know that she was alone."

"True. But who would help her commit a crime and why?"

"She'd do it for the inheritance," Helena chimed in. "If the Fortescues' estate was set up anything like my family's, then your father, as firstborn, would inherit the house and all its contents, along with his share of the estate. Since he's dead, his portion would pass to you as his firstborn."

"And skip Frances entirely?"

Helena nodded. "The house could, yes. And I'm guessing this place is worth a pretty penny."

Sabine repeated Helena's comments to Beau. "It reminds me of something Catherine said when she invited me to dinner. About being the 'firstborn child of a firstborn child.'"

"So quite possibly, a fortune at stake," Beau said, "and more importantly, her home. Maybe Frances was afraid she'd have to leave."

"I would never do that," Sabine protested.

"You and I know that," Beau said, "but Frances doesn't, and she's not exactly playing with a full deck. The more I hear, the less I like this idea of you playing bait, Sabine. I think—" He stopped talking as Adelaide walked into the room.

"If you are ready," Adelaide said, "I can take you to your rooms now."

Beau's mind raced with possibilities, none of them good. This situation had gone from bad, to horrible, to out of the fucking world in less than ten minutes time. If there was ever a situation where he needed to think quickly and clearly, it was now. But the overload of information, coupled with being stranded in Hell House—accompanied by a ghost, no less—had his mind racing out of control. Keeping Sabine safe, then getting her out of that house was his top priority and he needed a plan. Yesterday.

"That's fine, Adelaide. We're ready to go to our rooms now," Sabine said, and she took the lantern Adelaide held out to her.

"There's another in Mr. Villeneuve's room," Adelaide explained as they walked down the dark hallway and into the west wing of the house.

Beau committed every step of the hallway, every turn to memory. Knowing exactly where everything was located was key, especially if they needed to leave in a hurry. Adelaide stopped at the first room and motioned to Beau. "This one is yours, Mr. Villeneuve. There are some spare clothes on the bed, if you'd like to change. It's just a pair of shorts and a T-shirt, but it will likely be more comfortable than what you're wearing."

Beau smiled at the anxious housekeeper. "It's all fine, Adelaide, and I really appreciate all the trouble you've gone to."

"Oh, well," Adelaide said, apparently at a loss for not only being thanked but complimented as well. Even in the dim light, the flush on her face was evident.

"If you ladies don't mind," Beau said, "I'm going to follow Mr. Alford's example and check on my truck before I turn in." He looked at Sabine and inclined his head toward Adelaide, hoping she took the cue to try the Helena scam on the housekeeper once they were alone in her room.

"Mr. Villeneuve," Adelaide said before he could leave, "there's a big urn next to the front door that has some umbrellas in it. You help yourself."

"Thanks, Adelaide." He took the lantern off the dresser and headed down the hall, weaving his way toward the main entrance of the house.

He plucked a small umbrella from a large ceramic pot next to the door and stepped out into the hurricane. The wind and rain blew at an angle, making the umbrella more of a hindrance than a help, so he tossed it against the door and ran for his truck, holding one arm over his eyes to shield them from the worst of the pelting raindrops. Once in his truck, he tested his cell phone but wasn't surprised to find it had no signal.

He retrieved his spare revolver from the glove box and grabbed a backpack from the backseat. He pulled a pair of walkie-talkies from inside and checked the batteries. He didn't think the reception would be great, but the walkie-talkies might provide enough communication for him to stay in touch with Sabine. Despite Sabine's reassurances and Helena's dedication, Beau still wasn't convinced that the ghost was the best possible protection. But if she could shoot a gun, then his spare revolver might just come in handy.

He squinted in the darkness but couldn't make out the attorney's car anywhere in the front drive. Lucky bastard probably had an indoor parking spot. Although he didn't think it possible, the rain was coming down even harder now than before. He tucked the revolver in the waistband of his pants and slung the pack over his shoulder, then ran for the house, using the meager light of the lantern to help guide him.

He took a second to retrieve the umbrella and hurried inside, pausing only long enough to shake the water from his hair. He'd noticed earlier that the room Adelaide had prepared for him had an attached bathroom. Hopefully, the bathroom would have towels. After running in the monsoon, he was going to need one or two. Taking a right turn from the entrance, he stopped short at a door right at the edge of the hallway.

Figuring he could snoop as well as Helena, he peered both directions in the darkness. Deciding the coast was clear, he eased open the door and held his lantern close to the opening. A bevy of jackets and boots filled the tiny closet. He rifled through at least ten women's jackets, all too large for Frances, but then if you rarely left the house, Beau guessed you rarely needed a jacket.

He searched the pockets for anything interesting, but Catherine Fortescue was apparently not the type of woman who carried miscellaneous items in her jacket pockets. It didn't really come as a surprise.

At the back of the closet, he found a men's navy blue raincoat, likely William's. Beau stuck his hand in the two outside pockets and came up with a key. It looked like a door key and fairly new, but there was no indication what door it was to. He placed the key back in the front pocket, then slipped his hand inside the interior pocket. He felt something round and plastic, but couldn't even guess what it might be. He pulled the object from the pocket and lifted the lantern to see his bounty.

His heart skipped a beat when he realized he was holding a bottle of peanut oil.

He reached back in the pocket again and drew out a syringe. Beau slipped the peanut oil and the syringe in his pocket and started to close the door when he remembered the key. He'd seen that key before. Reaching into the front pocket, he located the key and pulled it out again. He lifted the lantern so that he could get a good look at it and in a flash, it hit him—it was just like the key Sabine had used to open her shop—the locks that had just been replaced by the property manager who worked for the estate that owned the building, which just might be the Fortescue estate for all anyone knew. Why hadn't anyone considered that before?

With a clear idea of exactly how Sabine was poisoned despite drinking from an intact bottle of wine, Beau closed the closet door. As he walked silently back to his room, his mind worked to make sense of what he'd found. Unfortunately, the only part that made sense was *how* William Fortescue had managed to poison his granddaughter. But why? Something to do with the DNA test results? Someone in the Fortescue family knew the truth about Sabine's parents, maybe the whole family, and for whatever reason, they were determined to keep that truth a secret.

Even if it meant lying about her being family until they could kill her.

As he turned the corner for the hallway to his room, he caught a glimpse of something white moving at the far end of the hall. He turned his lantern down as low as it would go and crept to the end of the hallway, then peered around the corner. He could see a lantern across the room, but the light cast from it was too dim to make out the person carrying it. Suddenly, a flash of lightning lit the sky and filtered through the far wall of what must have been a sunroom since the wall was all glass. In the burst of light, he saw Frances opening a door to the gardens. She was wearing a long white dressing gown and carrying a shovel. Without so much as a backward glance, she walked out into the storm.

Sabine followed Adelaide into a room several doors down from Beau. He probably wasn't going to like the distance between them, but there was really little she could do. "It looks fine, Adelaide. Thank you."

"Would you like for me to get you some hot chocolate, Ms. Sabine? I figured we could all do with a little warm milk and chocolate."

"That sounds wonderful."

The housekeeper nodded and started to leave the room.

It's now or never. "Adelaide, wait!" Sabine grabbed

the woman's arm and closed her eyes. "The spirits are talking. They said your name."

Sabine felt the woman stiffen and opened her eyes to see if she was up for the game. Adelaide stared back at her, eyes wide as saucers. "The spirits said my name?" Adelaide asked. "Why would they do that? I'm nobody."

Sabine shook her head. "You believe, Adelaide. The spirits are highly selective about who they speak to. It's an honor." Sabine waved one hand in the air, signaling Helena to get to work.

A dim glow began to form next to the bed and Adelaide grabbed Sabine's hand in hers and squeezed so hard Sabine was certain she'd broken something. "Look at that," Adelaide whispered. "You didn't say they'd show themselves, too."

Sabine shook her head. "They rarely materialize. I think it takes a lot of energy. This must be very important."

Adelaide nodded but never took her eyes off the expanding light. In the center of the light, two people began to come into shape, and Sabine had to hold herself back from giving Helena a high five. The ghost had chosen William's mother and father to create. Who better to get Adelaide to part with her secrets than the people she'd served the longest?

"Oh, my Lord," Adelaide said as the figures sharpened.

Sabine leaned toward Adelaide and whispered. "I think they want to ask you something."

"Anything," Adelaide said, "they can ask me anything. Aren't they beautiful? Just like in the picture over the fireplace."

"No shit," Helena grumbled and Sabine cut her eyes at the ghost. Helena huffed once and turned her concentration back to the apparition she was creating.

"I can hear her," Sabine said. "She's saying your name, Adelaide." Sabine closed her eyes for a couple of seconds, then looked at Adelaide. "She wants to know why."

"Why, what?" Adelaide asked.

Sabine shook her head. "I don't know. She's just saying 'why, Adelaide, why?'"

Adelaide dropped Sabine's hand and put her hand over her mouth. "Oh no! I'm so sorry, madam. I'm so sorry, but I swear I didn't know. Not until a long time had passed."

The possible scenarios raced through Sabine's mind, but she couldn't hit on one. She made the split-second decision to go vague again. "She wants to know why you didn't tell anyone when you found out."

"I wanted to," Adelaide cried. "Oh, I wanted to so bad, but Catherine told me that no one would believe me, and if I said anything, she'd just say I did it. That I hated you and wanted you gone. But I swear I had nothing to do with the car wreck." Adelaide let out an anguished cry. "Catherine said no one would take the word of a pagan housekeeper over the lady of the estate. And there was the babies. What would have happened to Frances and Adam? And my brother in that nursing home in New Orleans? Catherine was paying for it all. What would have happened to him? Oh, madam, please forgive me, I beg you."

Sabine's mind whirled with every statement Adelaide made. Surely she'd gotten it wrong. Adelaide couldn't possibly be saying that Catherine had killed

William's parents. What was the point? William was going to inherit everything. She would never have wanted for anything. Sabine searched her mind for the next question to ask, but before she could formulate the words, the door to her room flew open and Beau hurried inside.

"Shit!" Helena griped as she lost concentration and the apparition vanished.

"No!" Adelaide cried. "Don't go, madam. I'm sorry. I'll make it right. I swear to you."

Beau barely glanced at the housekeeper. "Thank God you're all right," he said to Sabine. "When I was coming back from the car, I saw Frances leave the house. She was carrying a shovel."

"Oh, no," Adelaide said, her face filled with fear. "I have to stop her. Her mind is so fragile. I can't let her do it again." Adelaide rushed out of the room, and they could hear her footsteps pounding down the hall. Sabine glanced at Beau and they ran out of the room in pursuit of the housekeeper.

"This way," Beau yelled at Sabine when they reached the end of the hall. "This is where Frances went outside."

The door to the sunroom stood wide open, rain pouring inside. Adelaide was nowhere in sight. Beau held the lantern out in front of them and they ran out the door and into the storm. "Which way?" Sabine yelled, straining to make herself heard over the wind.

"I don't know," Beau said, turning from one direction to another. "There!" He pointed to a spot in the far end of the garden. Sabine could barely make out something white before Beau grabbed her hand and pulled her with him.

The rain felt like needles on her skin and almost blinded her. Beau slowed and Sabine knew he was having as much trouble maneuvering in the storm as she was. She pulled her hand from Beau's and held it over her eyes, hoping to get a better look ahead. Beau glanced back, then did the same, and they crept across the backyard until they were close enough to see what was happening.

Frances was digging like a madwoman around some old blackberry bushes, and Adelaide was frantically trying to get her to stop. So far, it looked like she'd gone at least two feet deep. No matter how hard Adelaide tugged, Frances kept lifting more mud from the hole she'd created. Frances's eyes were fixed on the ground, never blinking, never wavering, despite the torrent of rain hitting her face. She didn't seem to hear Adelaide or feel the housekeeper's hands on her arm.

Beau handed Sabine the lantern and went to assist Adelaide. He tried to take the shovel from Frances, and Sabine saw the shift in her face. Her eyes went black as night and anger coursed through her. She screamed and tried to attack Beau with the shovel, but his hold on it was strong and she couldn't break his grasp. She let go of the shovel and launched at his face with her hands.

Before Sabine could even take a step to help, Beau had grabbed one of Frances's arms and twisted it behind her, then wrapped his arms around her entire body. He lifted her completely off the ground and turned toward the house. Sabine took a step toward them and stepped into the completely forgotten hole. She cried out as her ankle twisted on impact and Beau stopped short and turned around to look at her.

"I'm fine," Sabine said as she moved her foot around, making sure she hadn't broken anything. And then she hit something solid. She leaned over with the lantern and put her hand down in the water-filled hole, trying to locate what her foot had hit. Finally, she felt something long and hard and worked her fingers around it.

"Sabine, c'mon," Beau yelled over the storm.

Sabine pulled her bounty from the water, and Frances screamed. Then Sabine took a good look at what she held: a human bone.

Sabine flung it to the ground and jumped out of the hole. Frances thrashed about, screaming like a banshee, and Beau struggled to maintain his grasp. Adelaide instantly dropped to her knees, praying to God Almighty to forgive her.

"Go!" Sabine yelled to Beau, and he started toward the house, struggling to maintain control of Frances. Sabine pulled Adelaide to her feet. "Pray later. You've got to help with Frances." Adelaide nodded and hurried toward the house. Sabine grit her teeth and bent over to pick up the bone. The smooth, hard surface shouldn't have caused so much emotion, but it was knowing what that surface was that made Sabine almost wretch.

She ran to the house and into the sunroom after Adelaide, then followed the housekeeper down the hall and into Frances's room, where Beau was trying to keep the woman restrained on her bed. She was soaking wet, and the white gown clung to her scrawny body. Her hair stuck to her face, the silver almost translucent in the lantern light. She turned toward Sabine and Adelaide as they entered the room, but she looked right through them, her eyes wild with fright.

Sabine hid the bone behind her back, certain that Frances would launch off again if she saw it. Adelaide rushed over to the bed and rubbed Frances's head as if petting a dog. "Now, now, child," Adelaide said, "you're going to be fine. It was just a scare is all. You don't like storms, remember? It's just the storm."

Frances seemed to calm a bit at Adelaide's words and slumped back on the bed. Adelaide picked up a cup of water that was sitting on the nightstand and lifted it to Frances's mouth. "You just need to drink a little water and relax, okay, child? You'll feel a lot better once you've had your water."

Beau released his hold on Frances and stepped back from the bed. They watched as Frances took one sip and then another, then quietly drifted off in what appeared to be a restful sleep. "Drugs?" Beau asked.

Adelaide nodded. "She'd had some of the water before she went outside, which is why it kicked in so fast now. But she was so worked up earlier that her body was still moving even though her mind was shutting down. Poor thing. She's always been afraid of storms."

Sabine held the bone out to Adelaide. "Maybe this has something to do with it."

Adelaide nodded. "I thought she'd forgotten, but many years ago it rained so hard and for so long that one of the bones washed up from the ground. Frances ran out in the storm in a fit and saw it. I dragged her away, but it was too late. Ever since then, she's always been afraid when it rains. That's why I drugged her as soon as I heard the storm moving in."

"Who is . . . was this?" Sabine asked. "And why are they buried in the backyard? Don't lie to me, Adelaide. I know this is human."

Adelaide nodded and looked at the floor, her face full of shame.

Sabine waited a couple of seconds for a response, but when none was forthcoming, she pressed again. "You as much as admitted to me earlier that Catherine had killed William's parents. There's no way they were buried in the backyard, so this is someone else. Who, Adelaide? Who else did Catherine kill?"

"Lloyd," Beau said. "It has to be. He came home, and the family couldn't risk hiding him so they took the easy way out."

Adelaide lifted her eyes to Beau's. "It weren't that simple. Catherine killing the elder Fortescues was all part of her plan."

"Her plan to what?" Beau asked.

Sabine stared at Adelaide, and suddenly it hit her. "Her plan to marry Lloyd and still inherit everything."

Chapter Eighteen

"Lloyd?" Beau repeated. "Oh my God, you're right. Everyone thought he'd changed because of the war, but it wasn't the war at all. He'd changed because he was an entirely different man." Beau looked at Adelaide. "It's William that's buried in the backyard. You knew all these years and never said anything?"

Adelaide wrung her hands together, tears streaming down her face. "I swear I didn't know what they'd done until years later. It was Catherine who got Lloyd back from Vietnam and hid him at her family's lake house until they'd finished setting it all up. I mean, I knew Lloyd was pretending to be William. I'd practically raised those boys. They could never have fooled me, but Lloyd told me William was killed in Vietnam and that he'd taken his dog tags so that the military police wouldn't arrest him.

"I didn't know they'd killed William until Frances dug up the bones in the garden. My poor Frances. Her mind was already gone when Adam found her that night. She'd uncovered the bones and started screaming. That's how he was able to get you away. Oh, my sweet, sweet Adam. He tried to do right."

Sabine's head began to spin. "What are you trying to say—that Frances was going to bury me alive in the backyard? Frances is my real mother?"

Adelaide nodded. "Please don't blame her, Ms. Sabine. It weren't her fault. My Frances was crazy from the disease."

"What disease?"

Adelaide blanched. "Lloyd brought it back from the war and gave it to Catherine. She never knew until Frances's mind started going. When Frances got meningitis, the doctors found it. She'd had it since she was born—passed from Catherine."

"Syphilis," Beau said, the disgust in his voice apparent. "Adam had scarlet fever when he was an infant. That's what his medical records said, remember? They would have given him penicillin. Catherine had the scarlet fever too, so neither of them carried the syphilis any further."

Sabine covered her mouth with her hand. "Oh, my God. But Frances didn't get the scarlet fever, so she never got the drug. That disease ate away at her for all those years. And my father? Who is my father, Adelaide?"

Adelaide shook her head and rubbed the unconscious Frances's arm. "I don't know, I swear. Someone hurt her. I found her in the bath scrubbing herself with steel wool. She'd already started to bleed in some places. I'm so sorry, Sabine. I would have told, I swear, but someone had to take care of Frances."

"Adam knew, didn't he?" Beau said. "He saw the bones and knew his mother and father had killed someone. That's why he took Sabine and ran."

"Yes, and since he worked with the doctor, I'm guessing he peeked at Frances's medical reports and knew she was losing her mind and why." Adelaide said. "I begged Catherine to let him go, let them be, but she couldn't risk it. She tracked Adam and his girlfriend down and messed with their car. She never thought you'd find the family, Sabine, or she would have hunted you down, too."

"Is that why she's trying to kill me now? So that I won't find out the truth?"

Adelaide started to answer but then froze. A horrified look came over her face. Sabine knew even before she turned around that Catherine was standing in the doorway. What she hadn't planned on was the pistol that Catherine held, pointed straight at her.

"Don't flatter yourself," Catherine said, "I had no reason to harm you. You thought Adam was your father and had no reason to think otherwise. I would have settled a nice trust fund on you and you would never have been the wiser. Killing you would only have served to draw attention to the family, and that's the last thing I wanted." She stepped into the room, and Lloyd stepped in behind her. "It's a shame you couldn't hold your tongue, Adelaide. I knew it was a mistake to keep you all these years, but you were the only one who could care for Frances. She's been a trial since birth."

"She's lying," Beau said. "I found the peanut oil and syringe in Lloyd's pocket. They did try to kill you."

Catherine spun around and looked at Lloyd, who shook his head. "No way. Catherine's right. Sabine wasn't a threat to us until now, and if I'd tried to kill her, she wouldn't be standing here."

"Well," Catherine said with a smile. "It won't be for much longer." She motioned Sabine and Beau toward the other side of the bed. "I really don't want to get blood on this suit. I'm trying to avoid complications in my story for the police."

Sabine inched over to Beau. His jaw was clenched, and Sabine knew he was calculating every risk, every percentage of success if he reached for his pistol. But as long as Catherine was pointing her gun straight at Sabine, she knew he wouldn't take the chance. And that was most likely going to get them killed.

"I think," Catherine said, "I'll take this golden opportunity to clear up all my problems. I mean, I'm going to claim that Frances went crazy and killed everyone. When she wakes up she won't know whether she did or not." With that, Catherine whirled toward the doorway and shot Lloyd twice in the chest.

Sabine covered her mouth as she screamed. It was as if time hung suspended. The shock registered on Lloyd's face as he looked down at the red stain growing on his white dress shirt. He touched it and held up his hands, staring unbelieving at the blood dripping from his fingertips. He looked at Catherine, bewildered. He took one step toward her and stumbled, then crashed to the floor in a heap.

"Finally," Catherine said, "I can live the life I wanted without hiding in this musty old estate. Lloyd never could manage to act like William in public, so I had no choice but to become a virtual recluse. It's been like living in a prison. Worthless husband, crazy daughter, meddling housekeeper. But that's all about to change."

In the doorway, something moved, and Sabine squinted in the dim light, trying to make out what was in the hallway. A second later, Helena walked into the room and right through Catherine to stand between the murdering matriarch and her next victims.

"What a fucking mess," she said. "I can probably knock that gun out of her hand. If you want me to do it, blink twice."

It was a long shot, depending on Helena to get her ghost skills right on demand, but it still wasn't as long as the possibility of Catherine shooting and missing them from a distance of ten feet. Sabine said a silent prayer for all of them and blinked twice. Helena nodded and her brow wrinkled in concentration as she turned to face Catherine. At the same time, Catherine lifted the gun and pointed it directly at Beau's chest.

"I think I'll start with lover boy here. Might as well clear the room of men. And after all, if not for him, we wouldn't be in this position to begin with, would we?" She smiled at Sabine and her finger whitened on the trigger.

And that's when Helena struck. She jumped across the room, faster than Sabine would have ever given her credit for, and hit Catherine's arm with a semblance of a karate chop. The chop probably wouldn't have been hard enough to make Catherine drop the gun under normal circumstances, but being assaulted by an invisible assailant was apparently enough of a shock for her to loosen her grip. Catherine cried out as the gun fell from her hand and skidded a couple of feet across the floor.

"It's the spirits!" Adelaide screamed and threw her arms around Frances.

Catherine instantly recovered and dove for the weapon, but Helena drove her into the hardwood floor in a body slam the WWF would have been proud of. Catherine hit the ground with a thud and started to move when Beau said, "I wouldn't do that if I were you."

Helena rose from the floor with Catherine's pistol, a huge grin on her face. "How was that for a save? You owe me big, Sabine."

Catherine's eyes widened at what looked to her like a floating gun. Adelaide started to pray again, and Sabine had little doubt that the Catholic church was getting a new member come Sunday.

"Now, Helena," Sabine said, looking uneasily at the gun. "Be careful with that. The safety's not on. It could go off."

Helena turned to face Sabine. "What, do you think I'm stupid? I know how a gun works, see?"

Before Sabine could stop her, Helena reached up with her other hand and tried to engage the safety. She must have pushed too hard because she lost her grip on the gun and it spun around on her finger that was placed in the trigger hole. "Shit!" Helena said and tried to catch the gun, but instead, she pulled the trigger.

Luckily for all the good guys, the gun was turned backwards and facing straight at Helena's chest when it went off. The bullet passed right through the perturbed ghost and hit Catherine in the thigh. The murdering bitch went down with a cry and wailed as if she were dying.

Sabine took a step forward and grabbed the gun out of Helena's hand. "Give me that before you kill someone." She shot a look back at Beau, who was shaking his head.

Beau motioned to Catherine. "Move over by the bed. Sit next to the post."

"I'm fucking shot, you asshole," Catherine shot back.

"Then crawl, bitch," Beau shot back, "unless you'd like me to give the gun back to the ghost and have her put a bullet in your other leg."

Catherine shot daggers at Beau and pulled herself

across the floor to the bed. "You'll never prove any of this. Bunch of devil-worshippers, bringing demons into my house. I'll press charges against you, and the local police will never believe a word you say."

"Oh, that's rich," Helena complained. "The bitch killed half the local population but *I'm* a demon." She looked over at Sabine. "Can I poke her in the leg, please? Or maybe pour alcohol in the wound?"

"No, Helena, as much as I would like you to, I can't allow you to pour alcohol into Catherine's bullet hole." She looked down at Catherine and smiled. "I wouldn't keep calling her a demon if I were you."

"You're all crazy," Catherine said.

"No, they're not," Adelaide said, breaking off prayer long enough to put in her ten cents. "And the police *will* believe them, because I'm going to tell everything. Like I should have done all those years ago."

Beau motioned to Sabine. "I brought a backpack in from my truck and dropped it somewhere in the hall when I saw Frances with her shovel. There's a set of handcuffs in the front pocket."

It only took Sabine a minute to retrieve the pack and less than that for Beau to secure Catherine to the bedpost. Sabine looked down at her, still amazed and appalled all at the same time at all the evil stemming from one central source. All those people murdered, and for what—money . . . a title . . . a house? Sabine would never understand.

But Catherine had denied any attempt on Sabine's life.

"The least you can do," Sabine said to the murderess, "is tell me why you were trying to kill me. It's all coming out anyway. I deserve to know."

Catherine gave her a dirty look. "I already told you I couldn't be bothered."

"Then what about the peanut oil and syringe that were in Lloyd's jacket pocket?" Beau said.

Catherine frowned. "The jacket in the hall closet?"

"Yes."

"I'll be damned," Catherine said, a thin smile on her face. "Lloyd's jacket is in our bedroom. The jacket in the hall must belong to Mr. Alford."

Sabine stared at Beau in horror.

"Damn it!" Beau cursed and ran from the room, his gun in the ready position. Sabine rushed out behind him.

At the end of the hall, Beau pushed open the bedroom door and stuck the lantern inside. An open briefcase sat on the bed and Sabine could see a glow coming from underneath the bathroom door. Beau eased the bathroom door open and peered inside as Sabine lifted a folder from the briefcase.

"No one's there," Beau said.

Sabine opened the folder and looked at the black-and-white photo on top. It wasn't recent, if the woman's hairstyle and clothes were any indication, but there was something about her face . . . She flipped the photo over and read the penciled words at the top corner. *Mom, 1955.* She flipped the photo back over and took a second look. Still nothing. She handed the photo to Beau for his inspection and looked at the next document. It was a death certificate for a Sandra Franks, identifying the cause of death as drowning. Sabine frowned.

Sandra Franks was one of the names she'd found when searching for the women from her aunt's journals. But what in the world was Alford doing with her death certificate? *Mom, 1955.*

Sabine stretched her mind to recall the conversation they'd had at Alford's office. He'd mentioned losing his parents at a young age. She flipped to the next sheet and found a copy of a journal page. Her pulse began to quicken:

> *I'm afraid for me and my children. I haven't heard from William in over four months, and even with him in Vietnam, that's a long time. He promised to put a stop to this charade his family is putting on about his engagement to Catherine. He swears I am the only one he will ever love, and I believe him. He's told Catherine he will never marry her, but I think she has her mind set on being a Fortescue. I'm afraid for my babies. If his family finds out, I'm not sure what they will do. Even worse, I'm not sure what Catherine will do.*
>
> *She claims to love William and want a life with him, but I see the way she looks at Lloyd in church and I know the way the wind blows. There have been noises outside of my house three nights in a row, and now the dog is missing. I'm afraid someone has found out William is the father of my children, and that has put us all in danger.*
>
> *I pray daily that I will hear from my love, but there is a stone deep in my stomach that tells me it is already too late, and I will never see my William again.*

Sabine's heart pounded in her throat as she turned to the next page. A birth certificate.

Twins. A boy, Martin Samuel born at 10:10 a.m. and a girl, Mildred Grace born ten minutes before.

Sabine sucked in a breath as her whole world came crashing down around her. She yanked the photo from Beau, not wanting to see what she already knew was there, not wanting to believe that this was far from over. But it was right there staring her in the face. The curve of the smile, the wide-set eyes and upturned nose. Sandra Franks was Mildred's mother. The woman who had raised Sabine was adopted, and Mildred had never said a word.

Or maybe she hadn't known.

Panicked, Sabine shoved the folder at Beau. "It wasn't me!" she cried. "It wasn't me Alford was trying to kill."

Beau stared at her, wide-eyed. "Sabine, what are you talking about? Of course he was trying to kill you."

"No. Read the papers. Look at that picture. Catherine and Lloyd killed William's girlfriend in order to pull off their plan. But Sandra already had William's babies, so they gave them away. Twins. Martin and Mildred. *My* Mildred. She's been the target this whole time." Beau glanced down at the photo and his face instantly grew a shade lighter. "Holy shit! It was Alford who said the bridge was out."

Sabine grabbed Beau's arm. "We have to get to Mudbug! The phone lines are all down and the cells will never work, especially with the storm. We have to warn Mildred. He's probably on his way. Or already there."

They ran back into Frances's bedroom and Beau looked over at the stricken Adelaide. "Adelaide, I need you to watch Catherine for a bit. I'll send the police as soon as I can notify them, but in the meantime, I need you to stay here and keep watch. Can you do that?"

Adelaide nodded fearfully. "I think so. Do I have to use the gun?"

Beau shook his head. "Not unless you know how."

Adelaide blew out a breath. "I know how. And I'm a sight better than that ghost."

Helena huffed. "Look who's talking shit now. You were all frozen like a pack of steaks until I got here."

"Helena, we all know you saved the day," Sabine said, "now I need you to stay here with Adelaide and make sure nothing else happens. Can you do that?"

"Yeah, sure."

Sabine nodded to Beau and they hurried out of the room.

"But I'm getting a piece of that chocolate cake," Helena yelled after them.

Mildred sat in her hospital bed, staring at the static on the television and wondering if the worst of the storm was blowing over, or if this lessening was only a lull. She was worried about Sabine, about this dinner with her "family." Mildred was old-fashioned in a lot of ways, but family wasn't one of them. Blood didn't make someone love you. It didn't make someone treat you right. Not a single one of the people she considered family was related by blood, but when it came to family, Mildred considered herself the most blessed woman in Mudbug.

She had two beautiful daughters, who were fast becoming the women she always knew they'd be. They had integrity. They had respect for themselves. They cared about others and never even blinked at self-sacrifice for each other or for Mildred. They were her greatest joy, and when she was feeling a little vain, her greatest accomplishment.

She smiled as she thought of them, how they'd shown their character even in such trying times, and she knew without a doubt that no matter what happened, her two girls would survive and thrive. And that peace of mind was worth more to her than any amount of money in the bank.

"Lord have mercy!" Maryse burst into the room, both hands full and dripping water from every inch of her and the bags she carried. "It's a doozy out there."

Mildred glanced out the window and nodded. "I thought it was slacking off some."

Maryse dumped the bags on the floor and shook off her raincoat. "It is now, but when I left the hotel it was a torrential downpour. I deliberated between bringing your bags or just starting to build an ark right there in the middle of Main Street." She grinned at Mildred and tossed her raincoat onto the tile floor of the bathroom and grabbed a towel off a shelf next to the door.

Mildred laughed. "That would be a sight, wouldn't it? An ark in downtown Mudbug. And can you even imagine getting two of everything on board?"

"Yeah . . . two idiots, two fools, two rednecks . . . the hardest part would be narrowing it down to which two. And I don't care if they're God's creatures, I'm still not taking snakes."

"That's my girl," Mildred said. "I just wish Sabine were here instead of with those people."

Maryse lifted a duffle bag from the floor and wiped it with the towel, then handed the bag to Mildred. "Sorry about the wet part—couldn't be avoided. And I'm with you on the Sabine thing. I know the Fortescues are her family, but everything's been wrong since she found them. Well, and I guess even before."

Mildred nodded and waved one hand at the window. "Like the calm before the storm."

Maryse's eyes widened. "Shit. I didn't even think of

it that way. And I hope your poetic expression isn't lining up with our atmospheric conditions."

"Have you heard from her?"

Maryse bit her lip. "No. Cell phone reception's been spotty though, with the weather. Even if she tried, I don't know if she could get through."

"I don't feel right. I don't want to trouble you, Maryse, but I'm worried. I feel like something big is about to happen. And not something good, but I can't put my finger on what."

"Or why, or who, or how." Maryse sat on the edge of her bed, a worried expression on her face. "I feel it, too. Been feeling it for a while, but the truth is, tonight it all seems intensified somehow. I thought maybe it was just the storm. You know, like some creepy horror movie."

"The 'dark and stormy night' introduction. Makes for a great gothic tale, but a nerve-racking reality."

She sighed. "You know, it was always so easy for me to dismiss Sabine's beliefs about things we couldn't see. Not that I ever dismissed her or thought any different of her for believing. I just couldn't make that leap myself."

Mildred nodded. "I know. I have the same hesitation, but the older I get, the less inclined I am to say 'never.' It tends to come back and bite you." She paused for a moment, thinking about her next words, the best way to say them. "I know something has been going on with you and Sabine lately. Something that is bothering you both and that you don't want to tell me about. Maybe when all this has settled down, you'll think about letting me know."

Maryse looked stricken, and Mildred knew she'd hit a nerve. "We're not trying to leave you out or make you feel unimportant, Mildred. I promise you." She laid her hand on Mildred's. "But you're right. There have been some things happening to us that, well, we didn't really think you'd take the right way . . . or take at all."

Mildred patted her hand. "I know exactly what you're saying, and you were right . . . then. You were right until I woke up in this hospital and saw Helena Henry standing next to my bed big as life and the two of you talking to her."

Maryse's eyes widened. "You really saw her? We hoped it was the drugs making you confused."

"I saw her all right. At first I thought maybe I'd imagined it, but it was too vivid, and you looked too frightened when I said something for me to think it was just me being high."

Maryse jumped up from the bed and paced the tiny room. "That's not good. I have this theory, you see, that when someone sees Helena, they're in danger. That seems to be the pattern. That's why Sabine and I were worried. And since you saw her *after* your car wreck, it makes me think it's not over for you."

Mildred took in a deep breath and let it out slowly. "But that would explain this feeling we have, wouldn't it? Something's coming, and maybe somehow Helena is connected to it all."

Maryse stopped pacing. "That's what I think, and you're right, the three of us need to have a long talk when this is over. Whatever 'this' is. But not now. Right now, it would be overload, and we need to keep our minds focused on looking for whatever it is that's coming. Being blindsided sucks."

Mildred nodded. "We're going to be fine, Maryse. We may not know what we're up against but we know something's there. That makes us more prepared than most in our situation. I know I've sent you running all over tonight, but if you don't mind, would you pop down to the cafeteria and pick us up a couple of large coffees? I'm thinking sleep isn't really the best idea at the moment."

"Of course," Maryse agreed and hurried out of the room.

Mildred unzipped the wet bag she'd just gotten. She'd been carrying it around in addition to her purse for a couple of days—had been compelled to for reasons she couldn't attest to, but then things hadn't been normal in Mudbug for quite a while. Oh, there was a spare set of clothes on top to hide the real reason for the bag, but the cold, hard reason for it was nestled in the bottom. She pulled the pistol from its holder and carefully loaded it. A blast of thunder echoed through the room, and she looked out the window at the raging storm. Maryse was right—that storm was setting her on edge even more than before. She tucked the gun under the edge of her covers right by her hip and hoped to God she was faster than whatever the winds were blowing her way.

Chapter Nineteen

Beau pressed the accelerator on his truck, pushing the vehicle as fast as he could down the muddy road. "The storm is slacking off some," he said, hoping to reassure Sabine, who sat rigid on the passenger's seat.

"What if the bridge is out now? What if we're too late? What if he gets to Mildred?"

"Stay calm, Sabine. Mildred is still in the hospital, and Maryse was going to be there with her. It's not like she's alone, by any stretch. And maybe we're wrong about all of this."

"Mildred was firstborn. That must be important or Catherine wouldn't have mentioned it to me. As their attorney, Martin would know just how important it was. I'd bet he's been stalking the family his entire life, waiting for a chance to claim his rights."

"So why wait? Catherine would have paid him plenty to go away."

"I think . . . I know it sounds strange, but I don't think it was just about the money. I think it was about *being* a Fortescue. And if we assume Martin didn't know William was actually Lloyd, then the only way that would happen is if William admitted to an affair before he married Catherine."

"And since Martin knew Catherine, he knew that would never happen," Beau finished. "So he was biding his time thinking that when they passed, he'd come in for the biggest piece of everything as firstborn. But somehow he found out about Mildred. How do you think that happened?"

"It had to be that newspaper article—the same one Frances had. Remember, when we were at Martin's house, I brought a New Orleans paper inside. Mildred looks just like his mother. He would have seen the resemblance right away, and guessing that he had a sister out there somewhere wouldn't have been so big a leap to make."

Beau nodded, understanding Sabine's logic. "But that still doesn't explain poisoning you or the car bomb. That was your wine and your car, Sabine."

"That's just it," Sabine said, her voice growing more excited. "That bottle of wine was one Mildred picked up. I'd just gotten it from Mildred the day before. And since her car's been on the blink, she's been driving mine. If Martin came to Mudbug to spy on her—"

"He would have thought the car was hers," Beau finished, and his pulse began to race. "Shit, you're right. It makes total sense, as much as any of this does. And the break-in at your shop was probably Martin, too. It gave him a shiny new key to your building and access to anything you might have on Mildred."

"Oh no! I have a master key to the hotel. It's hanging on a rack in my kitchen with a label on it, plain as day. What a moron! I may as well have opened the door for him myself. And what do you want to bet that the whole dinner was Martin's idea. Being stuck at the Fortescue estate would have been the perfect alibi for him. If it hadn't been for Frances digging up dead people, we would never have known he was gone."

Beau nodded and felt his jaw tighten. It was very slick, very smooth. To have done all the things they imagined, Martin Alford couldn't be completely sane, but he wasn't all-out crazy like Frances. He was cunning and clever. Beau slowed as they approached the bridge, praying that Alford had lied and that the water hadn't risen since the attorney had made his escape. He blew out a breath of relief when he saw the water swirling just underneath the wooden structure.

"He lied," Sabine said. "Thank God, he lied. Now if we can get to Mildred in time . . ."

"We'll get there." Beau pressed the accelerator halfway to the floor and the truck launched over the bridge and onto the road beyond. "Check the phones. See if we've got a signal yet."

Sabine grabbed Beau's phone from the seat next to her and looked. "No, damn it." She pulled her own phone from her pocket and peered at the display. "One bar."

"Try it. Call 911."

Beau glanced over as Sabine punched in the numbers and was certain she was holding her breath. The relief on her face let him know right away that the connection had gone through. Sabine handed the phone to Beau. "You explain. I'm going to sound hysterical."

Beau took the phone and gave the local cops a brief description of the situation at the Fortescue mansion, then explained the situation with Mildred. The dispatcher was stunned, but he promised to get police to the Fortescue mansion and the Mudbug hospital as fast as humanly possible. Beau pressed End and handed the phone back to Sabine. "Call Maryse. Her phone might not pick up in the hospital, but it's worth a try."

Sabine took the phone and pressed in Maryse's number. A couple of seconds later, she shut the phone, the disappointment on her face clear as day. "It went straight to voice mail."

Beau turned the wheel hard to the right and the truck lurched onto the highway. "Don't worry about it. We'll be there in ten minutes." He prayed they weren't already too late.

Mildred was digging in her duffle bag for her mace when she felt the hair on her neck stand up straight. She looked up and sucked in a breath when she saw the man standing next to her bed holding a gun.

"Hello, Mildred," the man said, "or should I call you sister?"

Mildred studied the man, but didn't see anything familiar. "You're no one to me and I'm fine keeping it that way."

The man sighed. "I wish it could have stayed that way, but Sabine ruined it for everyone."

Mildred's mind raced, trying to make sense of what the man was saying. "What does Sabine have to do with any of this?"

"I was just waiting to stake my claim. I finally had the proof I needed after all these years to prove I was William's rightful heir. I could have left you alone, and you would never have known. But then Sabine turned up—questioning them about the family and the past, convincing them she was related. It was only a matter of time before they met you, and Catherine saw the truth."

Mildred's head swam in confusion. "There was a DNA test. Sabine told me."

The man shifted the gun in his hand, obviously agitated. "Adam was sterile. I read his medical records. There's no way he fathered a child. Why the Fortescues lied about the results, I don't know. But they'll pay—they'll all pay for what they did. I should have been firstborn. But that's something I can fix."

He leveled the gun at her head and pulled a syringe from his shirt pocket. "You're going to take a nap, little sister. One you won't wake up from, I'm afraid." He stepped closer to the bed, needle poised for injection.

Mildred's heart pounded so hard she thought it would burst. There was no way she could reach her gun. He'd won, even though she'd tried to prepare. She closed her eyes and began to pray.

A whistling noise echoed through the silence, and her entire body went stiff. She wondered for a moment when the pain would come, but suddenly a heavy weight fell across her. Opening her eyes, she saw the man who claimed to be her brother slumped across her, a single bullet hole through his temple. Raissa stood in the doorway, her gun still drawn, the silencer explaining the whistling.

"Who was he?" Mildred asked.

"Martin Alford," Raissa said as she stepped over to the bed and checked the man's neck for a pulse. "The Fortescues' attorney."

"Was he my brother?"

"Maybe."

Mildred slumped back on the bed, her pulse still racing. "How did you know? How did you know to come here?"

"I guessed."

Mildred stared at Raissa for a moment, then let out a single laugh. "That's one heck of a guess, Raissa."

Raissa removed her hand from Alford's neck and sighed. "I was really hoping I was wrong."

Mildred pulled her gun out from the covers and sat it on the tray next to the bed. "I'm glad you weren't wrong. It's over, and we're all still alive, and that's the most important thing."

Raissa glanced at Mildred's gun and raised her eyebrows. "You knew someone was after you?"

Mildred shook her head. "I guessed."

Raissa smiled. "That's one heck of a guess."

"Make that two of us who hoped we were wrong."

"Well, being as we were both right, I guess we need to call the police and get this process started before the nurse comes in to take your temperature and has a heart attack."

Mildred pulled her legs out from under the covers and climbed out of bed. She stuck her hand out toward Raissa. "Give me your gun."

Raissa stared at her. "What? Why?"

"Honey, I know what hiding looks like and you've been at it a long, long time. Are you going to tell me you want the police poking around into your background?"

Raissa's eyes widened and Mildred placed one hand on her arm. "I don't know what you're running from, and I don't care. I've known you for a long time, and you're a good woman. I know you have good reasons. You and I both know the police won't even think twice about my shooting a man who came here to kill me. It will all go away in a matter of weeks."

"I don't know . . . what if they guess . . . how are you going to explain . . ."

"I won't explain much of anything. I'm in a hospital, worried for my life, and on drugs—as far as they know.

Give me your gun, Raissa. I figure it's not registered to you, right? I can always claim I got it from Maryse's dad years ago. No one will think any different. Bayou men buy and sell this stuff all the time."

Raissa glanced at Alford then back at Mildred, obviously torn. Finally, she placed her gun in Mildred's hand. Mildred handed Raissa her own firearm. "I don't want you without protection, and I figure me toting two guns around might raise some eyebrows. If you wouldn't mind taking that with you."

Raissa took the pistol and slipped it in her purse. "Thank you, Mildred. I'll get this back to you as soon as I replace my old one."

Mildred waved one hand in dismissal. "Keep it. Mine's not registered either." She gave Raissa a wink and the other woman smiled. Mildred lifted the phone, dialed 911, and gave a brief description of the problem. Somehow it didn't surprise her to find out that Beau Villeneuve had already called the police and they were in route. She hung up the phone with a smile.

"What?" Raissa asked, and Mildred explained to her to Beau had already sent the police.

Raissa smiled and squeezed Mildred's hand with her own. "The house of cards is crumbling."

Mildred grinned. "We better get your prints off that gun, get mine on it, and call for the nurse. Tell her someone died in here and it damned sure wasn't me." Mildred reached for the phone as Maryse strolled into the room, wrestling with a cardboard coffee tray.

"Sorry it took so long," Maryse said, still looking down at the tray. "There was an incredible line down there and—" She looked up and saw Mildred standing next to the bed, pistol still in her hand, and the dead man slumped over her hospital bed.

All the color washed out of Maryse's face and the tray of coffee crashed to the floor, Maryse following closely behind. Mildred looked down at her and shook her head. "Sure, someone tries to kill her and she runs out of the hotel barefoot and not wearing underwear. Sometimes tries to kill me and she's a shrinking violet."

Raissa grinned. "Well, maybe we should get 'Violet' off the floor before the police get here."

Sabine bit her lip as Beau tore into the hospital parking lot and screeched to a stop in front of the main entry. They both jumped out and ran past a startled nurse who yelled after them. It seemed by unspoken mutual decision they both decided the stairs were the best choice, because neither even slowed as they passed the elevator. Sabine skidded on the polished floor as they burst out of the stairwell and onto Mildred's floor, but there was barely a pause before she picked up speed again and dashed down the hallway after Beau.

She saw him pull his gun from his waistband, and she pulled her own pistol from her purse and dropped the bag in the hallway. They rounded the last corner and burst into Mildred's room, guns blazing and ready to do some serious damage.

"Good heavens!" Mildred looked at the doorway as they burst into the room.

It took less than a second for Sabine to take it all in—Martin, dead on Mildred's bed, and Raissa standing over a white-faced Maryse, fanning her with a bedpan. She paused only long enough to click on the safety on her pistol, then rushed over to Mildred and wrapped her arms around the woman who had raised her and crushed her in a hug.

Mildred squeezed her back and rubbed her hands up and down Sabine's back, just the way she used to do when Sabine was upset as a child. "It's fine, honey. Everything's going to be just fine."

Sabine felt the tears surface and didn't even bother to try holding them in as she released Mildred and looked her in the eyes. "This has been the single most horrifying and terrifying day of my entire life."

"Tell me about it," Maryse mumbled.

Sabine looked over at her best friend and smiled. "Should I even ask?"

Raissa shook her head. "No, but it's worth a year of bribes later on."

Mildred cocked her head to one side and studied Sabine for a moment. "When I called the police, they said you'd already dispatched them here. How did you know?"

Sabine blew out a breath. "I found a bunch of papers in Martin's briefcase. They tied everything together. You were the one in danger all along, although I'm sure he would've come after me next. He was insane and obsessed with his quest."

"Is he my brother?"

Sabine nodded. "I think so."

"And you? Why did that man say you weren't Adam's child?"

"Because I'm not. Frances was my mother. Adam and his wife took me to save me from the Fortescues and oh, hell, it's a long screwed-up story that I'd rather explain after a hot bath and at least ten hours of sleep."

Mildred nodded and gave her another hug. "Of course, dear. What a shame. Like either of us cared about the Fortescues or their money."

"You might have to start caring," Sabine said.

"I'll deal with that when William dies."

Sabine glanced over at Beau, then looked back at Mildred. "You're right. No use inviting trouble."

"You're one to talk." Mildred glanced over at Beau, then back at Sabine, a smile on her face. "If you could have just seen the two of you, busting in here like something out of a movie." She leaned close to Sabine and whispered, "The two of you together looked right."

Sabine brushed a single tear from her face with the back of her hand. "Well, you always told me not to contradict my elders . . ."

Three hours later, Sabine crawled into her bed at the hotel, certain she was going to sleep for a week. Mildred was tucked in her bed at the hotel, absolutely refusing to stay in the hospital another minute. The hospital staff didn't argue over the release, probably glad she was going and worried about being sued for letting killers have free access to the patients. Maryse was asleep on her couch, refusing to give up her patrol duties, especially after passing out on the job.

Mildred had given her statement to the Mudbug police and explained how Raissa walked in after the fact, but Sabine knew she was lying about that part. Once the dust had settled on all of this, Sabine was going to get the truth out of her. She turned off the lamp and pulled up the covers. She was just about to doze off when she heard the connecting door open.

"Sabine?" Beau whispered. "Are you asleep?"

"About two seconds from being." She propped herself up on her elbow and looked over at him. "Did you get everything settled at the Big House of Horrors?" Beau had left for the Fortescue estate right after the police arrived at the hospital. Without a sane person in the mix, he was afraid the state police wouldn't have any idea what to do with a murdering socialite, a dead husband, an insane daughter, the terrified housekeeper, and the body in the backyard. Sabine only prayed that Helena hadn't decided to "help" while the police were there.

Beau walked over to the bed and sat next to her. "It's a real mess over there. Even the state police were blown away by all of it. Catherine's still tight-lipped, but Adelaide is singing like a bird. They had to sedate Frances again and cart her off to the hospital. I'm thinking she might need permanent care."

Sabine's mind flashed back to Frances, digging in the garden in the middle of a hurricane. The expression on her face was a mixture of so many things— fear, revulsion, horror, and not an ounce of sanity left. "After all that, it's no wonder."

Beau placed his hand on Sabine's. "I'm afraid you don't know everything. Hell, I'm starting to wonder if anyone does. That place was a regular house of horrors during Catherine's reign." He paused for a moment, the indecision on his face clear.

"What is it, Beau? There's nothing that could shock me now."

Beau nodded. "I know. And this isn't shocking as much as it makes sense but is incredibly sad." He took a deep breath and blew it out. "The police found another body in the backyard with William . . . an infant. I think Frances had twins."

Sabine's eyes clouded with tears. "Twins . . . yes,

that would make sense, given the family history. I guess Adam couldn't save the other baby."

"I guess not. It's all so tragic. I mean, obviously Catherine deserves no sympathy. She's been evil from the beginning, but Frances's mind eaten away by that horrible disease, William killed just because Catherine wanted more status and money than Lloyd would inherit, and Martin's mother murdered and her babies stolen. Then Adam taking you and hiding from his family because he knew it was the only chance for you to live." Beau squeezed Sabine's hand. "Adam must have been an incredible man."

Sabine brushed a tear from her cheek. "I think he was, and my mother. . . . well, the woman I thought. . . . oh, you know. I mean, she had to know what they were doing and she agreed to it to save me. They were still my parents in every sense of the word for as long as they lived."

Beau nodded. "They loved you enough to die for you. I'd say that definitely makes them mom and dad." Beau leaned down and wrapped his arms around Sabine. "I am so sorry, Sabine. I expected something bad when I took your case. That's why I wanted to stick around even after we found your family. I didn't want you working with someone inexperienced with these things."

Sabine gave a single laugh. "You mean inexperienced with an evil grandmother, a crazy aunt, and a gun-toting ghost?"

Beau released Sabine a bit and pulled back enough to smile down at her. "The ghost was more than anyone would want to take. I gave her a ride back into Mudbug. She was in my truck and passed me a note. I had to stop at the convenience store and buy her a dozen hotdogs and a whole box of moon pies. I didn't think the dead were supposed to be so expensive."

Sabine smiled. "Helena sorta operates by her own set of rules."

"Well, I never would have believed it if I hadn't seen it, and I like to think I'm fairly open-minded. All the same, I'm glad she's around."

"Me, too," Sabine said, "but don't you dare ever tell her that."

Beau laughed, and then his expression grew serious. "And what about me . . . have you given any more thought to having me around? I wouldn't bill you for it, of course."

Sabine sobered. "I don't know. I'm drawn to you like I never have been to anyone else. I care about you, and more importantly, I respect and admire you, but I don't even know what my own future holds. How can I ask you to live that way?"

"You mean one day at a time with you?" Beau placed his hands on both sides of her face and lowered his head, brushing her lips gently with his. He pulled back a bit and looked at her. "I love you, Sabine LeVeche. I don't care if we have fifty years together or two weeks. What I *do* know is that I don't want to live one more minute of either of our lives without you."

Sabine's heart pounded in her chest and tears filled her eyes. Everything around her seemed to blur, but Beau remained clear. It was a huge risk, but she knew she had to start living. It might be her last chance to do so. "I love you, Beau. God help us both. I don't want to spend another minute without you in my life, either."

Beau pulled her close to him and hugged her as if he

would never let go. And the wonderful thing is that Sabine knew he wouldn't.

"We're going to do everything possible for you, Sabine," Beau promised. "Even if it means extorting bone marrow from Frances."

Sabine leaned back a bit and looked at him, her eyes filled with tears but her heart full of the love for this man who had put everything on the line to protect her. "That won't be necessary. Mildred was tested last night in the hospital. She's a match."

Beau's eyes lit up with the hope and promise that Sabine felt for the first time in a long time. He lowered his lips to hers and she melted into his embrace, hoping she had a long, long time to feel as good as she did right now.

One week later

Sabine closed her shop and walked upstairs to her apartment. She could hear soft music playing inside before she even opened the door, but nothing prepared her for the gorgeous man standing in her kitchen, chopping vegetables and wearing nothing but an apron and a smile.

"I'm making you my famous spaghetti," he said.

She walked into the kitchen and pulled his apron to the side, laughing as he playfully slapped her hand away. "Tease," she said. "So does your secret recipe call for cooking in the nude?"

He pulled her into his arms and kissed her. "No. *You* call for me cooking in the nude. For some reason, when I'm around you I don't feel like wearing clothes." He eased back from her a bit and studied her face. "How are you feeling?"

Sabine smiled. "No side effects from the radiation at all. I think Maryse may be up for a Nobel Prize some day."

"And did the doctor call with your test results?"

"Just before I closed up. He said I'm responding well to treatment and everything looks great."

The relief on Beau's face was apparent. "Then I have a surprise for you."

"What kind of surprise?"

"The kind that involves you leaving this state for the first time. And it has a beach, and a private hut, and a minister waiting for a phone call from me. That is, if you're willing to marry a naked chef."

"Well, I don't know. You might want to put on clothes before we meet with the minister."

"Is that a yes?"

She leaned in and kissed him gently on the lips. "That's a definitely."

Who killed Helena?

It all comes down to a
Showdown in Mudbug

July 2010

"Craig's latest will DELIGHT . . . fans of
JANET EVANOVICH and HARLEY JANE KOZAK."
—*Booklist* on *Gotcha!*

Award-winning Author

Christie Craig

"Christie Craig will crack you up!"
—*New York Times* Bestselling Author Kerrelyn Sparks

Of the Divorced, Desperate and Delicious club, Kathy Callahan is
the last surviving member. Oh, her two friends haven't died or anything. They just gave up their vows of chastity. They went for hot sex
with hot cops and got happy second marriages—something Kathy
can never consider, given her past. Yet there's always her plumber,
Stan Bradley. He seems honest, hardworking, and skilled with a tool.

But Kathy's best-laid plans have hit a clog. The guy snaking her drain
isn't what he seems. He's handier with a pistol than a pipe wrench,
and she's about to see more action than Jason Statham. The next
forty-eight hours promise hot pursuit, hotter passion and a super
perky pug, and at the end of this wild escapade, Kathy and her very
own undercover lawman will be flush with happiness—assuming they
both survive.

Divorced, Desperate and Deceived

ISBN 13: 978-0-505-52798-1

INTERACT WITH DORCHESTER ONLINE!

Want to learn more about your favorite books and authors?
Want to talk with other readers that like to read the same books as you?
Want to see up-to-the-minute Dorchester news?

VISIT DORCHESTER AT:

DorchesterPub.com
Twitter.com/DorchesterPub
Facebook.com (Search Pages)

DISCUSS DORCHESTER'S NOVELS AT:

Dorchester Forums at DorchesterPub.com
GoodReads.com
LibraryThing.com
Myspace.com/books
Shelfari.com
WeRead.com

☐ YES!

Sign me up for the Love Spell Book Club and send my
FREE BOOKS! If I choose to stay in the club, I will pay
only $8.50* each month, a savings of $6.48!

NAME: _____

ADDRESS: _____

TELEPHONE: _____

EMAIL: _____

☐ I want to pay by credit card.

☐ **VISA**   ☐ **MasterCard**   ☐ **DISCOVER**

ACCOUNT #: _____

EXPIRATION DATE: _____

SIGNATURE: _____

Mail this page along with $2.00 shipping and handling to:
Love Spell Book Club
PO Box 6640
Wayne, PA 19087
Or fax (must include credit card information) to:
610-995-9274
You can also sign up online at **www.dorchesterpub.com**.
*Plus $2.00 for shipping. Offer open to residents of the U.S. and Canada only.
Canadian residents please call 1-800-481-9191 for pricing information.
If under 18, a parent or guardian must sign. Terms, prices and conditions subject to
change. Subscription subject to acceptance. Dorchester Publishing reserves the right
to reject any order or cancel any subscription.